HUXLEY X

AND THE SECRETS OF PLANET NEXT

J.P. MAXIMUS

I

III

A TRUE STORY, INDEED, IT'S NOT.

VI

SUMMER

FIRST DAY OF SCHOOL

HUXLEY X

Dear Parents,

We love you. But times have changed. We're tired. This ain't working. It never did. You just don't get us. You don't. Let's be frank: school is for losers. We're not losers, nor should you want us to be. That was never the plan—your plan. And if you spent time with our teachers, you'd understand why. But you haven't, nor should you want to. Indeed, a good choice.

Well, here is the thing: you taught us to be wise, you taught us to be smart, you taught us ... Wait a minute, what exactly did you teach us?

Now, hear us out. We want change: new rules. Ours. And good ones, too.

First off, bedtime is when we pass out from our creative labors, not when you wanna watch TV or whatever it is you like to do.

Next, we're not going to school. Uninspired, outdated, overly structured, assignment-driven—this is not learning.

So, let us make a friendly suggestion. We'd like to be responsible for our own education: no teachers, no classrooms, no school, no nothing—well, that is, nothing but *us* left to our own devices. Seems reasonable, right?

Moving along ... From now on, every night is Friday, and every day is Saturday. Why discriminate? We believe in equal opportunity for all days to be whole, and so should you. Besides, you always said so yourselves: be consistent. Dang, consistent, we shall be.

So, tell us, how does that all sound? Don't answer. We know. And you know, too.

Okay, so here it is: we're leaving. Starting today, we're beginning our own way of life. We'll be claiming our own land: Planet Next ... a planet for teens. It's now just *us*. Yes, don't doubt yourselves—you heard right ... *just us!* There'll be new laws, new ways of thinking, and new ways of doing things.

If you believe you raised us well (and you do), then give yourselves a pat on the shoulder. Here's your moment.

What's there to say? We tried. We saw the result: the end result, your result. Results tried and tested for centuries, you keep reminding us, results that, quite frankly, speak for themselves. Tell us, is the world a better place for it? Are we on the brink of world peace, saving the ice caps, or some other dang idea? Don't answer. Everybody knows.

With all due respect, as much as we can muster, we think we'd be better off in a zoo. At least there, monkey business is actually good business.

It didn't have to be this way, you know. It didn't. But it is. And now we'll be grounding ourselves elsewhere. Permanently.

Love you to death,

X.

On behalf of your kidz.

P.S. Hope you don't mind ... We took the cookie jars and left you our textbooks.

EARLIER THAT MORNING
PRINCIPAL'S HOME

The crimson summer sun sneaks up behind the forest on a beautiful Tuesday morning, punctuated by a few clouds passing through, just to ruin the moment. But, alas, even they can't blunt its light. Nobody can. Well and truly, it's the most marvelous morning for Mr. Wickly, the principal of the most prestigious school in Florida. This, after all, is not just *any* day but *the* day: the commencement of his cherished plans for the new school year.

Arising before the sound of his alarm, and looking at it with his customary calm: sitting, legs crossed, tapping his fingers, hoping, expecting, waiting for that expected hour to arrive, and, finally ... 6:15 a.m., it rings. And, one push, he turns it off, springing up.

Let the games begin.

Adjusting his suit that always feels right, he turns to the mirror, straightening his tie, staring at the image that never tires, never bores him; he moves one hair to the left—

4

perfect!—and admires the four remaining ones gracing his crown. The only thing more beautiful would be a younger image of himself.

His eyes narrow. He smiles. Who would he pick on today? A suspension, an expulsion, a lecture—his special lecture? *Good to have you back, Wickly ... so good.*

And with that, he walks down the staircase with a skip and a hop. Don't jump—that would be most unseemly for a man of his ilk, a man who shuns the central occupants of the bell curve.

But even he can't bury his joy on this day. He jumps, jumps, and jumps, but halts on the last step—his face stern, his smile flattened—a reminder to himself, who he is, what he represents, and who they're about to contend with.

With a mental call to order, he pulls his jacket straight and walks stately, stepping into the kitchen, and casts a disciplined eye: coffee brewing, microwave beeping, waffles popping out, the steam, the sizzle, the smell—*mmm!*—the day planned with precision ...

A good morning, indeed.

Jason, you'll be given one chance, just one. Sarah, that's it—detention! Be grateful, Lucas—I only said you'd be expelled from school ... not from hell.

In a series of pleasant rehearsals, he imagines with eyes wide open and takes his last bite, chewing dreamily ... a smile, a wipe, napkin folded—he's ready.

Efficient, Wickly, as always.

Time: 6:45 a.m. Time to leave.

Turning off the lights, he opens the door and stops. He hints a smile but manages his emotions. Looking forward, it's as though every tree is arched, bowing to the moment.

Could it be true ...? He shrugs. *If you say so.* Now that he's seen everything: chin up, deep breath ... "Ahh." *Duty awaits, and so does my scorn.* And with that, it's time to go meet the rascals! He looks down ...

Briefcase: check.

Glasses: check.

Pen: check.

Keys: check.

And feeling his pocket, the Knightlord ring: a delightful check. He puts on this distinguished prize for educators then raises it to the sun. It sparkles, a reminder of the standard, *his* standard, the Knightlord standard ... lest he forget.

Setting off, he begins to walk with his conventional, rigid stride. His four-door station wagon sits on the driveway. It shines, it's new, and it awaits his arrival, facing the road. Not a second to waste.

He opens his car door and sits inside. He looks at the mirror again, the hair not moved—*splendid!* With the engine turned on, his seat slides into position. Classical music plays, then, volume raised, bells ringing, shift gear—*easy does it*—he drives forward.

Smile, Wickly, smile.

On that happy note, driving on an empty road, a hundred yards into his journey—his home a shadow in the rearview—he nods to the summer and the start of his new year. Pleased as he is and lost somewhere in the bubble of his thoughts, without noise, without introduction, there is, suddenly, an unusual occurrence.

What was that?

He's not sure, but his eyes search for what they can't

see, and he wonders whether he's a victim of his imagination. He awaits the answer. It doesn't come.

A moment later, sliding back to fantasy, something else slides beside him, tickling his attention. His head turns, eyes sharpen—*goodness!*—in a sudden flash of understanding, the hubcaps of his car have spun off, jutting forward, keeping pace.

Stunned, his voice escapes him as he watches them find their way, sweetly, softly, rolling round and round with purpose, one aimed for Canada, the other pointed to Mexico—a North American endeavor.

And then—*click, snap!*

What was that? Looking left, looking right, he remembers: *blind spot!* Abruptly, the backdoor unhinges, bouncing into action, tumbling away.

This can't be ... But it is. *It shouldn't happen* ... But it has. And sensing a final act on the horizon, he flinches. He's guessed right: the wheels have come off, joining their hubcaps. The car bounces once, twice, and then again, with Mr. Wickly's classic concerto receiving a background base, a powerful staccato of: *clink, clank, clunk*, and then *BOOM!*

As his car meets asphalt, Mr. Wickly's eyes lock in a distant gaze. Steam rises in front, as does his fury. His eyes speak what his lips can't, and then his pupils dilate— venting more.

Music off, silence checks in, his eyes refusing to blink.

The hushed moment lingers and stirs the air. The muscles on his neck begin to quiver, slowly, then faster. And faster still, before migrating to his face. They cease.

It surprises even him. Pupils relaxing, neck slackening,

he says nothing.

As he is frozen somewhere in his thought, calmness ensues: one second, two seconds. "Three" never makes it. He *ROARS!*

TWO HOURS LATER
MADISON SCHOOL

Moving at the speed of an intoxicated turtle, Principal Wickly's car emerges over the hill; it struggles but manages to reach the parking lot. Doors duct-taped, wheels screeching, wobbling, it jolts its last stretch.

Journey completed.

Mr. Wickly steps out and stands, straight-faced and muted. Steam rises from under his hood. It doesn't divert his attention. With slit eyes, he surveys the premises and closes his door—*clunk!* His rear door pops out.

Distracted, he doesn't look back. He listens. *Something doesn't feel right.* He steps past the mist. The air is light, the sounds even lighter, and the parking lot strangely quiet. Keen as he is, he raises his head to the air, searching, his thoughts floating somewhere—stitching together pieces of a puzzle he doesn't have. Right now, this picture has a thousand pieces of a student crime.

Mr. Wickly knows his students: their strengths, their

passions, their resilience, their optimism, and their gifts. Indeed, he has reasonable grounds not to trust them.

Huh? He peers around again and begins his march. Viewing the school, he sees something—*Uh-oh*—and his stroll surges to quick strides, then a jog, a run, a sprint, bolting at full tilt now—*This can't be!*—he runs by window after window, shooting a glance at each room before storming inside.

In rushed steps, he trots by the first classroom. Empty. His stress barometer climbs, green, amber, his eyes flashing red now—the next one is empty, too. He rushes to another classroom, *empty*, and then another ... and another; his pace quickens until he is scampering, popping his head past each door.

What's happened? He can't believe it: No teachers, no students—the school is vacant.

Who? How? Why? Like a seasoned detective, he runs through his leads.

Daylight savings? No.

Power outage? No.

Morning traffic? No.

A mistake? A Wickly doesn't make mistakes.

Abandoning the thought, panicked, he scrambles to his office and finds his phone. Then he shuffles through his contacts, *her* name, a number, and—*There!*—he dials it.

A few seconds pass as he waits for a connection. He paces back and forth, impatient. Sweat drips from his temple as he looks to his watch and then scans the wall calendar, debating. *It should be ... It must be ... It is!* The first day of school.

"Mrs. Andrews. Thank God." He takes a deep breath.

"This is Mr. Wickly. Tell me … just tell me I'm not dreaming."

His face stern, eyebrows raised, he listens. At her garbled declaration, one eyebrow drops, and seconds later, the other one sinks to meet it. "What?" he shouts.

Mumbled words … then nothing; the phone then hangs. His heart plunges, and his tongue stills; the message refuses to sink in.

Emerging to reality—*No, no, no!*—he runs, sprints, skids around the hallway corner, and glides past classroom after classroom—all empty of souls and evil—and on reaching the gymnasium, he slides to a stop before slamming the doors open and striding in with the drama of a king entering his palace.

Like a throng of ministers, teachers line the side, awaiting his arrival.

"Speak. Hurry. Tell me. What's happened?" he commands while passing by, his words never far from his anger.

"We found this letter on the front entrance," Mr. Tepper mutters, timidly reaching out to pass the note. "I don't think the parents even know. We didn't wanna do anythin' until you arrived. Where have you been?"

Mr. Wickly locks an evil eye on the letter, unable to mount an explanation for his morning experience, not wanting to even if he could; he gently plucks it from Mr. Tepper's hand and opens the page.

Examining the contents, his eyes begin their hunt; he draws the letter closer, grimacing at intervals, methodically tracking each line—read, end, reset. Then he looks up, staring to nowhere, his heart racing, his palms sweating, his face a gateway to oblivion.

Who'd think of this? Nobody. Who'd even imagine it? No one. Then he remembers something—*Oh no!*—and unsuccessfully attempts to clear his throat. He tries again and looks to Mrs. Andrews beside him, his face now as pale as a spooked ghost.

"Sir, the letter is signed X. Who, if I may ask, is X? None of the teachers have heard of him."

Silence festers, and then a rattle and a rumble builds like a volcano ready to erupt, hinting its first sign, giving its first warning. Well, it would appear Mr. Wickly has already found his answer. He begins to shake uncontrollably; his face trembles, wildly, wrathfully, without limits. Glancing down to hell, he lifts his tongue with purpose and then raises his chin as well, finally erupting: "HUUXLEEEEEEEY!"

HUXLEY
X

ONE WEEK PRIOR
DRAGON DALE RESIDENCE

The music drones on, and it's as loud as it is outdated.
The house is filled to the brim—standing room only, some
in the pool, others upstairs, many dancing on the main
floor. It's one last party before the start of the school year.

Time: 11:00 p.m.

The parents: on holiday.

Supervision: none solicited.

Invited guests: only the cool.

Attending guests: everyone you can imagine.

Well, everyone except one. Shouts swim above the
crowd, arms raised, the celebration in full swing.
Everyone's waiting, everyone's excited; his name has been
bandied about all summer.

"Is he here?" a person yells.

"Who?"

"You know."

"Oh yeah ... No."

"I haven't seen him either," adds another.

"Is he invited?"

"He's invited."

"OH ... HE'S INVITED!" another voice adds.

"What does he look like?"

A shrug. "Dunno."

"I've seen him," someone confirms. "He's tall."

"Slim," another person chimes in.

"I heard he likes magic."

Nod. "He made the sky disappear once."

"Does he have long hair?"

"Yup, it's slicked back. No gel. See ... magic."

"Did you hear about his parents?"

A shout from upstairs echoes down: "He's here!"

"Where?"

"Down the street."

Everyone hurries to watch, and when a mirror falls inside, heads turn—it doesn't break. *Not tonight.*

The summer mystery is about to come to a climactic close. And there in the distance, the enigmatic figure strides forward, dressed in black, with something on his left shoulder and a caveman of sorts accompanying him on the right.

"Is that a grownup with him?"

"Nah, don't think so."

On the wall, a hanging horseshoe unhinges—its ends turn, point down, rock back and forth, and then spin back up. *Not tonight.*

With a confidant gait, he draws closer, and with each step, his presence looms larger. A black cat begins to cross his path, stops, changes its mind ... runs back. *Not tonight.*

"What's that on his shoulder?"

"Is that ...?" Someone points. "A stuffed animal?"

"It looks like a bird."

"That's ..."

The music stops, and everyone drifts closer to draw a glimpse of the moment. He's the newest member of the Madison School for the Gifted (and Rich). Of course, that last part is sort of like the "k" in "know"—silent and for unspoken accounts only. No one dares to ask, but everyone's curious to *know*.

Right now, everyone's curious just to see his face. Sounds descend to cricket chirps as he steps forward and onto the lawn.

The boy-man glances around, dressed in a black tuxedo, draped with a black cape. He looks puzzled. "I'm sorry. I believe I have the wrong place. I was told there'd be a party here," he states with a London accent. He turns to leave.

A moment later, a girl shouts, "Wait!" demanding his attention. "This is the right place!"

He stops, looks over his shoulder, and sees a young woman—fifteen, brown eyes, brown curls, and one sharp tongue—step forward.

"Really ...?" He swivels back, amused, curious for her to say more. "I guess a party here is different than where I'm from ...? Your *do* is quieter than a bookless library."

Wearing a red cap and white blouse, she takes another step forward, squeezing past the immovable members, elbowing her way through. "What's your name, magic boy?"

"I beg your pardon?" he says, slowly turning his head sideways.

She nods ... all smiles, all business.

"It's ... Huxley," he responds, sensing a challenge. "But, if you prefer, you can call me by my last name ... X." After a beat, he adds, "And whose presence do I have the bounty to be graced with?"

"Name's Chandler."

"Ah, yes ... I've heard. Your reputation precedes you. Oh right, I remember, a five-star humanitarian: environmentalist, animal rights supporter, peace warrior, children's rights activist ... and the fifth one escapes me, but I'm sure you'll remind us soon."

"We have vegetarian food inside, if I may offer you some."

"Marvelous."

"Who's the bird?" She points.

"That's Chester. He's a parrot."

"And falcon," Chester adds.

"Indeed," Huxley confirms, looking at his rare parrot-falcon hybrid, truly his treasured company. "Well, I believe an introduction is in order." He nods. "Chester, meet Chatter."

"It's Chandler," she corrects and asks, "Is he the prop you pull outta your sleeve?"

Taken aback, he bears no expression. A contemplative moment passes without a blink. Then he smiles. "Chester is no prop." After a second, he places a warm hand on the bird's feathers. "My sleeve is only to keep my wrist warm; I can assure you."

"Then show us some magic," she says, bouncing a look to arouse support and receiving a resounding shout from the audience:

"YEEEAH!"

"My, my ... aren't you all in a hurry. Perhaps, then, you'd like to take a seat?" he offers Chandler, pointing to the blue chair several feet behind her.

"No, I prefer to stand," she affirms.

"I'd prefer it if you had a seat for your viewing experience. After all, objects in the mirror are always closer than they appear."

"Thanks. I'll stand." She nods, defying him once more.

"Very well," Huxley says, reaching within his pocket and pulling out a stack of cards. "Pick one."

"You're not serious?" She huffs. "You're gonna give us a card trick?"

Everyone laughs, and she peers around at the crowd to join in with her banter before shrugging and pulling one out.

"Would you, at least, like to sit for the last part?"

"I'm good," she pipes up, rolling her eyes as if to get on with the lame trick.

"So, you're gonna tell me what card I'm holding, right? Finger on the pulse there," she taunts, flashing the card to the people standing behind her: the ace of spades.

Peeved, she awaits his response.

"Oh, no, that's just chocolate you're holding—for your delight, of course."

"Wha ...?" She looks, mulls, and then takes a bite. "Mmm, this ain't magic."

Huxley flaps open his cape and lets it float down, and then, lowering his axis, he gently sits. "Most certainly, it's not. But it's very good chocolate. Belgian, I believe ... quite unique—not too dark, not too sweet, and definitely not too nutty. Don't you agree?" He crosses his legs and leans back as though he's waiting for something.

Then, moments later: it happens. She takes another bite—*It's good*—before an epiphany occurs. "Wait, what are you sittin' on?"

"Finger on the pulse ... an astute question." He stands, raising his cape open and up again. Gently he steps to the side, and on the cape's descent, it reveals the blue chair.

Huh? Her head snaps back, looking behind her—*The chair moved.*

"Well, I did offer it to you first ..." he says, "as any gentleman, magic boy or not, should," and steps past her with his crew.

Everyone's astonished, and they swap stunned looks as Huxley paces forward, parting through a wave of silent shrugs.

As he reaches the doorway, someone murmurs, "Wait, is that a grownup?" breaking the silence.

"No, he's forty-two." Huxley nods. "He's my uncle."

"No grownups allowed," the voice states louder, and then he edges forward, uncertain, afraid of some impending doom. His eyes search surrounding stares for support.

There's none.

The teen's name is Dragon. Sixteen, six feet tall, three hundred pounds, thirty sacks and sixty tackles last year. And yet none of those statistics matter at the moment, nor does it matter that his twin brother, Dale, steps into action beside him. Their chests flutter, though not with muscle.

Huxley throws a glance at his uncle, Jed Jules, and then suddenly they burst into laughter, with Jed hunched over, holding his stomach.

"I mean it," Dragon mumbles in nervous tones, more uncertain, placing a hand on Huxley's chest to hold him back. Jed, almost choking with laughter, drops to the ground and rolls side to side.

"Is this your home?" Huxley wonders, calmly looking about before staring at the teen's hand in pity.

"Yes."

"Are you their president?"

"No."

"Are you their luminary?"

"Uh ... no."

A moment lingers before Huxley cuts his eyes to his amply padded shoulder. Then he parts his cape open, and Chester flies off. Flapping his wings, the bird arcs up and soars—wings spread apart, beautifully checkered black and white.

"Chester?" Huxley calls out.

"Aye, master."

"Shall we play a game of *Ches*?"

"With pleasure," he responds, soaring higher.

Everyone is muted, mesmerized, captivated as much as they're confused, watching as the bird circles above, pushing higher.

"Chester ...? Can you please put the 'mister' in Chester?"

And with that, Chester surges even higher, circles once more, and then wends back on a direct aim toward his victim, his wings tucked in, before suddenly halting and dropping something, something that, moments later, is quite clearly a bomb of excrement, pasted on their faces.

"UHHHHHH!" the crowd collectively exhales before

joining in with Jed for a hysterical laugh.

Finally, Jed dishes out, "That's the first Jules Rule: never underestimate the X factor," reaching out to Huxley for a fist bump.

"All right, all right ... you can go in," Dale says. After wiping his face, he looks at his hands with shame, as does Dragon.

"I feel so relieved." Jed laughs.

"As do I," Chester confirms.

And on that note, Huxley steps inside, commanding their respect, commanding their interest, commanding to be heard, with Chester once again adorning his shoulder.

"I need to speak to your leader," Huxley says, treading in, glancing back at Chandler.

"Uh ... hello ... This isn't prehistoric man; we're not some primitive tribe," she retorts. "Not sure whatcha talkin' about. There ain't no leader here."

"Okay, then I'll speak to everyone."

He drifts forward, past their awe, as if in slow motion, and makes his way to the heart of the party. And like an invisible force, the crowd parts, lulled by his mystic calm.

Huxley stops at the head of the room, on elevated ground now, and steps up on a table to address the crowd. He lifts an arm to beseech their attention and invoke their silence, and finding what he seeks, he begins.

"Good evening, everyone!"

The audience claps, and their cheers rise to greet the moment.

"Are you all enjoying the party?"

Sealed with a rocking nod, mouths cupped, the crowd roars another cheer, which echoes off the walls.

21

"It'd be a shame for all this to end tonight, wouldn't it?"

Pumping their fists up, the reveler's shouts boom out as their voices gain momentum.

"In fact," he tosses in, "it would be a shame for this to end at all."

The crowd's cheer crescendos louder and louder, with clapping, stomping, whistling, before Huxley raises a suggestive hand, merging their focus to listen to his next words.

After a hushed second of riveted attention, a mental drum roll ensues, and looking left, looking right, with a decisive nod, Huxley frees a smile and finally delivers, "I have a plan."

HUXLEY'S PLAN
GROUND ZERO

It's 8:30 a.m., the first anticipated day of school—anticipated, of course, not to be fulfilled. No worried faces. No nervous speeches. It's still early.

Students roll in near the docks at Meyersville Harbor: shorts, sandals, t-shirts, and no cell phones. What a wonderful morning. A cool draft surrenders a breeze, adding to the moment.

The yacht's waiting, Jed Jules is at the ship's wheel, his thoughts lost somewhere to ecstasy—his timeless occasion now arrived.

"I pasted the letter on the school door," he finally says, laughing, his mind flipping through the memory before taking a respite. Jed passes Huxley a copy of the message, and curiously, he's made a small modification.

Reading over *their* chosen words, Huxley notes a peculiar line added at the end, penned in a closely matching handwriting. "Cookie jar …?" he mutters. "Jed, we're not children anymore."

"Hey, the Jules Rules: cookie jars aren't just for kids!"

"Indeed, Jed. Indeed. And the gingerbread?"

"Covered! Mailed out of state yesterday with the second package. The chocolates will be sent later from overseas."

"And the phone call?"

"I'll do that just before we leave. Payphone is over there."

Yes, it appears it will be clear sailing, with every detail thought out in advance—equipment, supplies, cargo shipments—and now just waiting to consummate the plan. It's time.

More students arrive, excited, luggage in hand. Chandler wanders in, smiling, cheery as ever, removing her red cap, ready to unleash every thought on her mind. Or so it seems.

"Nice necklace." She points.

Huxley attempts to look down at his chest for a peek, forgetting he can't. His face pops up, and he grins. "Yes. I'm glad you like it. Handcrafted, I imagine."

The silver necklace is a peace symbol with the wings of a soaring bird, laced with gold.

"By the way," she wonders, casting a glance at Jed. "How come your uncle doesn't have a British accent like you?"

"He grew up in Santa Monica."

"Well, that certainly explains a few things." She laughs. A moment passes in confirmative silence while she mulls another inquiry. "Why does he have a different last name?"

"Too many questions," Chester chimes in, watching droves of people rush into the yacht.

"Yes, I forgot again," Huxley fires back. "Is your name Chitter … or was it Chatter?"

As her frown sets in, Chandler stares, visibly miffed.

"One at a time!" Jed calls out, directing students onto the boat, giving each a high-five, a twist, a low one, and then a wiggle.

"So, he's not your real uncle?" Chandler digs in, bouncing back to her earlier thoughts.

Headshake. "Yes, he's my maternal uncle."

"Oh, then what's *your* last name?"

"If I actually thought you could pronounce it, I'd tell you. As it stands, X, it is."

"Try me. I'm good at pronouncing. Everything."

Interesting perspective, probably correct. Huxley, though, is not amused. "Well, I'm certain you have many talents. But there are exceptions."

"You might as well tell me. I'm good at finding things out. You know I'll figure it out eventually."

"Yes … that's what I'm afraid of."

A moment passes in silence as Huxley looks to magically disappear.

"By the way, what happened to your parents?" Chandler asks, realizing only after she's raised the matter that it is neither smooth nor the sensible thing to say.

Huxley sits frozen, his face vacant of expression, his eyes zoned out to nowhere.

"Okay, okay," Chandler concedes with a voice infused with regret, her eyes roving, searching to change the subject. "So, tell us"—she tilts her head sideways, smiling—"did you get into our school because you're a genius, or is it because—"

"I'm rich ... very rich," Huxley breaks in, aborting her question. He's in no mood to wrangle. Standing up, he searches for an escape, and after a moment, he bounces a glance to his bird and calls out, "Chester?"

"Aye, master."

"Shall we play a game of *Ches*?"

"With pleasure," he says, flapping, ready on demand.

And moments later, Huxley makes good on his promise. "What's so special about the knight?"

No response. Chester flies behind Chandler, soaring, twirling, wending above, twisting higher, the sun blinding, flooding her eyes. With her attention deflected, Huxley quietly steps past her, squeezing forward and pushing through the crowd.

Then he casually arrives at the ship's end and waits. No more questions, no rehearsed answers. His mind is at peace when, finally, he looks up and sees Chester arrive.

"And what's so special about the knight?" Huxley repeats aloud.

"It hops its enemy without a fight," the bird answers, descending to perch once again on Huxley's shoulder.

"Fabulous, Chester ... well done."

The yacht's lineup is long, but it comes to pass, and the Dragon Dale brothers dash in. "All aboard!" Jed announces, one fist raised, his other hand firmly on the wheel. They're all set. Cheers rise, excitement fills the air. At last, they're ready to sail to their untold, fond-of destination.

"How long before *he* finds out?" someone shouts.

"Who?"

"Wickly."

26

Emotions buried, nobody responds. A few buzzes and swapped glances, and someone rumbles. A smile emerges, and it's contagious. Indeed, it spreads to a row of smiles, and that's where they'll leave it.

Hopeful and stirred, a new adventure awaits.

YACHT RIDE
ATLANTIC OCEAN

The hour-long journey passes as quickly as their words, accompanied by nothing but the sun, the water, and their excitement. It's summer.

Destination: Planet Next ... A new life, a new beginning, just teens and teens alone, with, of course, Jed. What could possibly go wrong? Or maybe the more relevant question is what could possibly go right? Today it's simply ... everything.

Alas, at some point, every teen daydreams about escaping home. Equal to that force, and often unmentioned, is the parents' fantasy to run away from their children. Percentage of success of each: zero or hovering closely above. The percentage today: one hundred percent.

Chandler does another headcount. "The whole school is here." She smiles, holding back her thoughts for a brief tortured second before relieving herself of the torment. "What a surprise no one called in sick."

Indeed, no one had. It's perhaps the only time the students have all been present on a school day, and maybe the only time they've all been smiling, united in purpose.

Music rings above, a dance floor lies below, while a cool breeze gusts through the deck. The surrounding music ... still outdated. That doesn't sit well with Jed. A frown sets in; his party-loving, happy-go-lucky gospel is all but losing its luster, and so, too, is his patience.

He rises. "They need a lesson in music history, not the history in a music lesson," he mutters as he approaches the deejay, Jaxston Jansen.

He leans forward, cups his mouth, and whispers something; then, with a smile and a wink, he flashes a thumbs-up and treads to the dance floor.

Suddenly the music stops. Heads turn, cheers fade, everyone stares at Jed. He holds court, leading their eyes and their imagination. He's ready. Shades on, face to the sky, he points. "Hit it!"

Jaxston nods: one track—A good one—music floods their ears. Then the medley begins, as does Jed's shuffle. The crowd cheers, hands to the horizon, snap, clap, tap, and the temperature rises ... salsa, mambo, rock and roll, and tango ... popping, locking—Hot damn!—that's disco dancing.

Turntable sounds, new rhythm rounds, he's krumping, stomping—Arms up, everybody—robot dance is coming.

Collective claps reach a fever pitch; next glance, breakdance, next thrill, windmill, then jackhammer and headspin.

The music changes, excitement rages—howling, smiling—a few students start talking.

"The moonwalk again!"

"Yeah, came back in style."

"Whoa ... the running man."

Led by the crowd's roars, he tours music history, each track, new class, before, at last, he cycles back to hop, bop, a jig, and a twist ... and he's done.

Cheers roar.

Chants of their excitement surge above, filling the air.

He nods to their applause—then nods again. In an epic moment of enlightenment, he's living proof that age is just a number; his is just a high one.

The crowd shouts for an encore and endlessly echoes, "Jed! Jed! Jed!"

If they weren't learning, they were certainly entertained.

Concluding the ovation, Huxley turns and views the horizon. "The smell of freedom," he says, shaking his head, stirred with rapture.

"Yes. I imagine it as pizza, burgers, and unlimited hot dogs," Dale tosses in, his head popping up beside Huxley's.

"There's gonna be burgers there, no?" Dragon chirps, his head sliding into the fray, next to Dale's, speaking with an optimistic undertow.

"I don't know." Huxley shrugs. "Chandler is managing the food."

Silence descends, brains churn, and distractions wither before the coal is pressed to a diamond, producing: "Wait ... she's vegetarian, right?" Dragon shoots a glance at Dale, with a sudden screech to their thoughts and a sudden dash to their hopes—their faces robbed of their earlier promise.

The twins stare at each other and then back at the sea, imagining how far a distance it would be to swim back and wondering more measurably if they are of the breed that will float ... or sink.

Deferring to their better judgment, they turn back, silent, forlorn, eyes glazed, empty of pleasure. "Great," they whisper under their collective breaths.

"We'll be there for how long?" Dragon wonders.

"Six months was the plan," Dale mumbles, lost in obscurity.

After a moment, change of mind. Dragon turns and climbs the rail, his sanity lost to the sea, held back only by Dale's arm. "It's okay—don't do it."

He stops and climbs down, and they slowly turn away, with Dale's comforting arm slung around his brother's shoulder. But alas, it's now Dale's turn; he quickly spins back and climbs up, but then Dragon's discovered sanity holds firm, and he pulls his brother back.

"WOOOOWZERS!" Jed shouts and lifts his cap, letting everyone know something monumental is in view. They're home.

"Cheerio," Huxley smiles and turns to the twins. "Come."

Everyone looks to the front where Jed stands, yet no one can see anything but a vast body of blue water, calm and pathless, and a few boulders.

The yacht stops. "We're here," Jed says and turns to the crowd.

"Where?" someone mumbles.

It's a stunner.

Jed ignores the voice and steps forward. "Before we get off, there are a few Jules Rules everyone needs to know." He elevates his chin and thoughts and then begins his party sermon.

Preach. "First rule: tonight we bunk together. Afterward, everyone builds their own tree house. You can work in pairs, or you work in groups, but no matter where you are, we come together for dinner every evening."

Discipline. "Two: if you plan to sleep early, you'll wake up at midnight in the middle of the party."

They cheer, arms raised, clapping, their excitement mounting.

Redemption. "Three: the only thing to wash down a party with is a beach party."

Everyone roars, though nobody's sure where they're staying. Everyone looks out again: there's nothing but blue shimmers, the sun's reflection, and rocks.

Love. "And four," he says to make his final point, "the island is shaped like pi, and that only means one thing." Jed pauses a moment just for the dramatic effect. He's never liked math, and he's never understood pi (π), but if he had to guess, "It's 3.14159265 times the fun!" he booms, throwing up both arms to a score of high-fives from the surrounding students.

Carving out his mantle of provisions, he steps back to the control room and then presses a button, and after a mystic moment, the ship turns 60°, 120° ... 180° ... *What's happening?* It shifts past the boulders and stops. Straight ahead, in clear view now, an island emerges.

"Wow ..." Chandler murmurs.

Jed chuckles. "We passed it while I was dancin'. Just checkin' to see if you were all payin' attention!" he shouts.

They all gaze with fervor, their focus now fixed on the island and its patchwork of hills. The ship drifts closer and closer, and moments later, a freshly painted sign at the dock is spotted. On closer inspection, it has a rustic charm, and its misty words can now be seen more legibly:

PLANET ΠEXT.

Chandler appears next to Huxley. "I like the name."

He nods. "Yes, I thought you'd approve."

This island is draped with a braid of forest as wild as an untamed jungle, and at its center, it's charmed with lake-like waters.

At last, a planet for us, a planet of bliss, a planet without limits.

Imagine that. A place where everyone gets their share and their pi of life.

The yacht docks, and a single file forms. Cheers rise. Anticipation mounts. Everyone's ready.

Phase I of Huxley's plan is now completed. Not that he's keeping score. *Not today.*

He looks to the skies. It's sunny. It's blue. Not a single cloud to blemish the moment. Alluring to one's eyes, it's as peaceful as it is deceptive. A hurricane is on the horizon. There's no time to enjoy this marvel; there's work to be done. They know it. And, quite truly, their lives may depend on it.

PLANET NEXT
FIRST DAY

10:30 a.m., everyone offloads shipping container number one. It arrived from Mexico just a few days earlier. Students lounge around, exchanging jokes, yapping away. Eventually, on Huxley's reminder, they get started: building floodwalls and strategic embankments and clearing the front landscape. There is no wind yet, but it'll come. That's a promise.

Many of the designs were previously conceived and implemented by Jed, but the science aficionados in the group wanted something different. They submitted their proposal, Jed agreed, and the necessary productions were set in motion, along with their delivery to the island.

Seven hundred and fifty-one students: one mission. It will get done in teams of fifty, with Huxley leading the charge. Of course, that's the plan. Jed, as expected of any good host, is putting the final touches to tonight's accommodations and food.

Each student was delegated a task prior to arrival, and Huxley wants everything to flow like clockwork, racing to deadline. It's worth an attempt. Nothing ventured, nothing gained—though it appears the students have their own ventures in mind, schmoozing, slacking, and mingling their way through their work.

Will it be done? Odds of success: zero.

In truth, they debated coming to Planet Next a few days later, but no one was ready to pass over the look on Mr. Wickly's face on the first day of school as he imagined them enjoying themselves as they are now, bantering away.

They are, after all, Floridians. Who are they kidding? In good days or bad, hurricanes are a part of life. Why brush aside such a fortuitous opportunity?

"He won't even think to look for us on an island," Coco murmurs, hoisting a floodwall with a group of ten.

"Who?" Jaxston asks.

"Who else?"

Knowing nods wave through the circle of people. Jaxston's the last to clue in, but he finally gets it.

"With a name like Planet Next, they'll probably think we're leaving the solar system," Coco quips.

Laughter rings out. All cheers, all smiles, everyone takes another break.

The time now: 3:00 p.m.

The sun has already disappeared, hiding somewhere in the sky. Clouds rush in, and in the distance, drapes of black take shape. It's coming.

On the south side, the brainiacs are hosting an argument with the floaters, the floaters are blaming the naturalists, and the naturalists are blaming the clouds.

Worried now, Huxley looks to his leads:

Coco signals thumbs down: Eastern floodwalls not done.

Chandler signals as well: Western floodwalls not done. Not even close.

It's a tidy disaster. Thankfully, no walls are needed for the north. The stopbanks should be enough. The south side, however, needs work, and Huxley would like to direct some members to fortify their efforts there. He can't.

With sunset a few hours away, he's concerned. Alas, there's never calm before a storm; there's wind. And it's already started.

One hard gale, and the eastern floodwalls topple over. The surrounding members watch in shock, their lackluster effort confirmed.

Huxley reminds them they can't quit—failure is not an option. Not on the first day. Not to their teachers. Not to Principal Wickly. The last thing they want to see is a wagging finger tagged to an I-told-you-so moment.

They know.

The time: 7:15 p.m. It's darker; the rain has arrived. It's hard to hear what anyone is saying. Strong winds gust through in stacks of three pulses. The ocean waves rise, crashing against the embankment in stacks of four. Each round, Mother Nature echoes a burst of excitement rumbling through the island. Chester looks north and stares. Huxley knows what that means, but he ignores it.

An hour later, the wind battles harder, revealing its unmatchable force. The western floodwalls drop down like a curtain, succumbing to the waves. Huxley knows what that means. He ignores it again. Jed can't. How could he? Then he raises the call.

The horn sounds three times. How can anyone ignore that? They can't. No compromise, no exceptions. Jules Rule: drop everything and run back.

Jed stands at the edge of the doorway of his underground storm shelter, waving them inside. Everyone rushes in frantically, walking down twelve steps and into the vast space.

They're all dripping, but it doesn't matter. Chandler marches through and does a headcount.

"Two missing."

That matters.

"Are you sure?" Huxley laments.

She nods.

"Who?"

Holding his lantern high, he swings it left and right and paces forward, wading through the crowd, the light casting shadows on their soaked heads. Chandler follows, crossing off names on her list as they elbow past drenched garbs.

Huxley's eyes rove wildly, uncertain, but he has a hunch. Minutes later, in a moment of epiphany, he looks at Chandler, and they chime, "The Dragon Dale brothers."

Worried, angry, and shaking his head, Huxley thinks, *Surely, it's no coincidence.* He's been expecting this one: By accident or intent, if anyone were to challenge a Jules

Rule, it'd be the twins. In defiance, they were never too enamored with a grownup on the island.

Huxley runs and bursts up the stairs in a flash, and on the last step, he calls out, "Chester?"

Prepared as always, his bird responds, "Aye, master."

"Shall we play a game of *Ches*?"

Chester looks to the storm, and despite his DNA telling him to lie in the shadows, his answer, truly and verily: "With pleasure."

Huxley challenges: "Done and gone. Where must we rise to find our pawns?"

A moment later, he thrusts open the door and steps out to disaster. Fighting the wind, he closes the door. At last, Chester flies off and rises, pushing against the gales, bucking his instincts, ascending higher; he circles once, looks, circles again, and then suddenly he descends like a bullet, skimming by Huxley's ear and then flying north.

As with most falcons, he's blessed with night vision and can see ultraviolet light. Nothing is missed.

Following his lead, Huxley sprints as fast as he can, keeping one eye on Chester and the other on the trail, which is marked with sticks, logs, and stones.

It's dark. Huxley's primary visual aid is Chester; his secondary aid is a flashlight.

Meanwhile, at the north end, the Dragon Dale brothers take shelter under a tree. They're lost.

"That dinner wasn't worth this," Dale says, looking at the blustering ocean.

"Nope," Dragon concurs. "And it will be our last one."

They mull their situation—*Perhaps it was worth it, then*—while taking the last bites of their roast beef sandwiches brought from home.

It's dark, it's windy, and they're scared. The rain pounds against their heads. Alone, they huddle, watching the winds swirling around them as water drips from their faces.

"We made a mistake," says Dale.

"Shoulda never come here," agrees Dragon.

"Who comes to an island during a storm?"

"Next week, we invent an excuse and leave."

They nod. It's a sobering realization, or perhaps it's just second thoughts. The idea seemed promising a few days ago. Not anymore.

"I was lookin' forward to Project X."

"Me too."

A clap of thunder lights the skies with a deafening boom. They're petrified. This wasn't what they'd envisioned, and they don't know what to do. Distracted, they suddenly feel something zip past them; then, seconds later, they see it again, flying above.

"What's that?" Dragon points up.

It whizzes by once more, this time circling the tree. It's black, it's white, and it's fast. Before they have a chance to say his name, a flashlight soaks their faces, blinding their eyes.

No voice, no shouts, someone steps closer. Another thunderbolt blasts it fury, lighting the sky, and now they can see his eyes—steeled with purpose. It's Huxley. He's disappointed, and they know it.

They struggle to explain. "We were just … um …"

"Come." Huxley waves, shooting a glance at the food wraps. He already knows.

Walking back with muted steps, no one talks. The only sounds are the cries of the sky.

Finally, they reach the underground bunker. They knock twice, the panel opens, and they hustle in, closing the door after them.

Jed looks at the twins but says nothing. No lectures, no sermons. He's not interested. Their defiance scents the air. He takes a deep breath, smelling onions and something else. With no expression, he nods. Surprised, the Dragon Dale brothers look at each other and add nothing more.

Outside, the rain rages its war, wild and ferocious, battering against the grounds. It's not the start anyone was anticipating. Not like this. What were they expecting? A party? A fantasy land? Whatever they were hoping for, this wasn't it.

Muted emotions define the moment as fear, awe, and adrenaline beat through the chamber. An impending argument is brewing; the teamsters swap stares with the floaters, with everyone else looking on. Their glares hold court, and eventually, eyes drop; nothing transpires. An hour rumbles along, tickling their angst until they are in the throes of despair. Jed reminds them it's happy time. Why pass on happy?

His attempt misses the mark. No one responds. Regret grips them like never before and overtakes the vibe. *What have we gotten ourselves into?* Their imaginations skip along in pixilated colors, pondering the possibilities, knowing the results. Lost in the abyss of their thoughts, they wonder what scene they'll wake up to in a few hours. Will there even be an island?

The winds howl and whistle the night away in high and belligerent tones. No doubt, they're restless, at times fighting to stay alert, now and then fighting to sleep, but more than ever fighting to not surrender to calamity.

Two days later, morning arrives with a curious sound: silence. Students wonder what that implies.

"We might be underwater?" someone says.

"Beneath a tree, more like it," warns another.

"Nah ... under the sand," a voice chirps.

Whatever it is, they're about to find out. Huxley walks up the steps. He gently pushes the bunker door and then stops. He's surprised. It jutted forward with ease. Curious now, he thrusts it open, and much to his delight, a flood of light pours through, unrestrained.

He looks back to a row of smiles. He nods. Stepping outside, he quietly gazes about, adding his grin. Chandler and Jaxston stand beside him, and other students follow. They can't believe it: no rain, no wind, just clear skies. The sun has returned, and so have their hopes.

All around are broken branches, sand piles, damaged docks, and no floods. They'll take it. It could've been worst. For sure, there's work to do. They messed up; they know it, and they've seen the result. But they also know they've survived, perhaps, an even bigger test: living together under one roof.

Nodding at the opportunity and grateful for their good

fortune, everyone knows what they must do.
   It's time to build their new home.

PLANET NEXT
DAY SIX

Tucked in bed, forty feet above sea level, Huxley claps his eyes to the stars and reflects on the week gone by: dodging a tornado, completing his tree house, offloading cargo, storing food, allocating resources, deploying students, determining future occupations. It's been an interesting week.

The midnight moon glows like a projector, arcing higher and higher before dimming, sinking, and bowing back to the horizon. Charming.

Tonight is the first night they sleep in their tree houses. Tired and worn out, he closes his lids, listening to nothing but the melody of birds, the waterfalls nearby, and the evening's cool breeze. Indeed, it's calming.

He smiles. "Goodnight, Chester."

"Goodnight, master."

"Sleep tight."

They intend to. A few minutes pass in silence. Soothing

as it is, Huxley drifts deeper into sleep, his thoughts drawn to heaven. Then, almost as though abruptly awakened from a vivid dream, hoping to close his eyes and immerse back in it to its conclusion, he hears that peculiar sound:

"Huuuuxleeey."

The name is pleasant, the melody soft, the tone stretched, the voice eerie familiar.

"Huuuuxleeeeeey." The tone stretches longer; the voice is more than familiar.

Ignore it. Sure enough, denial sets in before indecision overtakes him. *Impossible.* Then he reasons, *this* impossible is still possible. A quarrel is brewing in his mind, digging, defending, pondering, sorting the logic—*the Dragon Dale brothers are my neighbors. How can this be?* The voice once again calls out, "Huuuuuxleeeeeeey ..." leaving no doubt.

Chandler! His head lifts, but he's too timid to peek out. Frozen in thought, his eyes lock onto the vines and lianas hanging softly outside his window.

"HUUUUUUXLEEEEEEY."

This will not end.

Rubbing his eyes now, he pretends that he's just woken up; he needs a good show to avert a longer discussion. But, alas, even Huxley can't avert this surprise.

"What are you doing here?" he mutters, peeking through the window of his tree house at the adjacent one. "I've could've sworn Dragon and Dale built this tree house. If I recall, you were assigned the northeast side of the island."

She smiles, perched on her window, leaning on the ledge. "I can only sleep with a south view ... and since

Dragon and Dale moved in with Jed, this room was, well …"

"Wait … did you just say Dragon and Dale moved in with—"

She nods. "Jed."

"But I thought they didn't like him?"

Shrug. "They seemed pretty upbeat when I saw them."

It doesn't make sense. Cutting his eyes away, Huxley slowly lies back on his bed. He has the look of someone attempting to decode a riddle that can't be solved.

"Huuuuxleeeey."

His head pops up, and he shoots her a glare. "Yes, Chandler?" he says in a resigned tone.

"I can't sleep. There's too much moonlight."

Huxley looks to the skies and nods. "I'll turn it off in a couple of weeks. I promise."

A minute passes in rumination before she remembers. "Wait … there won't be a moon in two weeks. It will be a new moon."

"Yes," Huxley mutters. "Precisely."

"But—"

"Goodnight, Chandler."

"Don't you think—"

"Goodnight, Chandler."

At 7:00 a.m., the sound of the breeze wafts through the jungle, as does the chirps of the birds and the cicadas, echoing from dwelling to dwelling. It's a delightful morning.

The air: crisp. Its heat: comforting. And oddly, in light of the season, it's not yet moist. There's still time.

The morning cocktail of nature and beauty is stirred to perfection with one exception: a fly is sitting on Huxley's nose, and several more hover above, looking for a runway to land.

His eyes flick open, his arm lifts, his hand opens ... tracking ... tracking ... and snatch; it's captive, now locked. At last, Huxley is alert, his reflexes fine as ever.

Silence resumes, and rolling over, he lifts his head to look through the window and stare at the world beyond, now a world of wonder.

The island is a masterpiece of colors, with trees and nature acquired from every continent on the globe. It's truly a mosaic of the world.

A new civilization begins: theirs. First, though, he must pay a visit to Jed and ensure that he's certifiably safe from the hands of the twins, who suddenly have struck a friendly chord and nestled and cozied up with his uncle. It's a bizarre turnabout of disposition; they weren't so welcoming at the opening party and their first night on the island.

Rising up, stretching, muscle knots and everything, he steps out to the window, stands, listens, and smells the trees. Then he peers across the waters at the adjacent homes.

Though it's still incomplete, Jaxston's tree house looks stunning. There's a man with a dream. Mulling in silence, Huxley wonders if it looks like a country home, or perhaps a villa. He settles on a Roman villa. Still, he debates further ... well, definitely European.

Situated beside it, the series of tree houses are distinctly

Mediterranean: windows, skylights, open spaces, sharp lines, and spiral staircases—inviting as ever and truly a visual renaissance of the imagination.

To the west, there's a dashing attempt at innovation. Huxley appreciates the challenge of the architecture. Difficult? Yes. Impossible? No. Asian tree houses decorate the horizon: blocky, symmetrical shapes and multi-inclined rooftops, as alluring as the hemlock and vines that grace its foundation.

As for the north, well, that's interesting, quite remarkable, actually. It's big, huge, quite frankly. *What would one call that?* he wonders. *Oh, yes ...* American as ever. The vibe is somewhat overwhelming.

Huxley turns to the south, listening to the charming sounds. Atop the central hill, the waterfalls crush through the adjacent rocks, splashing down, burbling, bubbling, and rippling over the waters below.

Turning slightly, Huxley shifts gaze to the sundial clock tower, anchored in the open space. It's still unfinished, visible from most of the island ... which reminds him, *Yes, that's right—time to see Jed.*

Stepping away, he sees a friendly face. "Good morning, Chester."

"Good morning, master."

"Shall we go for a walk?"

"Aye, master," the bird chimes, flapping its wings to perch upon Huxley's shoulder.

In measured steps, Huxley treads down the stairway. Then he reaches for a woody vine and ropes down the last segment before jumping on the soil below.

Alone, he roams through the jungle, overstepping logs

and passing orchids, mosses, bromeliads, and ferns. One mile into his journey, away from everyone else, at last, he sees Jed's tree house.

Huxley ponders the structure. He's not quite sure what to label this one. Interesting, yes; simple, no. It's definitely creative. And it's definitely Jed. A moment passes ... *Ah, the citadel,* and debating further ... perhaps he'll just leave it at that.

He marches up the hill and draws closer to the fortress, listening to the birds' murmurs morph into tunes of pleasure.

Then, curiously, he also notes a detectable smell, and after a second take, he sniffs. *Smoke?* he wonders. Alarmed, he looks up and sees dots of mist floating to the sky.

What's happening? There's no time to ponder. In a flash, he races up the hill to find Jed, Dragon, and Dale, laughing, exchanging humor, sharing food with arms slung over shoulders.

It's as relieving to the eyes as it is bizarre. On closer inspection, it's not just any food they're sharing: more precisely, it's steaks, burgers, and hotdogs.

On seeing Huxley, Dragon and Dale stand straight, stop speaking, and look around. They seem panicked.

Huxley nods. "No worries, mate. The food police are not with me."

A collective, "Phew," escapes from their relieved mouths, and they sit down. Jed smiles and stands at the BBQ grill, armed with a spatula and looking much like a general preparing for battle.

He flips a burger and winks. "S'up?"

"Nothing," Huxley mumbles, still surprised by the sight—unexpected and pregnant with oddity. "Is that a barbeque?"

"It's electric. No fire. Don't worry. We'll live."

"Indeed."

"Man, you got the coolest uncle," Dragon chimes in, slinging an arm around Jed's shoulder as he watches his wizardry with the spatula ... a twirl, double flip, triple axel, and then back on the grill, squeezing down ... more heat, more sizzle ... *Ahh* ... before throwing in, "We learned more from Jed the last few days than our whole time at school." He reaches out to Jed for a fist bump.

"He sure is a bag full of tricks," Huxley affirms. "A wealth of wisdom ..."

"We'd give anythin' to see him surf again," Dale says, pointing to a stack of pictures of Jed in swimwear.

Huxley looks on, amused at their sudden spell of ardor. *Fascinating, no doubt.* He smiles, still trying to digest the moment.

Dragon nods. "When we get the windmill runnin', we'll have enough electricity to power the waves."

It was installed earlier in the summer, and there's obviously some work to do before its deployment.

"So, you're all bunking together?" Huxley asks, changing the subject. He clearly underestimated the twins.

"Uh-huh ... we sleep downstairs." He points above. "Jed only sleeps penthouse."

Staring at the grill in disbelief, Huxley reminds them, "You realize it's probably time for breakfast?"

"Actually, we didn't sleep last night." Dragon laughs. "Technically, this is late supper." He reaches up to Jed for a high five.

The brotherly interlude is suddenly interrupted.

"What's goin' on here?" a soft voice declares in the distance, joyously coming up the stairway.

Huxley gives a quick to the twins. "Sorry, my mistake; the food police, the mob—"

"And the mighty falcon," Chester cuts in.

"Are all here."

That distinguished honor, of course: Chandler.

Jed's wizardry turns into sorcery of closure and, more succinctly, the hiding of all evidence: food wraps, smoke, the various scents, as well as their excited and ardent expressions.

Walking onto the patio, she winces, takes a deep breath, and mulls things over. She says nothing.

Neither does anyone else.

She looks around, and noting the portable BBQ, she wonders a little and points. "What's cookin' here?"

A reasonable question, no doubt. And she's good for a few more.

Raising an eyebrow, Dragon does a headshake. Emotions sealed, only his thoughts march freely with fear.

"Oh, nothin' … just havin' an early breakfast," he remarks, standing in front of the grill, blocking her view.

A curious look dawns on her face. The scent: familiar. Its memory: distant. "Smells good. What is it, if I may ask?"

They swap looks, their eyes bouncing around like they're in a pinball machine. No one says a word.

Silence hovers.

Dragon nods to Chester, as does Dale. "Does Chester

want to play *Ches?*" they chime.

Unfortunately, no magic, not even the *Ches*-master, can save this moment.

Chester doesn't move, doesn't reply. He's not amused. He stares, darting a scornful eye, mounting a response with just his inaction, and with every passing second, the tension rises.

Chandler notes the peculiar behavior, and drawn by a premonition, she reaches for the BBQ grill handle. But then she stops. Waiting a beat, she begins to lift the lid, her eyes open—no judgment, not yet.

Jed reaches out and lightly grabs her arm. "It was supposeta be a surprise," he reveals with his good guy accent. "But go on. It's okay ... We did this for you."

Curious, suspicious, yet enamored by Jed's chosen words, she slowly lifts the cover and sees the various food items she never eats.

Swinging somewhere in the jungle of her thoughts, chilled to the marrow, she stares, her lips sealed.

Jed stares on, and if he had to guess—and he might as well do so—he'd arrive at: "It's Texan." Adding a nod, he tosses in, "And it's tofu."

She looks with wonder, her thoughts floating somewhere, somewhere that neither Jed nor the Dragon Dale brothers care to speculate about. She smiles. It's as transformative as it is infectious, and it overlaps with their relief. They all look to each other and grin.

Texan tofu.

A nod, a shrug, Dragon drops his chin. "Would you like some?"

MADISON SCHOOL
DAY SEVEN

In the full auditorium, parents bustle in with hurried faces, cramming inside, looking for seats. None are available. It's standing room only.

This is the fifth gathering this week. They're worried.

Time: 6:00 p.m.

Anxious voices sputter to hushed whispers as the parents sense the start of the evening meeting. Mr. Wickly marches to the podium, his gait still rigid, his heart frail with doubt, his eyes lit with anger. *Huxley X.*

"Thank you for coming tonight," he announces, speaking above the reach of their fear, gulping down what's left of his saliva, gazing about.

Unclenching his lips, he tilts his head and says, "We still have no word on your children."

The crowd responds with an outburst of cries.

"They're starving,"

"How are they going to survive?"

"Where are they gonna live?"

Guilty. The room comes alive: headshakes, angry gestures, parents throw up arms in outrage. It's time to vent.

"They'll be lost without us," a man frees from his lips.

"What'll they do alone?" an unidentified voice shouts from the back.

"They'll go crazy!" a woman yells in front, adding to the soundtrack.

The sobs drone on. Indeed, the daily gathering with Mr. Wickly has produced no clues, no results, and the police chief, Nelson Ross, who'd previously dismissed the letter as a prank, has now, after much pleading, conceded to meet the parents.

Amidst gestures for calm, the voices fade, but the stares remain, fixed on one man: Mr. Wickly. "I know you're anxious," he resumes, "and that's why I called the local police to come tonight to say a few words. Please let me introduce to you ... Chief Ross."

A few claps, a few whispers, nobody is calm.

Chief Ross yanks up his pants by the belt, but they meet a formidable barrier, his gut, and drop back down like a rock. With a businesslike manner, as much as he can drum up, he steps to the podium and leans into the lectern. After reflecting for a second, he starts to speak, hesitates, and then reflects some more before finally announcing, "You didn't wanna spank your kids." He shrugs. "This is what happens."

His counsel falls short of the mark. The room explodes: parents yelling at the chief, parents shouting at each other, fingers pointing, teachers refereeing. It's a mess.

"Order ... we need order!" Mr. Wickly shouts, lifting up a decisive hand. "Everyone ... please sit down."

After some semblance of peace, the voices surrender, and the chief, shifting his tone, carries on. "The important thing is ... we know they've done this by choice. They weren't kidnapped. No ransom, no hideous crime. And let's remember, they did begin and end the letter by saying they love you. C'mon, you know them better than anyone else," he says, striking a more conciliatory pitch. "You know how lost they'd feel without you. And how do you figure this will end? What exactly happens when you have a group of teens livin' together?" He doesn't wait long to deliver his answer. "Chaos, that's what happens."

Adding a reassuring nod, he continues. "There's a reason Florida is shaped like a gun. We know regulated order. We'll get 'em, don't you worry. And keep in mind ... they did say they're grounding themselves. Why would they say that? Why, because they know they're wrong, that's why! Give it some time. They'll miss you. When that happens, and it will, they'll be beggin' to come home. You'll see."

MEANWHILE ON PLANET NEXT

"PAAARTYYYY!"

With hugs aplenty, the crowd cheers as lanterns light the skies, blue, red, gold, and white—each filled with wonder. It's a blast. And the evening is not yet dark.

There has been nothing but rain for a few days. Although it's hurricane season, the island, so far, has been mostly outside its destructive grip. Having repaired what's marred, they now make up for lost time.

Tonight they celebrate. Hopping, bopping, everyone is dancing away—the music current and delightful. Jed's message has finally hit home.

As they dance on the shore, heads suddenly turn; a sea of eyes looks up. Descending the stairs, Huxley appears, wearing bowtie and tuxedo, with Chester nestled comfortably on his shoulder.

"There's Hux in a tux!" someone shouts.

"Lookin' good, my man."

"Broooo ..." chimes in another.

Reports come in sequence as he passes each student.

"We've planted vegetative farms on the north side of the island; it will keep us sustainable, once our food supply runs out," Chandler says.

"Well done," Huxley replies.

Coco steps forward. "Our compost is biodegradable now, and our new clean-up device will be clearing the ocean of the debris arriving from the mainland."

"Wonderful."

"The windmills are ready. The solar panels will take a few more weeks, as will the hydroelectric power," Dragon says, his toe bleeding from a long day of labor.

Huxley's quite pleased.

"We've planted seeds to help support the existing wildlife to maintain our ecosystem," Jonathan explains.

"Splendid! Good work."

At Chandler's suggestion and Huxley's direction, she advocated that each student dedicate themselves to one task for the betterment of their new planet. Point taken, point received. And the students were allowed to volunteer their services if they desired. At the last count, participation was thirty percent.

Feeling a wave of satisfaction, Huxley walks down the last few steps. Suddenly he sees a campfire. He stares, silenced by its glow. "Who started this?" he finally mutters. "I thought everyone knew … no fires."

"We've had nothing but rain the last few days," Coco tries to explain.

Huxley gazes at the trees. "Fire and forest make a precarious mix. If you don't mind, put that out. Our lives may depend on it."

Coco nods.

Huxley smiles, not wanting to cast a pall over the moment. Tonight, of course, they party.

Uncle Jed asked Huxley to arrive by 8:00 p.m. to unveil his latest invention. Anticipation has swelled, as has expectation. Everyone's curious; no one underestimates. Not anymore. This is Jed. Say his name.

"What does your uncle do for a living?" Jaxston asks.

"I think that's what he wants to show you." Huxley nods.

Indeed, Jed is a man of many thoughts, many talents, Santa Monica's own five-time surf champion. He promoted his sport to unexplored markets, and his first entrepreneurial endeavor: selling bathing-suit underwear. It never gets wet. An undiscovered market, as he called it, for the conservative and imaginatively discrete.

His calculated pitch evolved to his next endeavor, saucier, gutsier ... the surfing Vibeboard. The reassuringly conventional choice: surf in your business attire without swimming, without touching the water, riding the board, riding the air, riding nature. A pioneer? Sure. Audacious? Why not? One thing they know for certain: This man has vision.

And today he will unveil his latest, grandest invention. Speaking with his customary charm, Jed announces, "And now the newest Jules Rule: What do you do if you're bored at a party?"

A trick question, yes, but perhaps one that is not meant to be answered, one that's best left to be answered by the man himself. That being noted, despite conventional wisdom, Jaxston attempts anyway.

"You can't be bored? Not at a party."

"Nope," Jed replies.

Jaxston tries again. "You stand outside."

Jed shoots back a glare, muting Jaxston with his look.

He looks around as everyone thinks, and a hint of a smile creeps onto his face. The answer will likely arrive shortly. A purr is heard, then a hum, mounting to a buzz, and his smile widens, showing his teeth. Emerging behind him, something slowly rises, inch by inch, and stops. Covered by a tarp, it seems to be a disk-like object forty feet in diameter.

Jed's smile curls now; he's not even tempted to glance over his shoulder. He's taking pleasure in seeing the clueless expressions pasted on their faces.

Thanking the waters, he repeats his question, "What do you do when you're bored at a party?" He turns to Huxley. "Will you please do the honors?"

And without further delay, like he's unveiling a Michelangelo statue, Huxley pulls the tarp off just as Jed chimes, "You step on a Partyboard."

As everyone watches a series of breath-holding moments kick in, someone lets out, "Whoooaaaa," followed by a chorus of inspired words:

"Damn!"

"Sick!"

"It's a beast!"

"Un-be-*lieve*-able."

It arouses the imagination, as it should. White lights trim the perimeter, above and below, lighting the ground and the surrounding waters. A few lights flash, arm rails come up, and the music turns on. Jed presses a button and steps majestically descend from the saucer and stop. It's time to get on board.

"Fifty at a time," Jed says as people excitedly jostle to look over rival shoulders.

Party members step up, one by one, hoping to be the first to be thrilled, helped by none other than Huxley X, who provides, as always, a gentlemanly arm.

With the first batch on deck, Jed shouts, "It's party time!"

The Partyboard glides around the waters within the island's pi. It fluidly roves, ascending higher. Every witness is spellbound. The music is calm, and it's as soothing to the ears as the lanterns are to the eyes. Stars drape the skies as sunset nears. Truly, the night has just begun.

Dolphin tails join in. Their beaks emerge, as do their smiles. They swim. Stop. Submerge before a leap, a dive— and then a few more. Their movements: synchronized to evoke wonder.

As the dolphins capture everyone's attention, with peaceful steps, the partygoers drift to the rails and lean forward, enjoying the friendly creatures of the water. And with the next breeze, all their senses fill with life.

"They're gray," someone mentions.

"So beautiful ..." says another.

Staring curiously, deep in thought, Dale mutters, "That one has big teeth."

"That one's a shark," Huxley calmly utters, perched on the rails.

"Wait a minute ...?" Dragon says, peering closer at the creature surfacing beside the first shark, realizing that it's actually a second ... "SHAAAAARK!"

Panic sets in, and every member pulls back from the rails, bracing themselves as one shark emerges higher and looks up with an open mouth.

"What's the matter?" Huxley gazes about, confused, uncertain about everyone's bizarre reaction.

"Look!" shouts Chandler in fright. "Dragon's foot ... it's bleeding!"

The screams that erupt from the group are punctuated only by their gasps. "They! Can! Smell! Blood!" Everyone points.

Huxley walks to the ledge and stares down—fright has not found him. He smiles. "They can't smell your blood, I assure you. But they can smell your fear." After a beat, he adds, "There is no need to be worried."

Heeding his words, they embrace, lost in terror; the reassurance does little to bring calm, and they step away, not trusting the ledge, dread pasted on their faces. Dale holds up an unsettled arm, still pointing at the unwelcomed creature. He's not sure what to say.

Huxley mulls things over for a moment, sensing an obligation to do something, anything, perhaps everything to ease their minds and those riveted stares. Not an easy task.

Bouncing a look to his shoulder, he calls out. "Chester!"

With delight, those falcon eyes lock on Huxley's. "Aye, master."

"Shall we play a game of *Ches*?"

Flapping skyward, the bird pipes up, "With pleasure."

A moment passes as everyone watches him fly in circles, and as he wends closer, Huxley asks, "What must be done to capture the queen?"

Simultaneous to his command, Huxley pulls a lever, lowering the Partyboard closer to the water, and seconds later, the shark emerges—its eyes lidless, boasting a full smile. Delightfully, each tooth is as white as the next. Huxley holds his arm out to capture its focus. Can he do it? Believe it! His fingers are drawn together like a lotus flower waiting to be unfurled. Gliding his arm to and fro in arced motions, he opens and closes his fingers, slowly directing the shark's attention to Chester, who is now flying in circles above, his wings stretched to the limit. The checkered black and white wings mesmerize and mellow the shark, as every so often they retract and extend, morphing squares into diamonds, back and forth, in reciprocal series.

As Chester circles, he winds lower, and on each round, the shark watches, increasingly sedated. When it's finally motionless, Huxley moves closer and closer, and at last, he can view his reflection in those marbled, stock-still eyes.

It's hypnotic.

Huxley reaches out with a gloved hand and gently pats the shark, calming it with his touch. Beneath the bitterly angry face, beneath the knife-like teeth, and beneath the bone-crunching jaws, Huxley senses something more, a deeper emotion, something sinister. There's hurt. There's resentment. There's the torment of centuries of human mistreatment: overfishing, finning, the shark's distorted portrayal, the insidious rumors, and remorseless condemnation.

"More than anything, they need our love," Huxley murmurs, bringing his nose to touch the shark's snout, rubbing gently, and pulling back an inch before being magnetically drawn back.

"Huh …? What the hell?" Dragon mumbles, finally opening his eyes.

"Geez, you gotta be kiddin' me," Dale says, and he draws closer, as does his brother, with the others trailing behind.

Nothing can underscore the moment. A mixture of fright and curiosity crosses their faces, and as they come forward, their fear melts away with every small step.

Huxley watches them, amused at their interest. Regrettably, he underestimates their marine insight and turns his head back, oh, so briefly, to passively wave Chandler closer.

Kneeling close to the shark, Dale murmurs, "Wow …" and stretches forth a hand to gently feel its teeth.

Dragon smiles and nods. "That's one helluva …"

Just as he utters those words, in a swift motion, the shark's mouth opens wider than Dale's head, and in one quick snap, it abruptly clamps down, slicing into action.

Screams ring out, and Huxley turns as Dale yanks back his hand. It's bleeding.

Stirred by fear, more screams roll in, this time from Dale. His mouth is wider than the shark's.

"It's just a graze," Huxley says … *Phew* … his mind now at ease. "Thank goodness."

A collective gasp of relief sweeps through the group, and Huxley adds, "Never put a hand in their mouth … I said they need more love, not more food." He resumes his healing, soothing stroking of the hypnotized shark.

Seconds later, a pod of dolphins draws closer, also entranced by the moment, while Chester concludes his efforts. At last, the bird rests, once again, comfortably perched on Huxley's padded shoulder.

Huxley stares at the sharks and wonders. He has something in mind. It's crazy yet charming. *Can it be done?* He's not sure. But it does serve a purpose. And if anyone can do it, well, it might as well be him.

He doesn't say anything; he just looks up. His gaze is cryptic, but his smile is even more mysterious. Jed knows it, and the Dragon Dale brothers see it, too, but they all know better than to ask him what he's thinking.

Soon enough, they'll find out.

MADISON SCHOOL
DAY FOURTEEN

The night is young, but regrettably, the parents are not. Every day, every hour, they feel more restless and further away from joy. Solemnly they sit. The auditorium is full.

"They're hungry," one parent sobs, comforted by another.

"My daughter would never do this," laments a mother before shooting an angry eye at a familiar parent.

After a confused moment of swapping stares, the blame game officially begins, with each parent faulting the other for their child's influence on their offspring. The floating accusations bounce about, member to member, like a game of tag that never ends ... always a moving target, always a moving narrative. By design, everyone is *it* except themselves.

Ignoring the pandemonium, Mr. Wickly approaches the podium, smiling, a self-satisfied expression on his face. This is the first manifestation of joy he's demonstrated since this fiasco began. He has news.

He raises a hand to beckon for customary silence, but nobody pays attention. At last, shouts calm to hushed voices. He begins.

"Mothers, fathers, grandparents, thank you all for coming tonight on such short notice. We know you're concerned, and we appreciate your patience. It's been a long week, but I believe we're on the cusp of turning the corner. Your children have made contact."

One sigh, two claps, fifteen hundred stares, no one is relieved. They're not out of this mess. Not even close. Everyone tunes in to his next words.

"We received a package today. While it may not be what some of you may want to hear, it's a start. More important is what it signifies: an attempt to establish a dialogue. It appears your children have also chosen their medium for these negotiations. As such, I will ask the chief to share with you the letter we've received."

Chief Ross steps forward but then stops; he nods to the audience, his eyes roving about, unsure if he actually shares Mr. Wickly's enthusiasm. Relieving himself of his dilemma, he shrugs. "The morning package had various boxes of gingerbread cookies—and a letter attached to it." He waits a moment and then jaws on. "There's something … something important your children want to be known."

Feeling the weight of the moment, he's uncertain how to proceed. After a headshake, he looks down and struggles to unfold the letter, but ultimately opens it. Then, he puts on his glasses, stares at the page, and after some musing, decides it's best to deliver it … unfiltered. He shoots a glance at the audience and then drops his eyes and reads:

Dear Grandparents,

We adore you ... forever! You're the only ones who actually get us and understand where we're coming from. We miss you. A lot!

Our only regret in leaving and doing what we did is, well, *you*. Just *YOU!*

You, it is, who symbolizes our fondest memories. *You*, it was, who ceaselessly sheltered us from our mutual villain. *You*, and always you, understood what it meant to have common sense ... and used it.

Truly, our most valued lessons in life were learned with our palms comfortably nestled in yours: curiosity, compassion, kindness, understanding ... You're the best. And it is with these lessons in mind that we begin our journey—a journey to enlightenment.

Our parents griped about you. They whined. They scorned. Shhh ... we didn't listen. How could we? After all, it was *you* who shone a light into our lives— brightly and for eternity.

We didn't choose our parents, but if we had to choose our grandparents, we would choose you every time.

Please don't be upset. We never wanted to leave you, not like this, not ever ... which is why we're sending you the gingerbread man—our common friend—in loving memory of our times.

Hugs and kisses from afar.

XOXOXO ... to infinity,

Your Grandkidz

P.S. We always understood why you spanked them. Always.

Resting the letter on the lectern, the chief stands stoically before looking up and removing his glasses. He holds back his thoughts against the silence, but he can't resist the temptation. It's too much. He finally doles out, "I rest my case."

An outburst of anger rings through the auditorium: shouts, curses—the blame game now drives full steam ahead.

The chief shrugs and calls for order. After a few seconds, the sounds finally wither to chirps, and then, the last of the purrs subside, and there's silence once again.

"Look on the positive side," he says. "They seem like bright kids."

"They're minors—bring them home!" someone shouts to rounds of claps, cheers, and one thumbs up from a mother sitting in front, swinging it left and right.

Nodding his head and readjusting his pants, the chief continues. "Yes, they may be minors, but you gotta admit … they're damn smart. These ain't no lunatics for us to run out and save society from. Their words, their views, are well thought out and have a premeditated purpose. And I want ya to think about this. What happens when we bring 'em home? They'll just run away again."

The crowd replies with grunts and murmurs.

Sensing this is a good moment to intervene, Mr. Wickly steps forward as the voice of reason and leans over to the microphone. "For every weakness," he declares, "there's a challenge to reveal it. We're still trying to understand why this has happened. Our school, our curriculum, our technology, our behavioral expectations of our staff are unprecedented in their scope. This outburst has many unspoken layers that must be explored. But rest assured ... we'll find your children."

Gesturing her agreement, Mrs. Andrews indicates to Mr. Wickly that she desires to come to the front, discerning a need to disclose her sentiment.

"Good evening," she says loudly, speaking too close to the microphone. Her voice echoes. Inching back to a safe distance, she carries on. "Many of you know me. I've worked at this school for more than twenty years. I know almost all of your children."

Nodding, she continues. "As much as I don't want to say this, I feel it'd be dishonest not to share my feelings." After gaining everyone's full attention, she adds, "I think that more than anything, we have to start asking the tough questions. Why did they do what they did? What led them down this path? If it was just the school they were frustrated with, there are other solutions than running away. Solutions they chose not to explore. Solutions they didn't express to us."

One parent shouts, "You're forgetting that they said they hate their teachers!"

Everyone claps. Mr. Wickly stands quietly, his head hanging low, his emotions sealed.

Mr. Farnsworth steps forward, tilts sideways, and pushes his face in front of the microphone. "Hi, I'm the school psychologist. Most of you don't know me ... though ... by now, most of you should," he utters in hesitant tones. "I agree with Mrs. Andrews. We can't have a constructive discussion about this matter without looking at the genesis of the problem and, of course, its psychological implications."

Frustration stirs, and angry eyes rivet on him. His collar begins to tighten as he suddenly feels a lump in his throat. Beads of sweat line his brow; one begins to drip down. Feeling its trickle, he stutters, "I-I'm going to-to suggest we take a break ... perhaps meditate on the problem, meditate on the solution, and possibly meet again in a few days."

At last, the chief steps forward and puts a friendly arm around Mr. Farnsworth, directing him to step aside. His time is up, and the chief will fittingly cap off the evening with his wise words.

"That's a good suggestion." The chief nods. "In the meantime, we're gonna try and track down where this letter came from. But like I said, you can curb a person's freedom and constitutional rights only so much. They will do what they will do." He shrugs. "This is one of the great things about our country: freedom." Quite candidly, if there's one thing the chief wishes for the parents, it's that the call of freedom echoes in their ears—from now to eternity. But he leaves them with one conciliatory note. "Wherever they are, whatever they're doin' ... they're bored. They'll be comin' home any day now. Trust me."

PLANET NEXT
DAY TWENTY

Five days of anger management, and that's all it took, just five. Group therapy, as Huxley called it.

Now everyone's eager to see its ultimate result.

In tux and cape, Huxley descends the stairs of his tree house and, with purpose, runs toward the water. The crowd cheers him on. He's made them a promise. So far, there's been no magic, no charm, no nothing. It's time—Huxley time—to deliver.

At last, today is a day reserved for respite, and it's as good a time as any for Planet Next to enjoy the moment. Jaxston holds court on stage, singing a slow song that shifts into a fast one. He dances and jiggles, moving his feet faster and faster. Capping off his song, he throws an arm up like a rock star and points to the sky. Then he cuts his eyes to the deck and runs, and when he reaches the end, he jumps, knees up, and lands in the boat.

Meanwhile, making his way down the hill and bolting

with steam, Huxley signals to Jaxston to start the engines.

Thumbs up, a fist, and then the motorboat rumbles, rousing the crowd to revelry. Revving sounds—*vroom, vroom*—echo above their roars, and he's off! The boat spins, picks up speed, and bursts forward, towing a water-ski rope that unrolls from the docks.

Everyone rises from their seats and goes nuts.

Huxley reaches full tilt, and on nearing the ocean, he whistles, nods, points. He's set. He hits the docks, and in one fluid motion, his left hand grabs the water-ski handle, and he reaches above for the lianas with his right and swings above the water, dangling to heaven.

Airborne and at his peak, he lets go, landing flatfooted—a splash—in the water. Then he blasts off, moving at warp speed, pulled only by the towrope.

The flood of water sprinkles sideways, tracking his path. The crowd roars, hopping, clapping, and yelling in excitement.

No kiteboarding, no kneeboarding, no hot-dogging, no spotter, no slalom. Huxley has something else in mind.

"Wow, he's barefoot waterskiing," says Chandler.

"Nope, he's not actually barefoot." Dragon smiles. "His skis are white."

Don't trust your eyes. She squints against the sun. The odd shapes under the water roam curiously to meet Huxley's feet. They move in unison, and on close inspection, she realizes they're gray, big, and certainly not white.

Dragon and Dale high-five and cheer, fists raised, cycling madly, pointing back.

"Wait, are those sharks?" she wonders.

"Uh-huh … great *whites*." Dragon high-fives Dale again.

Chester flies above, charming the air, swirling as expected, keeping a close eye on Huxley.

Someone throws a hat … a leap, a stretch… Huxley grabs it with a perfect snatch. Winking, he puts it on and waves. Then he takes it off again, and wouldn't you believe it: two doves are sitting on his head.

The crowd laughs and then claps, and the doves fly by, wending to the skies.

Two acts done, but he's good for a third. The boat takes another turn, this time closer to the crowd. Removing his bowtie, Huxley raises it in the air: a shake, a wiggle, and— take a close look—out pops a bouquet. Laughs and cheers echo, and he throws it to the young ladies sitting in the sand.

Then Huxley cues the twins, and Dale, looking to the control board, pulls a lever. Dragon presses a switch. Waves motion in, and now the third act begins.

The crowd applauds with hands above their heads, sensing something grand. They want more.

Huxley arcs behind the wave and disappears from view; seconds pass in silence, and as the wave fades … *What?* He's vanished, and so has Jaxston.

Time rumbles with the audience in suspense—no Huxley, no boat. *Where have they gone?* The crowd watches at the edge of their seats, and now, as a second wave rolls through, suddenly emerging from the deep blue wave, a boat crashes through … Everyone blinks. *This can't be!* Huxley's on the boat, driving, his attire now swimwear. Jaxston sits in the rear, fishing, wagging the rod and waving at their ovation.

Everyone goes wild. Huxley throws up two fish, and great whites emerge. They jump, snatch, and, noses down, splash. It's a beautiful morning.

The crowd screams with relief. Was that enough? It sure was. But they want to be thrilled again, and Huxley will give them something nobody expects. And they know it.

Another wave appears ... larger. Emerging on his surfboard, Jed pops into view. *You don't say!*

The crowd goes bonkers.

Jed paddles with his arms, not looking back. Instead, with his eyes closed, he feels the water and then rises to his feet to form a perfect stance, a perfect view. He leans forward, and feeling the vibe, he rides the wave.

The crowd roars, throwing up fists, shouting his name. The water surges higher, and the wave creeps above, but Jed is more defiant, more at ease; he intends to champion this wave. He ducks low, keeping balance.

Another roar, and then Huxley leaps into action, cutting the wave and jumping out ... twisting six feet up—*The air is nice*—deep breath, somersault, feet down ... he lands on Jed's board. Together they stand, arms out, managing the wave, bursting ahead ... And seconds later, another smile, and they're done.

Never to be forgotten, never to be seen again, this one's for the books.

Droves of salutes greet their arrival, uncle and nephew riding together, riding to shore. Arriving wet, they're soaked by the crowd's embrace. Jaxston joins in, and together, clasping hands, they stand ... then bow. As the applause presses on, they bow once more ... then again.

Huxley nods at the crowd's praise as shows of support shower down from above. It's a celebration, no doubt, but beyond their cheers, beyond their smiles, there's something more, and he feels it. There's camaraderie. There's solidarity. There's a cohesion of purpose. It's clear. It's palpable. Who can deny it?

The people are becoming citizens—citizens of a new planet, a new vision. Theirs. Unparalleled in its scope, unmatched in its possibilities, it's morphing into something different ... and something truly wondrous. But more than ever, Huxley knows this'll be essential before any attempt is made at the most critical phase of his plan. That's next.

Phase II of Huxley's plan: completed.

MAINLAND
DAY THIRTY

The week passes without further news, as does the weekend. The chief, at times forgetting there's even a matter to contend with, ignores Mr. Wickly's calls and the families' concerns and provides no updates, shrugging things off with the thought, *There's nothing to be done.*

As for the parents, it's Thursday morning, and each passing day is a grim reminder: no kids, no love, no one returning home. Thankfully, a weekend of shopping cures all ills, even this one, and most certainly, there's no better way to spend away the grief than some healing time in Milan, Paris, and Singapore, with a stopover in London. *Oh, what a sale it is.* The end-of-summer clearance is truly worth it.

Mr. Wickly conducts his daily meetings with his staff, reviewing each student's psychological profile—looking for disorders. Apparently, when one examines carefully, each student has one. Look closely; it's all in the details.

Sure enough, they've got them all:

"Anxiety."

"Bipolar."

"Depression."

"Attention deficit—"

"Obsessive-compulsive—"

"Oppositional defiant disorder ..."

They reel the list off in a reported series, like the credits of a good movie, scouted and recited with investigative diligence, naturally.

"Huxley ..." Mrs. Andrews reads. She pauses and wonders, staring at her page. "How do you pronounce his last name?"

Mr. Farnsworth tilts sideways, adjusts his glasses, and brings the page closer. He says nothing at first. Then he frowns and murmurs, "Huxley X ... I dunno how to pronounce that."

"What diagnosis would you say we should we call him?" she asks. This is a bit of a tough one.

Heads pop up around the table. Eyes merge to assist with the heavy thinking. It'll be a team effort.

"The report says he likes magic ..." She glances around at her peers. Deep reflection reigns over the room. They're having a faculty puzzler. The seconds tick down as everyone waits for someone to untangle this Gordian knot.

Mr. Farnsworth shrugs. "A psychotic disorder?"

Teachers nod; there's agreement. *Truth!* Heads sink back to their pages.

"What's the point?" Mr. Tepper chimes in. "You reap what you sow; if the kids wanna run away, let 'em run. That's what you raised."

That may be the case, but Mr. Wickly is neither fluent nor is he literate in the language of failure. He slowly turns toward him. One look, no words, and there it is: he's earned a Wickly lesson. Mr. Tepper's eyes swiftly drop back to his notes. Lesson learned.

CHIEF'S OFFICE

Meanwhile, at the police station, the chief arrives, coffee in hand. He finds his desk, takes a seat, leans back, and raises his feet, resting them next to a peculiar package addressed to him. The box has been perched on his desk for five days.

Taking a sip, he casts a glance at the package. Ruminating as he is, the thought of its origins pops into his mind, but then it recedes, emerging somewhere else—assigned with a rain check.

Minutes later, placing his mug on the desk, he glances at the box again, and a curious look dawns on his face, a look that only a keen detective would know, would identify with. The chief leans forward, mulling in silence, noting with clarity: the package has colorful markings and is addressed with youthful writing. *Who? What? Where?* The moment is gripped with his stare and his astute investigative attention.

Another minute passes in silence … his gaze becomes more intense, and his lips relax as his mind grows entangled in the mystery. He reaches for his mug, takes another sip, and focuses his gaze even further.

Finally, his face thaws, and all doubt melts with his nod. He rests his mug on the package, looks away, turns on the television, and snacks on a donut. Cartoon reruns. They never get old.

As he stands up to adjust his pants, gently gripping the Boston cream between his lips, his elbow drifts forward—a light tap, the mug tips, the coffee spills ... He yells a curse, and the donut pops out.

While using his hand to curb the spill, he blames the table in the series of shouts that follow.

What's more, the package is now wet, and his hand is soaked. After he wipes it down, he lifts the package ... Coffee is seeping through. In a moment of epiphany, staring as he is, he wonders, *What's inside? And does it need to be dried?* But first, napkin. He reaches back and dries it off.

Satisfied at last, he sits and looks around. *Where to begin? Oh, yes*—his to-do list. It was provided by his newly graduated officer, Ms. Angelos.

He eyes the list, but he's distracted. Some temptations are hard to ignore. He glances at the fallen donut, and a dilemma stirs a tussle in his mind. Shunning the thought, he resumes reading. Then he stops and looks at the donut again. Alas, this is not a battle he's prepared to win. Reaching over, he raises the donut like an abandoned trophy and takes a bite. *Scrumptious.* He closes his eyes in bliss. Everything's calm now—back to normal.

"Chief ...?" His eyes pop open. Ms. Angelos is standing at the door. "Did you get a chance to see that package?" she asks. "Its postage is from Cuba."

Indeed, this is unusual. They've never had a package arrive from Cuba before.

ONE HOUR LATER

In a surprise move, the chief calls Mr. Wickly for an urgent meeting tonight, and he requests that some extended families attend along with the parents. Proactive as he is, he wants this meeting as soon as possible.

At 7:00 p.m., the auditorium is full. No one speaks.

Chief Ross steps to the lectern and waits, with the teachers and Mr. Wickly standing behind him. He glances back, nods, and then looks forward and begins. "Thank you all for comin' tonight on such short notice," he says, playing with the microphone, up and down, before angling it up.

"It's been a while since we've met, but I wanted to reassure you we've done everythin' in our power to find your children," he says to an auditorium of heads nodding back.

"At 9:00 a.m. this morning, we opened a package at our station. And it contained a letter."

He reaches down, raises a folded page, and opens it. Strangely enough, it's marked with a large brown coffee stain at its core, which his hands unsuccessfully try to cover.

He puts his glasses on and then flattens the corners of the letter as much as he can. Anticipation ripples through the hall. Everyone is on the edge of their seats, waiting. The chief glances up, looks back down, and then finally reads:

Our dear aunties and uncles,
God bless you ... and often. As we have already written our grandparents, we didn't want to seem

impolite and make the unpardonable omission of leaving you out. Now, that wouldn't be right, would it?

After all, if our vision has reached as far as it has, it's because we've climbed up on your neck and shoulders—literally!—and quite truly, we were unspeakably delighted with the best views.

You were the ones we'd escape to in our times of mischief, which often included the obligatory depletion of your reservoir of chocolate.

Because of you, we increased our vocabularies to include ice cream, popcorn, tacos, and pizza ... and tireless as you were, in due time, we discovered your other treasured words: arthritis, tendonitis, disc herniation, and chronic fatigue syndrome.

In a world of madness, you taught us the code of life: to keep smiling, to have patience, to be fair, to find balance. You were our role models, reassuring voices of all things practical, and, as always, you bought us the coolest gifts.

Please excuse us for not saying a proper goodbye. We've sent you chocolates, the sweetest kind, as belated amends for our mistake and to replenish your supply.

We know you understand. You always did.

Love you forever,

Your nieces and nephews

The chief puts down the page, nodding. He's not certain if he should share his feelings. Well, he decides to anyway. "I think they've clearly marked who their enemy is."

The auditorium is silent. No one blinks. The parents stare at the teachers, and the teachers at the parents, still wondering. *Who's the culprit, again?*

"Like I said before," the chief jaws on, "this is what makes our country great: the freedom to make our own choices. The package, by the way, was sent from Cuba. Your kids knew exactly where to go so we couldn't find 'em."

Silence captures the moment. No one says a word. Everyone ruminates.

The chief is ready to close the books on the matter when suddenly a man stands up and shouts, "I will pay a ten-thousand-dollar reward for the return of my son!"

Everyone in the audience turns, searching for the voice that tendered the proposal. The man sits in the left corner, wearing a tracksuit. He seems pleased with his offer.

Intriguing? Yes. Will it change the outcome? Probably not.

The chief looks on quietly, amused. Chirps echo through the auditorium.

A moment passes before another parent rises. "I'll pay or donate—whatever terminology you wanna call it—to any civilian or law enforcement organization a hundred million dollars to find my child."

The chief's stunned; his jaw unhinges. "A hundred ..." he confirms, almost choking, clearing his throat. "That's the other thing that's great about our country."

Another parent stands and motions like they're raising a

paddle at an auction. "I'll pay two hundred million."

Everyone gasps. Heads turn. The chief's eyes refuse to blink. A sigh of disbelief rings through the hall as everyone debates if, indeed, they heard it right.

"Three hundred million!" another voice shouts, and just like that, everyone has already forgotten the last bid.

Shaking his head, the chief whispers under his breath, "Freedom be damned ..." before suddenly losing his voice.

Their imagination doesn't have a chance to absorb that bid; another man gets up, wearing a flat cap. "I'll pay four hundred million for my daughter's return—or, for that matter, any other child," he adds with a menacing tone. "But on one condition: we also get that Huxley X."

Well, he certainly knows what he wants. His enemy has been clearly marked, and the bounty carved on a stone of vengeance. The auditorium is silenced by his words, astonished.

Then the chief steps back and doesn't say a word. His eyes rove, searching the crowd, before he softly says, "Do we have ... five hundred million?" Leaning forward, he pauses. "No?"

Being the methodical man he is, he glances at his page, takes out his pen, and does the arithmetic. Seconds pass, and with a nod and a smile, he writes ... He's done. "So, we have, let's see ..." He does the math again just to be sure. "Yep. We have one billion and ten thousand dollars."

Staring at the numbers, he waits a beat and looks up. His eyes search for the man in the tracksuit, and hitting his target, he mumbles, "Did you wanna come up on that ten thousand?"

At that moment, Mr. Wickly steps forward and reaches

for the microphone. He's poised, and his voice is sharp with purpose. "I think it would be most prudent not to advertise this." He takes a second to think, or perhaps he's just taking a moment to seal his argument. "If the media gets wind of this, it would give your children a fresh opportunity to escape once again. We wouldn't want that, now, would we?" he says in a cautionary tone.

"I agree," Mrs. Andrews says, jutting her head in front of the microphone. "For this to succeed, it must be kept in-house. I can't stress this enough."

The chief steps in, taking back the microphone. "I'm on board with the school on this one. They may be in Cuba. Once you step outside our country, it can be tricky. You may endanger their precious lives just by making a public announcement."

A parent shouts, "Why should we listen to you? If you coulda found them, you woulda done so already!"

Everyone claps. Heads nod.

The teachers all trade glances. Mr. Farnsworth steps in and tilts sideways to the microphone, grabbing it from the chief's hands. "I understand your frustration, but you must understand … this takes time. As is evident, your children have already designated us and the police as their preferred choice to communicate with. Why would they do that? There is a reason: there's a psychological drive to where they deposit their message. We understand them. They wouldn't speak to us if they didn't want us to negotiate with them."

"It's you they're runnin' from!" an angry voice yells. "That's what they wrote."

Everyone claps again, louder this time. Heads nod more

wildly; gestures of agreement move through the audience in waves.

"Yes," Mr. Farnsworth says, reaching to find a solution, speaking above their ovation. "But they're still writing us, so not everything is lost. They want to negotiate. We'll negotiate. And, think, who knows your children better than us? We understand their psychology. We're familiar with their needs better than anyone. In some ways, we know them even better than you."

The last message strikes a conciliatory tone, and all appears calm.

The man wearing the flat cap stands up. "You have two weeks."

Chief Ross protests, "Sir, with all due respect, if they've gone to Cuba, two weeks is not enough."

Probably true. It certainly sounds reasonable, but will it be enough? After a moment of reflection, the man can't refute the logic. "Very well, you have one month. That's it. Then we take it public."

Eyes stare forward: teachers, Mr. Wickly, the chief. Though awake, they cannot see, and they cannot hear; their minds were lost somewhere between the fourth and fifth bid.

Beyond measure, each one is already plotting a clearly constructed plan, and more pleasurably, something else is also cooking in their minds—something indescribably wonderful.

One month.

Parents and family members leave in an orderly file, no curses, no arguments, no fights, amicable as ever. Mr. Wickly holds open the door, shakes hands, and nods to each as they depart. Formal, dignified, and courteous, he holds no outward expression. He's professional. He's Mr. Wickly.

At last, with perfect door-side manner, he nods to the last person leaving: the chief. Yes, it's business as usual.

Everyone's now gone. Doors closed. He looks back: teachers stand, as all good soldiers would, lining the front, ready for his command.

One second of silence.

Two seconds of silence.

Three seconds ... he smiles.

They smile.

His smile widens, showing every tooth ... as do theirs.

Faces glow. They should. Their love knows no bounds.

Make no mistake—it's time to bring the kids home.

PLANET NEXT
DAY FORTY

It's morning, and all is silent. Huxley sleeps while Chester looks on. It rained last night. The fresh scents of trees and moss fill the air. The sun's rays peek through the clouds, work past the branches, struggle through the leaves, and make their way into the tree house, where their heat gently touches the face of Huxley, who is immersed in an unremembered dream about fire.

Suddenly his eyes spring open. "They're coming."

He repeats it, this time in his mind.

Arising, he climbs above his tree house, spiraling to its balcony rooftop. It's Planet Next's highest point and definitely his favorite spot. The tree house is spread across three trees—Huxley's triangle. With a suspicious frown, he gazes about, beyond its shores, beyond the horizon, but sees only water: no swimmers, no ships. The ocean is blue and tranquil, untouched by visiting hands or ships.

The sun's beam is warm, but for how long? How much

further can this fight press on?

His sits. He doesn't want to think about it, even though he's thinking about it. Feeling his necklace, his fingers roll along its edge, back and forth, and he mulls the situation longer. Finally, sensing a need to do something, he calls out, "Chester?"

Listening for his command, the bird chimes, "Aye, master?"

"Shall we play a game of *Ches*?"

With beak to the skies, the bird says, "With pleasure."

Looking to his shoulder, Huxley asks, "How many pawns can orbit the king?"

Chester lifts off and wings forward, gains height, gains speed, more view, more momentum, then wends, soaring skyward, cutting through the clouds, disappearing from view ... Time rumbles ... Then he emerges back, circling the perimeter, soaring higher, circling again.

Huxley stares below, as farsighted as one can, past the surface of the ocean, past the fish, imagining as he is, peering deep within the ocean, to its seafloor, and there he mulls over its secret, its treasure, and the mystery it encloses. *Not the right time*, he wonders. *Or is it? But if not now, then when?*

Flashing his gaze to the island, he turns back and admires its nature, the unfinished work, the envisioned plans, all admirably in progress: the growing crops, the renewable resources, the utility infrastructures, and, of course, Chandler's plans for their civilization.

Looking up, he sees Chester returning, having scanned the oceans, and when the bird finally sits on Huxley's shoulder, he's prepared to deliver his answer. "No pawns, master."

"Perfect," Huxley says with relief. "It must be just a bad vibe."

Stepping away from his rooftop, he descends the stairs and walks onto the wooden suspension bridge linking tree house to tree house. These bridges arc across the island, held up by ropes and cables.

Chandler suggested their construction, as well as ziplines to cross the water. Community building, she called it … fostering social connectedness and a sense of togetherness. It seemed like a remarkable idea at the time. But, alas, little did Huxley realize it would unwittingly imply daily visits, sometimes more than once, by none other than Chandler herself, seeking, asking, wondering about, well, just about anything to clear her mind.

All is peaceful this morning. She's sleeping, snuggled in bed, windows jutted open. Huxley tilts sideways and takes a glance. After a sigh of freedom, he walks by with a bounce. His arms stretch out; he holds the handles. He's happy. There's a buoyancy to his walk.

The view is as rich as it is raw, and he enjoys the jungle, the birds fluttering across, and the feathery leaves of the trees as they gently brush against his head. Truly, it's a marvel. And then:

"Huxleeeeey."

He freezes in his tracks. He assumed too soon, quite naturally, a common misgiving. To err is human.

"Lovely," he whispers under his breath. Debating whether or not to answer the call—*This might be a call to disaster*—he weighs on his choices, afraid to decide.

A second wave arrives. "Huxleeeeey."

The voice: unmistakable. The pitch: high. The tone: silkier than one can hope to imagine. There's no doubt, indeed, that a third wave will arrive shortly.

Mindful, and in measured movements, his head slowly turns, and as the seconds tick by, he wonders if he'll regret this. A gallery of possibilities flashes through his mind, none of it worth a second look. Yes, he'll regret this.

Her neck stretched, her head lifted above the pillow, her eyes half-closed, barely awake, she looks through the crack of the window, desperately trying, telepathically attempting, as much as she can, to establish a connection.

Please don't fight it, he pleads. "Shhh ..." he hushes amiably, stepping forward. "Go back to sleep," he adds in a faint tone. "It's early. I'm getting water. We'll talk later."

For a suspenseful moment, she holds her head still, pondering, and then, much to his surprise—and even more to his relief—her head finally descends in an arc, and she falls back to sleep.

Phew.

Huxley turns, resumes his walk, and reopens his thoughts, gazing at the jungle, the trees, the plants, the flowers, the birds, the stream, the sea, and everything wild and everything alive.

Then something flies by, a curious little creature, gray-brown, long legs, short wings, big eyes, rounded tail. It perches, unafraid, on a rope in front of him.

"Well, who do we have here?" Huxley smiles and stares with wonder, listening to its *churring* sound. "Would you like to introduce yourself?"

The bird stares with its dark forward-facing eyes.

Huxley looks to his shoulder. "What do you think,

Chester?"

No response. Chester's not in the mood.

Huxley bounces another glance to the bird and then Chester. "Nothing …? That's the first time I've seen you so quiet. I think you might be smitten."

"The name is owlet-nightjar," that unmistakable voice murmurs from behind.

Huxley turns, surprised. Again.

"Do you speak to all birds?" Chandler asks. "It's a little cuckoo, if you ask me. No pun intended."

"Do you sneak up behind all lads?" Huxley nods. "It's an odd peek-a-boo, if you ask me, no pun intended, most certainly."

Huxley allows a mischievous smile to emerge. "I thought you were sleeping."

"I thought you were getting a drink," she says and waits a beat to repeat, "Name is owlet-nightjar."

"Owlet-what …?" *A peculiar hyphened name,* he thinks.

"The bird." She points. "It's an owlet-nightjar. There are less than fifty of them in the whole world. It's an exotic bird."

Huxley smiles and looks to his shoulder. "Well, well, Chester, I didn't think your choice would be of the exotic variety, but I must say, I'm not surprised."

"Don't step too close," Chandler cautions. "They're quite territorial. I've seen a few more of them here." Then she looks around, silent with hope, admiring the beauty of the island. Overwhelmed, her voice trembles with emotion. "The greatest miracle of Planet Next is these birds. It's truly another world here. There are no words to describe it.

Do you know what this means?"

Huxley lets her question sink in for a moment, moved somewhat by Chandler's emotions. Then he clears his throat. "Well, I could venture a guess ... but I'd be more delighted if you tell me."

"It means this place is special. The endangered species have found sanctuary here."

"Indeed," Huxley murmurs and looks to his shoulder, perplexed at Chester's silence. "Did you hear that? You're in elite company ... as you should be."

The owlet-nightjar turns its head and gazes at Chester. Then it steps closer on its dark, stout legs, continuing to stare mysteriously. There's an exchange of sorts between the birds. It's odd, and it's indecipherable to everyone, including Huxley. Moments later, the owlet-nightjar flies away.

Undoubtedly, it's a welcome addition. There is no place like home.

POLICE STATION
DAY FORTY-SEVEN

It's 7:00 a.m. Chief Ross has arrived early. No coffee, no donut, no distractions. *Dammit, there's work to be done.*

"Hell or high water, we're bringin' those kids home." He pounds his fist on the table, and his voice echoes down the halls.

The police station has hired five new staff members in the past week. The normally quiet office is now bustling with footsteps, ringing phones, investigative leads, memos, letters, and frequent call-outs across the room. It's a businesslike atmosphere. This is surprising since crime has been low recently.

"These kids are the trust of our nation, the bedrock of our hopes. No child will go missin', not on my watch," the chief commands to a roundtable of officers, all shuffling through papers with their heads down.

"Okay, what do we know so far?" he yells to the row of faces tilting up to meet his; their expressions are solid as a rock.

"This scheme is led by this kid named Huxley ..." Officer Jefferson says, quickly glancing at his notes. He pauses to read the surname. "Huxley ... uh, Huxley ... I still can't figure out how to say this last name."

Chief Ross tries to help, tilting sideways, looking on. "It's Huxley ..." He stretches his neck closer to the page. "Um, Huxley ... uh." He cuts himself off on that note, giving up.

It's long. It's hard. And it's challenging them as much as his disappearance has. Officer Jefferson shakes his head and resumes, "He's fifteen; just moved from the UK this summer." He lifts the page to read the remaining details. "It says here he's scared of fire. His parents died when he was seven years old. He's been raised by his uncle, a mister ... Jed Jules."

Chief Ross nods. "What do we know about *him*?"

Officer Jefferson looks down at his report. "I'm not sure what his vocation is at the moment. He's a five-time surf champion ... and apparently, after his surfing days, he invested in swimwear underwear; a business that had revenues of about a million dollars ... but lost over ten.

"His next business venture was a Vibeboard surfing device. It says here the board had many problems managing waves. It lost close to eighty million. That was, of course, followed by an investment in appliances for tree houses: solar fridges, battery-operated stoves and microwaves." He pauses. "That gamble lost him forty million."

"His next startup, *Globack* ... was styling gel for back hair. Strangely enough, that venture started off well, but after its rippled buzz, that too lost another forty million.

Thankfully, Mr. Jules's parents were well off, and he inherited nearly five billion dollars, as well as six homes, a cottage, a yacht, seven cars, and a few international properties, including a private island that's an hour west of here."

"Wait!" the chief commands, raising his palms, his ears perked, his eyebrows raised. He's intuitively stumbled on a clue, oblivious to everyone else, but when you've served as the city's chief for nearly twenty years, battling the nation's worst criminals, standing at the frontline during every perceivable calamity, well, you see hints others miss, clues many can't imagine, and without a blink, you can link facts that amateurs can't even see.

In a moment of epiphany, he lifts his chin and smiles as all his detective senses come alive. "Find me," he whispers, "the license plates of those seven cars."

"That's brilliant ..." Officer Jefferson mumbles in awe, and as he leans back, the page slips out of his hand.

Suddenly the room door jerks open, and Officer Angelos pushes in. Her expression is stern. "Sir, we got him."

No one speaks. Heads turn as they swap looks—then they freeze. Lulled in the moment, a second passes for her words to enter their thoughts. They all pop up, pushing their chairs back, revealing their delight.

"Heaven be praised!" the chief yells, stepping forward.

They march out and down the hallway in single file, and then they turn the corner and pick up their pace. They chime together like drums in the opening notes of a suspenseful tune. On reaching the end of the hallway, they open the door to find Officers Higgins and Sanchez standing there, awaiting their arrival.

"We found him this mornin' as he stepped off his boat."

Chief Ross turns and gazes at them, still surprised at their luck. The interrogation room is dark, with just a few scattered chairs and a table. He steps closer to the one-way mirror and stares. "So that's him, huh?"

"Yep ... no doubt about it. We got our guy."

"Damn, he looks young," Officer Jefferson says, shaking his head and stepping up next to the chief.

"You could never tell he's forty-two by lookin' at him," Officer Higgins says, glancing over.

"What has he said so far?" the chief asks.

"Nothin'."

"And the kids?"

"He's not sayin' a word."

"Well, we'll just have to find creative ways to get him to speak, won't we?" And being the creative man that he is, beyond question, he knows a few.

Everyone puts on their headphones. The chief rolls up his sleeves, cracks his neck, and adjusts his belt before treading to the door.

Officer Higgins trails behind, mimicking the chief's every movement, and then, they swap stares. They know it. This is the turning point they've been waiting for. Exchanging confirming nods and leaving their reservations behind, they signal, *We're ready*, and open the door.

Armed with a strategic acumen, they gaze at their enemy and put on their good-cop-bad-cop faces, hoping to end this case and its unwelcome drama.

No doubt about it, they understand what needs to be done. Yes, indeed. It's now time to deliver.

MOMENTS LATER
PLANET NEXT

"Where's Jed?" Dragon asks. "It's not like him to be late."

It sure isn't. This, of course, is no ordinary day. They are as confused as they are worried.

Dale opens the BBQ grill's cover, flips the steaks, closes the lid, and shakes his head. "Jed knows better than anyone that Chandler walks past here at 12:30 every day." Indeed, there's not much time left before she passes on her way to the fields to collect fruits.

Dale looks at his watch. "The smell has to be gone by the time she arrives."

"Man, we're gonna be in trouble. There's only so much finger-lickin' Texan tofu one brings to an island."

"This baby is well, well done."

Dragon smells. "Mmm ... damn well."

"Call him."

"You call him."

"You kiddin'? The last time I walked in, he was workin' on that Vibeboard. You know better than anyone that he doesn't wanna be disturbed."

"Yeah, I was lookin' forward to the lessons. Our luck that he brought the board that's broken."

"Christ! It's almost noon. Maybe we should start?"

"Can't do that … Jules Rule: we break bread and steak together."

"Okay, we'll both go up."

Good enough, it would seem, so why do they doubt themselves? In an attempt to delay, they're coming up with excuses. They know that. But they also know … Jed is sacred. Don't disturb sacred.

Fighting the temptation and their hunger, they nod. A decision has been made. Dragon turns off the grill, and they tread up toward the tree house, step by step, listening attentively for his voice, his footsteps. They hear nothing. Making their way, they arrive at the penthouse and stop. Shifting sideways, they tilt and look through the window.

His bed is empty: no Jed.

Should they knock? What if …? They don't want to imagine. Following a swap of nods, they each point to the knob and then at each other. After headshakes, a muted argument, and three rounds of rock paper scissors … *Dale, you're it.*

Pushing his anxiety aside, Dale will take one for the team. Inch by inch, he turns the handle as slowly as one can, and on wedging open the door, their heads jut inside in sequence, and they gaze about.

Oh, no! Glancing at each other, neither can believe it. The room is messy. A trail of hair products lines the floor.

Jed is asleep, lying flat on his Vibeboard, wearing nothing but his underwear.

Worried now, they push open the door and run up. "Jed," they call, tugging on his shoulder.

"Poor guy was up late again, fixin' the Vibeboard," Dragon says, attempting to wake him.

"Jed," Dale repeats louder. "There are twelve ounces of love waitin' for you downstairs. Chandler will be here soon. Come."

Jed's lids flick open. The words had meaning. Their impact was felt, for sure. He says nothing and doesn't move; he just looks around. Clearing the lump in his throat, he finally mumbles, "I think ... I'm stuck." With his back against the board, looking at the Globack tin cans scattered beside him, he doesn't move an inch.

"Did you pull your back?" Dragon asks.

Jed shakes his head. "No ... back is okay."

"Did you sprain your neck?" Dale chimes in.

"No, that's fine, too."

"Your hip?"

"No ... all is good there."

"What did you hurt, then?" they ask.

Not tempted to answer, Jed lifts both arms. "Here, you boys will have to pull me up," he affirms before adding, "Keep your foot on the Vibeboard."

Confusion crosses their faces as they clasp hands with Jed. *Why step on the Vibeboard?* they wonder.

No time to explain. They'll find out soon enough. Jed nods and winces. "Alrighty, boys, on a count of three: one ... two ... and—"

POLICE STATION
INTERROGATION ROOM

"Let me ask you again: Where are the kids?"

Chief Ross's eyes are swelling with fire. He circles around the man, stepping closer with each round.

The suspect sits handcuffed, says nothing.

His name: Jose Garcia.

Nationality: American.

Country of birth: Cuba.

Employment: commercial fishing.

Everything matches the identification provided by the Cuban authorities: the name, date of birth, eye color, hair color, his date of travel, and, most critically, the photographs of his appearance at the post office.

"We've been at this for two hours now," the chief says, frustrated, bending forward to look Jose squarely in the eyes. "If you don't speak, I'll have you deported from this country. Do you understand?"

Jose makes no sounds; his feathers are not ruffled.

"DO. YOU. SPEAK. ENGLISH!" the chief shouts in a punctuated manner. It's a good question, he reasons.

Everyone watches from behind the one-way mirror, their headsets on.

No answer comes.

Then Officer Higgins leans forward to take another stab at extracting information from their speechless suspect. More pressure, more sound ... they're frustrated.

Still nothing.

Their full-on attempt continues for another thirty minutes, taking turns, before, foiled and denied, they step out and, at last, join the others in the back room, lamenting the failed task.

"Not sure anythin' can get through to this guy," the chief mumbles, scratching his head.

"Sir," Officer Angelos chimes in, "I know I'm just a rookie, but perhaps it might help if I spoke to him."

"Be my guest." He points. "Officer Higgins can accompany you inside. My only advice: no matter how frustrated you feel, no matter how angry you are, don't let them see it. They know its scent, they taste it, they feel it, and they'll never let you win."

"Understood, sir." She nods and then turns back and enters the interrogation room. Wasting no time, she parts with her doubts and begins her questions.

Depleted of hope, the chief is reluctant to watch the encounter. As the minutes pass, the officers continue to watch.

Suddenly Officer Jefferson blurts out. "Look ... he moved his lips!"

The chief turns, surprised, and steps up to the window,

staring, curiously waiting for the attempt to fail.

"Wouldn't ya know it ..." another office chimes in. "I think they're now having a conversation." He puts on his headset.

The chief searches his mind for an answer he doesn't have, but then he finds it. "Well, it certainly helps that Ms. Angelos speaks his language."

"Actually ... I think they're speakin' English," Officer Jefferson says with one earphone on. Glancing over his shoulder, he nods to confirm.

"Yep ... it's all in the Latin connection," the chief goes on. "They understand one another's vibe, pulse along on the same wavelength. Their cultural ties are so, so strong and run ... ah, so deep."

"Sir ... I believe Ms. Angelos is from Greece."

Five minutes pass in a rapid-fire, back-and-forth sequence, and then Officer Angelos walks out and circles to the back room. "Sir, his contact person was not the kids, nor was it Huxley X. It was the uncle: Mr. Jules.

"Apparently, they met by the docks just a few weeks ago. After he mentioned to Mr. Jules his intended family visit to Cuba, he was offered a hundred dollars just to mail the package of chocolates from a Cuban post office.

"Chief, he doesn't know anything else. He knows nothing about the kids, nor does he have any information regarding their whereabouts, or for that matter, anything else pertaining to Mr. Jules or Huxley X."

The chief looks on in awe, his tongue tamed, his eyes searching, and his mind focused on one certainty: beginner's luck.

After mulling things over for a moment, he grumbles

out, "Good job." But he doesn't know what to think or make of this.

Could it be? Would a grown man actually plot a runaway with a clan of teens? Why would he do this? Every crime has a motive. There's no motive. This can't be. It shouldn't be. No ... it's just wrong.

But there's a way to determine for sure. The chief frees a smile. He knows where to seek his answer. Thinking ahead, as all great commanders do, he nods to his thoughts. Indeed, there's a place to find out.

BACK ON PLANET NEXT

"Ahhhhhhhhhhhhhhhhhhhhhhhhhhhhhhhh!" Jed's mouth is wide open, and the flap at the back of his throat vibrates like a clapper. He pauses to catch his breath and chimes in for a second round of screams.

Dragon and Dale look at the surfboard, and—curious little thing—there's a new rug covering its surface: it's brown, curly, and moist.

Huxley walks in. "What happened?"

Jed pants, preparing for a third round. With a comforting arm on his shoulder from Dale, he finally relents and waves away their concern. "I'm okay. Really, it was just a twitch," he mutters and lies on the bed, his back shiny, smooth, and red like a beet.

"Wait, wait ..." Dragon suddenly remembers. With concern, he scans the perimeter. He darts a glance at Huxley. "You know the Jules Rule: you're not supposed to visit here from eleven to twelve—the Huxley blackout zone. Oh, c'mon, you know what happens. Every time you come, she follows."

"Huxleeeeey." That sweet, soft voice jingles in the background like an angel of death swirling the skies.

Dale glances over at Dragon. "The food!"

"Huxleeeeey," it echoes again, louder.

The moment is ripe with failure. There's no time. Huxley looks at his shoulder and says, "Chester?"

"Aye, master."

"Shall we play a game of *Ches*?"

Ready as always: "With pleasure."

Waiting a beat, Huxley asks, "Steak and bake … What do we say when they say 'Checkmate'?"

Chester flies off, bolting out the window, wending his flight, soaring high. He disappears from view.

"Huxleeeeey," they hear again; the beats of fear in their chests surges stronger as the voice draws closer.

Dragon and Dale storm down the steps, with Huxley trailing, running as fast as one can. Turning the corner, they run along the deck, reaching the grill just as Chandler arrives.

"There you are!" she says, skipping up the steps, smiling. "I thought I heard a scream from over here."

"Everything is fine now," Huxley says. "I'll be leaving. I can accompany you to the orange trees if you like."

Slinging a comforting arm around her shoulder, he starts to escort her out.

Suddenly she stops. With eyebrows raised, she sniffs a few times. "Wait," she says, looking over at the BBQ grill, musing studiously, "what are you cookin'?"

Drawing closer, she turns and places a hand on the grill handle, ready to lift. Just as swiftly, Dragon reaches out and gently holds her arm down.

"I wouldn't do that," he implores.

"Why not?"

He shrugs. "I just wouldn't."

One would assume that after all this time, he would have a ready-made answer. He doesn't. Dale looks over, words having escaped him, too.

Chester reappears in the skies, flapping, descending, and sliding in an arc to perch upon Huxley's shoulder.

"Now, Chester, what do we say when they say, 'Checkmate'?" asks Huxley.

Sitting comfortably, the bird pipes up, "Check *again*, mate."

Chandler is baffled. She doesn't get it. She looks at Dragon and Dale, who shrug, innocent of any knowledge.

At last, she looks back down, and pondering a moment, she nods and opens the barbeque. The twins cringe and tilt over to confirm, resigned to doom, but—wouldn't you know it—there's nothing there: no steak, no food, nothing but a juicy grill.

Surprised yet confused, Chandler thinks, *Huh?* Then she looks at Huxley. "Should we leave now?"

"Yes, go on ... I'll meet you in a minute. I just want to have a word with my mates," he answers, looking at Dragon and Dale.

As she walks away, Dragon leans over and whispers, "That's a neat trick," and then he throws in, "We're gettin' back the steaks, right?"

Huxley says nothing, Dale looks at Chester, and Chester adds no further comment, conveniently looking away. His response portends an ominous conclusion.

"That was my lunch," Dale protests. "C'mon, man!"

"And it's now his lunch." Huxley smiles. "Chester is part falcon. Never trust a carnivore with your food. All in all, it was a fair trade, don't you agree?"

Their faces don't. Dragon and Dale swap glances. Glum expressions mark the experience as neither speaks, swallowing nothing—nothing, that is, but their words.

MADISON SCHOOL
TEACHERS' LOUNGE

Mr. Wickly paces the floor in silence, ruler in hand, his footsteps clicking to the rhythm of his movements. "For every weakness, there's a challenge to reveal it," he whispers, looking out the window. "We must first unravel the weakness before we can unravel where they might go."

Teachers circle the table, shuffling through every bit of last year's homework completed online: each assignment, each essay, and whatever writing, cryptic or intelligible, they can find.

They battle on, searching widely. There are clues to be found, and Mr. Wickly wants to ensure that the teachers know they must do their homework, too.

Working together, their back-and-forth exchange of views skips wildly, as do their fingers across the pages on their screens.

"Charming ..." someone notes with a teacher's insight. "Nope, candy canes will not cure diabetes."

"Interesting ... those Dragon Dale brothers," Mr. Tepper wonders.

"How so?" another teacher asks.

"They have a curious take on how to incarcerate your parents."

Mr. Farnsworth looks up. "Huh? What do you know about them?"

Mr. Tepper thinks for a moment. "Well, they certainly like to eat together. Good at IT, real good. Oh, yes, and they play football."

"Found it!" Mrs. Andrews shouts, swiveling her laptop and flashing its screen at the surrounding teachers.

Heads turn, and Mr. Wickly steps forward, locking a keen eye on the screen. Everyone draws in, listening with fervor.

"It's an assignment from Chandler Collins ..." Mrs. Andrews explains, spinning back her laptop. "Check. You'll wanna hear this one. It's a poem she wrote called 'The Planet Dreams.'"

Looking at her screen, Mrs. Andrews does a once-over and then glances up.

Mr. Wickly arrives behind her, eying the display. Then he motions, beckoning her to continue.

"This was written just before the end of the school year." She nods and, wasting no time, leans forward to read.

THE PLANET DREAMS

There once was a planet, more than four billion years old, and every so often, she'd share her story, one that's untold.

She speaks at night, and she speaks alone; her message is our planet, a planet that's dying, a planet that's home.

Confusion, illusion, delusion, and diffusion, wake up and stand up. There's only one solution.

Your kingdom is dying. The mighty are lying. Prepare for calamity—your calamity is perilously coming.

Believing out loud, believing with sight, believing together, we see her light, that star-like light, that unearthly light, something that's right.

We must not bow. We must act now to vow for what's next; it's really not complex. The planet dreams, dreams aloud, dreams ahead, and dreams again for Planet Next.

Everyone is silent. Mr. Wickly gazes away, muses, and finally turns back. "Oh, the remarkable words of naïve minds ... And how, may I ask, is this relevant?"

Mrs. Andrews reflects a moment, forgetting what had seemed important. Then she remembers. "Planet Next ... that was mentioned in the students' original letter."

"Wait ..." Mr. Wickly chuckles, shaking his head. "You're not suggesting she's the one who spearheaded this project? You realize her father is the one who provided the highest total of that billion-dollar reward?"

"Well ... does that make her involvement more or less probable?" Mrs. Andrews asks.

Raising a corrective chin, he chides, "If you think this is

the doing of anyone other than Huxley X ... then you're not paying attention. And let's presume she's a coconspirator; where would there be such a planet? Did they go to Mars? Or, remind me, was it Venus? I suppose it's a bit warmer there. Saturn ... oh, yes, it has a nice ring to it, wouldn't you say?"

Mrs. Andrews looks at her screen, and everyone waits for her eyes to bounce back. "There's nothing in this poem that suggests they'd leave earth. Planet Next is right here." She nods, looking up. "I think they'd go somewhere walled off from adults, for privacy, and perhaps, judging by this poem, someplace where there's nature."

"Where?" Mr. Wickly asks, not tempted to venture a guess.

"It's gotta be close. They're kids. How far could it be?"

"But we've checked everywhere." Mr. Tepper shrugs.

Mrs. Andrews shakes her head. "Or ... we've checked everywhere we thought they'd be. We have to think like they do. They seem pretty confident we won't find them. Why? How can they be so sure? If it's somewhere close, it must not be accessible to us."

"Teens will always prompt before launching a disaster. How did we miss it?" Mr. Farnsworth adds, and then he gazes back at the pages of his notes scattered on the table.

"Hmm ..." Mr. Wickly ruminates on the possibilities, staring outside, reflexively playing with his Knightlord ring. A thought crosses his mind. It fascinates him for a moment, but then he abandons it. Another one crosses shortly after, like a shooting star. *Strike that.* Suddenly he smiles, more interested, more promising, but after a second, that idea fizzles, too.

A rebellious band those teens are. Are they smart? Sure. Does he want to give them credit? Not entirely. And so he asks, "Who is the only parent ... or guardian that hasn't shown up to the meetings?"

"I thought everyone had." Mrs. Andrews looks up. "We contacted them all."

"No ... definitely not everyone, I can assure you."

They all glance up, unsure what Mr. Wickly has in mind. His face: certain. His eyes: focused away, naturally, waiting for others to chime in with wrong guesses before he unveils the right answer.

After a few shrugs, no attempts, and a moment of clueless silence, he says over his shoulder, "Mr. Jules." Then he slowly turns back and resumes his stare.

Mrs. Andrews is perplexed. "But I remember speaking to him the morning it happened. I left him a message, and he called back ... right away."

"Most certainly," Mr. Wickly confirms. "But did you see him at the meeting that evening?"

An unexamined question, but obviously well examined by Mr. Wickly. Everyone searches their mind. Truly, no one actually remembers. Mr. Wickly, though, seems sure. He looks at his reflection in the window and lightly adjusts his tie, impeccably tied in a Windsor knot, dimpled, oh so perfectly, at its center. One more touch, flawless.

Then Mr. Wickly turns, tilts his head forward, and peers at the others through the top of his glasses. "Peculiar, wouldn't you agree? A curious no-show."

No one answers. No one cares. What's the connection? Not everyone sees past the colored facts. He does.

Time is short. The current plan is not yielding results.

Mr. Wickly, though, has something in mind—something he knows will bring him informative answers.

Picking up his suit jacket, he shoots a glance at the others and nods. "I'll be back. Keep searching." And storming out with determined steps, he leaves the school.

MAINLAND
JULES RESIDENCE

It's almost sundown. Ten miles outside the city center, a trail of five police cars arrives. The mansion's gates are mysteriously open. The driveway is long, the route is scenic, and their cars move too fast for them to keep track of what they're passing. So, they slow down to watch with captivated interest. It's a fantasy land. On reaching the residence, they stop.

In sequence, the car doors fly open, and officers step out. They bunch together, side by side, taking off their hats, facing the estate. As they gaze with open mouths, no words can express their thoughts. They're impressed.

"Holy smokes!" Officer Jefferson finally cries out, turning his head to look at each side of the fifty-thousand-square-foot fortress.

"How many homes did you say he has?" the chief asks.

"Six."

Swapping looks, they tread toward the door and up ten

steps, still amazed, eyes roving. On reaching the top step, the chief snaps his mind back to reality and rings the doorbell.

Time passes; no one answers.

He tries again.

No response still.

He makes four additional attempts and confirms what they already suspect: Jed's not home.

Hands cupped at the side of his brow, he leans over to the window and looks inside for some clue. No hints, no sound; no one's inside. Then a shadow moves in the distance. The chief looks closer, past the empty foyer, the grand hall, and through the kitchen window, into the backyard. He waits for it, and then ... the shape quickly moves again, left, right, and then stopping. He looks back before darting left again.

The chief runs to the side of the building, stops, and slants laterally to inspect. He sees a man in the back doing a one-eye peek, his face partially hidden behind bricks.

"Mr. Jules?" the chief calls, uncertain.

The man darts right and races to the other side of the house. The chief follows from the front end, running to the same side. He does a quick look, and in a back-and-forth game of tag, they run east–west at their respective ends.

Tired, the chief lifts two fingers and signals Officer Jefferson to go left; he will go right.

Taking slow and measured steps, Chief Ross calls out, "Hello ... we're just here to talk!" He stops at the side of the home.

Stretching his neck past the edge, the chief casts a glance and sees the man standing at the other end, hiding behind the pillar. The person slides his head sideways, and indeed, it matches the pictures. It's definitely Jed.

"Mr. Jules ... we just wanna have a word with you. That's all."

The chief hears an echo: "Mr. Jules, we just wanna have a word with you. That's all." It's Officer Jefferson's voice, shouting from his end.

They both turn and swap glances, confused. Officer Jefferson points as if to say that Jed is on his side of the building. Chief Ross is adamant, *No, Jed is on my side.*

There's no time to debate. Jed's head peeks out again ... and he runs.

"WAIT!" Chief Ross gives chase, his hand reaching for his gun, his pulse rising, his body moving faster than it should; he gallops around the corner, panting as fast as one can, and sees a figure running for the pool.

Then, he has a flash of bamboozled realization: *Whoa, an identical person is running from Jefferson's side ... they're both Jed!*

Officer Jefferson also darts in pursuit, his steps mirroring those of the chief. Finally, in a watershed moment, the two Jeds merge and dive into the water in a no-splash event. The chief and Officer Jefferson stand by the pool. They're as baffled as they are amused. Then, emerging from the water, a large Jed soars, twelve feet tall.

"Are you lookin' for me?" He laughs hysterically, towering above them.

The officers look around, speechless. Officer Angelos, who trailed behind the chief, chimes in, "It's a holographic image. Look, over there ..." She points. And sure enough, the image is being projected from Jed's upstairs balcony, and the sounds are coming from the speakers outside. "There are motion detectors at both ends," she explains. "They sensed your approach."

Jed grows larger, his smile swells wider, and then he soars up until he's twenty feet tall. At last, he bends forward to the officers. "You wanna know what it feels like to be a little munchkin? Someone has been naughty!" He laughs. "And by the way, you're all trespassing. Look." He points. "Smile for the cameras."

The officers turn, and Jed dips down, puts his holographic arms around their shoulders, smiles, and photobombs them.

Flash! Flash! And another Flash!

"Welcome to Jed's palace!" his voice proclaims. "Where the grass seems greener than the other side, but only because the soil is browner. Now, remember, there are rules." After a moment, he motions to the door. "And here's your first one for the day. There's a gift inside that box. Go on, it's yours to open."

Disoriented and uncertain, they're not sure what to make of this entertainment, or rather, *his* spectacle; the officers begin to slowly walk to the back door of this pleasure dome, exchanging glances. They don't trust it.

On their way, they turn to look around at this beautiful, well-lit yard: the flowers, the landscape, the back yard, the pool, the pond, its bridge, the water fountain. It's a work of wonder, or perhaps the work of Jed.

All the lights slowly fade except the one under the box. On opening the lid, the box floods the skies with light. There's an envelope inside. As the chief pulls it out of its holder, the lights fade and another one waxes above.

The chief slowly opens the envelope, looks around, and pulls out a folded page. His thoughts are scattered, but he's curious. The surrounding officers nod in support, urging him on.

Shaking his head, he opens the note and takes a glance. Puzzled, he looks to Officer Jefferson for affirmation. After a concurring moment, the chief gazes back at the letter and reads aloud:

Dear Grownups,

Thanks for stopping by, and when you're done, please smell the roses before you clean up. It's a Jules Rule.

What lovely children you have. Truly. They took me as ransom: a ransom of mercy, a ransom of justice, and possibly a ransom of the heroes of a forgotten dream. Yours.

Let's be honest. The neglected dreams of today are the realities of the storm of tomorrow—and our generation has many. Tomorrow is here. So is its storm.

Thankfully, in the unfiltered light of their vision, I've rediscovered my dreams, and although, at times, I've been condemned to look like you, after a gratifying moment of truth and a game of jacks, I've been accepted as something different, but definitely not you. And being the great soldiers they are, I'm indebted to your kids for not leaving me behind.

As they called it, this will be the coming-of-age journey for Jed. But, frankly, I also like to think

of it as a becoming-like-Jed journey for them.
You may have concerns (not sleeping). You may
have intrusive thoughts (can't work, either). You
may even have sudden flashbacks (PTSD). And
who could blame you? But you need not worry.
I'm in good hands. These are wonderful kids.

Respectfully yours ... for the purposes of this letter only.

Jed Jules

The chief seals his lips and puts down his arms and the letter. Moments later, the sounds of shots roar behind them. Surprised, they all pull out their guns, turn, and lift their arms up and watch.

An array of fireworks lights the skies with orchestral music. Their eyes drift upwards, dazed by its beauty before they slowly put their guns back into their holsters.

After a deep sigh of relief, and perhaps a sigh of wonder, the chief eventually folds the letter again and darts a knowing glance at each of his officers.

Every suspicion is now confirmed: Jed is involved. The kids have an adult on their side, which expands their possibilities and their resources—Jed resources. And even more powerful and more dangerous, they're in peril of a Jed vision.

"This story gets more bizarre by the moment," Officer Jefferson complains.

Turning, they march back in businesslike sequence and with hurried, formidable steps, their eyes lock onto their cars. Comments shoot back and forth in a series of rapid shouts.

"We need to visit every one of his homes," the chief begins.

"But some of them are in California."

"Find a way—get it done."

"We need to trace everywhere his phone has been in the last three months," Officer Jefferson suggests.

"What about his cottage?" the chief wonders.

"That's three hours northeast of here. It's next to a conservation park."

"And the island ...? Do we know where it is?"

"Yes, sir. It's just twenty-seven degrees north, seventy-nine degrees west," Officer Angelos chimes in. "About an hour from Meyersville Harbor."

"Great. Let's start with the cottage. That's our best bet."

Their to-and-fro soundbites continue during their orderly march to their cars. Then doors open, they slide inside, ignitions are turned on, the hums of their engines echo, lights flash, the cars pull out, and finally, they drive off in a procedural series.

As the vehicles drive away, the rumble of their engines fades to a distant whir. Seconds later, stepping out from behind a tree, Mr. Wickly emerges, his eyes glazed, gazing at their cars, thinking of something ... truly wonderful.

Reflective and creative, he whispers, "Twenty-seven degrees north, seventy-nine degrees west," and it echoes in his mind, where it stays.

In a moment of bliss, his mouth curls into a smirk whose ends point skyward, to where his thoughts have risen.

Island.

PLANET NEXT
DAY FIFTY

It's midday, and it's humid. The sun blazes—its heat offers no mercy. Huxley, Jed, and the Dragon Dale brothers work on their mutual project. Beads of sweat adorn their heads, the occasional one trickling down the side, pausing, taking a tangent, and then dripping down further.

A week before their arrival at Planet Next, Jed transported the necessary items for their envisioned project—tools, motorboat, and these panels.

They're tired. Huxley's worried. The panels are inserted into the ocean floor, creating a field. The device worked when tested on the mainland. It's not working now. Too much sunlight, too much water, and they didn't account for the sun's reflection. And like a secret weapon, the cornerstone of a beautiful scheme, this device was the signature move for their covert plan.

Time is short, and soon enough, their enemies will be near, and so will calamity.

"There ..." Dragon says, "I think this might do it." Putting the final touches to his effort, he reinserts the motherboard and taps the panel.

"Shall we give it another try?" Huxley asks.

Dale nods.

Suddenly Huxley stops and looks skyward, and the others follow his gaze. Something has caught his attention. In the distance, Chester flies, his wings flapping vigorously; he's not stopping to glide like he normally does. Each second he draws closer, the moment looms larger, and as he descends with purpose—*No doubt about it*—Huxley knows what this means and puts on his falcon glove.

Chester's legs arc forward, and with wings outstretched, he floats down to land on Huxley's arm and stares at him, preparing to deliver an answer.

"One pawn, master."

Huxley's eyes flood with fear. "Sound the horn!" This has been rehearsed. Everyone knows the signal, and everyone knows what to do. A visitor is on the horizon. It's happening.

Ready or not ... "We must turn this on now," Huxley urges, anxious to do something.

The device: a radar and optical camouflage. It hides the island from visitors, extending hundreds of feet from shore. "It's just filtered light and sound. Don't worry, Hux. We'll be fine," Dale says, though he's not entirely convinced of his own words. This is their first test.

The horn sounds, and people rush to their positions. This is not a drill. In a heartbeat, everyone settles, hushed, not daring to move. The device is turned on. They look on with fear; once any ship passes the boulders, the island will come into view.

They wait in silence, and at first, there's nothing. Then, seconds later, a boat arrives, sailing by the rocks, gliding freely. Alas, most ships change course on seeing the boulders. This one seems determined.

Though journeying on an unconventional route, it still appears to be cruising by, but then suddenly it turns, aiming straight for Planet Next.

It draws closer and closer, and holding their collective breaths, everyone hunkers down, waiting ... At last, it slows as it nears their shores, winding left to drift by.

There's no sound. It floats quietly.

Feeling lucky, Jed whispers, "I think it's workin' ... It can't see us."

Huxley nods. Dragon and Dale swap glances and signal a thumbs-up.

Roaming leisurely, the boat slows even more, and then ... it comes to a halt.

Everyone clears their throat, holding firm.

Silence lingers. Nothing happens.

Finally, a man emerges on deck. He searches, gazing about, before coming closer to the rails, sheltering his eyes from the sun.

Everyone takes a deep breath, hoping for the specter of his presence to pass, but suddenly there is a call:

"Mr. Jed ...? Is that you?"

Standing beside a tree, apparently in clear view, Jed is surprised. His eyebrows pop up, and he quickly steps back behind the tree and peeks around it.

The man waves. "Mr. Jed ... Mr. Jed!"

Cupping a hand above his eyes, Jed squints against the sun. "Jose? Oh my God … what are you doin' here?"

Jed, outing himself, runs into the ocean, taking high steps in a theatrical rush. Water splashes as he pushes through, not letting up as though he's attempting to reach an old, lost friend.

"Jose," he echoes, sprinting faster, challenging the unstirred waters.

Everyone steps out from their hiding posts, and Huxley indicates to the onlooking students that they're clear of danger. Relieved, he turns to Dragon and Dale. "But it didn't work. Next time, we may not be so lucky."

It's back to the drawing board.

Lending a helping hand, Huxley ascends onto a motorboat, opens the panel, and heads toward Jose's ship. Jed is still wading through, but he jumps on the boat as Huxley passes by.

On reaching the ship, Jed steps up and embraces Jose, still curious about his appearance.

Jose looks around. It's the first time he's seen the island. After he's done pleasing his eyes, he explains, "The police took me in for questioning. I didn't tell 'em anything important, but they are looking for you. They were planning on goin' to your house."

"Thanks, Jose."

"I overheard them talking when I left. Apparently, there's a reward for your safe return."

"As there should be," Jed chimes in, smiling. "How much am I worth?"

"Actually, I think it's more for them. They didn't say how much, but it sounds like a lot."

Jose reaches inside his boat for a large cooler bag. "I can't stay long, but I brought you somethin'," he says, turning back. "I thought your supply might be low. These aren't Texan like the last ones, but the bacon chips are."

"Thanks, Jose."

Huxley is suspiciously quiet, and he watches the exchange with his customary courteous manner; his response belies what is percolating in his mind as he waits for Jose to conclude his conversation and visit.

A few minutes are spent in the traditional swapping of stories from their earlier surfing days. They shake hands, Jose waves to Huxley, and then, as quickly as he arrived, he leaves, turning his boat and sailing off.

Huxley ruminates on thoughts his lips can't utter. Speechless, he gazes at Jose's boat as it glides off into the distance, watching it shrink smaller and smaller before waning to a speck.

He eventually asks, "Can we trust him? There is now a reward for our capture?"

Jed seems surprised by the question. "Who? Jose? C'mon, even if you offered him ten thousand dollars, he wouldn't blink in his loyalty."

"Are you sure ...?"

Jed lifts a hand and gestures. "Cross my heart. Hope to die."

"I hope you don't." Huxley nods. *I hope we're not captured, either*, he hedges in his mind.

PLANET NEXT
DAY FIFTY-FOUR

The day arrives with one certainty: they'll be coming, if not today, then perhaps tomorrow, but definitely soon. Word of a reward has spread on Planet Next. Undoubtedly, it's a challenge. And the challenge has been accepted. The collective response is one of solidarity of interests, a fellowship of spirit, and cohesion toward a common goal.

Captured? Who, us? Reward …? Keep dreaming. Which parents? Ours? Who's the culprit here?

Doubters, be gone! They will beat this, and they'll beat it together.

After the Jose mishap, it's time to double down and increase the security measures for their island camouflage: expanded circumference, better filter, no distortion. The Dragon Dale brothers work around the clock with Jed, performing trials and retrials. This has to work, and soon.

At all costs, reward-contending parties cannot know, cannot detect, and cannot be clued in to Planet Next's location. And it's not just the interested parties they're concerned about—the casual passing boats should also not see the island, tipping off would-be seekers.

It's morning, and it has rained, so the air is cool. The day hasn't had the opportunity to unleash its damp excitement. Huxley sits on his rooftop and stares at the waters; he knows the time is close, the risk high, and any mistake will certainly be punished.

Playing the soundtrack of the debate in his mind, he realizes that, without camouflage, the secret of the waters, Project X, cannot be divulged. Alas, it may serve as a summons for unwanted investigation.

Lost in his thoughts, he hears a familiar murmur below. Chandler is speaking, though this time it's not with him.

She looks with admiration at a bird, her head slanted, smiling as though she's seen a long-lost friend and is offering her blessings.

Though he knows he might regret this, his mind is tickled at the curious sight, and he can't resist tossing in his thoughts. "Have you found a new friend? Seems like an interesting chat."

She rolls her eyes up. "And this is comin' from a guy who talks to his bird all day and plays *Ches*, right?"

Very true, Huxley thinks. He smiles. Chester, though, is not amused and tilts his head forward, flashing her a skeptical eye.

"You're not the only one who likes rare birds," she says, staring at this interesting creature of nature perched upon her window ledge.

After a moment, she whispers under her grin, "Wow … this must be a sign."

Indeed, the heavens are shining their light, and destiny is tapping her on the shoulder. This is the signal she's been waiting for, possibly, her whole life. Motivated, as always, for the good of humanity, she accepted Huxley's offer to come to Planet Next to see if the planet could offer the social and environmental good she's been seeking and, perhaps, be a symbol, a model, and in due time, a motivating force for the rest of humanity to follow.

Driven by a singular goal, a plan, a concept—her concept—she delineated her intentions, carefully elaborated their implementation, and submitted a formal proposal. Though of a slightly different mind and with different motives, Huxley accepted her provisions, including wearing the peace symbol necklace she provided, simply her reminder: keep your promise.

For her part, Chandler had a deluge of supporters, and her voice was a leading mouthpiece amongst her like-minded peers. Securing her allegiance was critical to any success for this endeavor.

Since childhood, Chandler has identified most with endangered birds, figuratively seeing herself as one. Backed by her moral code, she knows she's not liked by all, that her views are odd to some, that her perspective is opposed by many, and that her ideology will not win a popularity contest anywhere, not even with her father. But much like an eagle flying above the storm, driven by its inner compass, she soars high, over and beyond the reach of their ridicule, their defiance, and the groundswell of their condemnation.

Today she's found a rare friend in her visionary quest. Huxley leans over and stares with wonder at this unique bird. "Would you care to share?"

"This is the second endangered species that has chosen Planet Next to be its home."

"Really?" Huxley says, intrigued, beckoning her to say more. After all, he feels he has partnered in this fascinating occurrence, and as any true champion of justice would, he gazes curiously at this emblem of their mutual triumph.

"This is a Cuban kite."

"Well, we certainly have been having Cuban visitors lately."

"No, no … this is different," she says, resuming her stare. "It's rare to see them even in Cuba. You won't see them anywhere else. There are less than a few hundred of them."

Indeed, it's a fine moment for Chandler, for Huxley, and for Planet Next. Not only have they charmed the birds, but they've also stoked the fire of the students' imaginations. At the last count, they'd garnered more than sixty percent interest in collaboratively laboring to advance the planetary goals toward their climate-friendly, philanthropic target.

"What do you think, Chester?" Huxley darts his eyes to his shoulder before glancing back at their welcomed visitor.

Chester looks on, his expression stoic, his thoughts unspoken. He adds nothing more.

"Well, you're definitely at a loss for words where exotic birds are concerned."

After a moment, Huxley stands up and steps closer. The small gray-white bird has an interesting hooked bill; yellow, it seems. Huxley draws forward for a better view, amused. Holding out a twig in his palm, he closes his hand;

then, blowing at its rim, he opens it ... The twig has turned into a flower.

The Cuban kite just stares.

"Not impressed?" Huxley asks. He closes his fist again, shakes it, and then opens it again. This time, there are seeds.

"I hope you don't mind me sharing your food, Chester." Huxley glances at his falcon eyes with a smile.

Strangely, the Cuban kite is not interested in the seeds, and Chester doesn't appear pleased, either.

"Tough crowd ..." Huxley says, looking at them both. Then he leans forward for something more daring.

"Be careful ... don't get too close," Chandler pleads. "We don't wanna scare it away. This is precious."

Surprised, Huxley draws back and glances at Chester, trying to decipher his cryptic gaze. He waits for him to warm up. It's taking longer than expected.

"You don't mind sharing Planet Next with a few friends from the skies, do you, Chester?"

Noteworthy, and rather mysteriously, the bird offers no response—just as with the owlet-nightjar.

Huxley stares at Chester, bemused.

Really, Chester?

MEYERSVILLE HARBOR

As Mr. Wickly sits at the docks, waiting for the teachers to arrive, he glances at his watch. Eager and uptight, he stands up, looks about, and paces to and fro before staring at his watch again. The time: 10:00 a.m.

The teachers, the school psychologist, and Mr. Wickly have agreed to reel in the kids and for the earnings to be split, much like their weekly lottery at work, fairly and evenly ... by Mr. Wickly.

Trapping the students is a daunting task, and Mr. Wickly knows that, alone, it would be a challenge, even for him. He needs the teachers' help, their influence, their muscle, and much like cowboys rounding up cattle, they must work together to converge, direct, and push the cows to a corner one by one.

In anticipation, Mr. Wickly has made arrangements for a large ship, and he trusts and hopes it will be filled, and filled to the brim, upon return—and, of course, that his pockets will be filled ever so prolifically after.

Alas, Mr. Farnsworth is the only member licensed to take them on such a trip. And he's not here.

Teachers roll in with bags in hand, rubbing on suntan lotion, chatting with elation, their exuberant voices ringing above the docks.

Fifteen minutes pass, and Mr. Wickly impatiently paces, awaiting Mr. Farnsworth's arrival, scanning the docks.

Then, far in the distance, a figure appears, leisurely walking, whistling, unhurried, arms lazily swinging, turning here and there and gazing about.

Tilting his head forward, Mr. Wickly narrows his eyes. Like a laser beam, his sight pierces through the haze of a hot summer day, penetrates through a stack of heads as well as a child's skipping rope, and then slides between a hotdog stand and the ice cream parlor before abruptly meeting the eyes of Mr. Farnsworth.

Bullseye.

Terror grips his face. Mr. Farnsworth suddenly stops, frozen in his tracks. He understands precisely what that look means. How can he not know? Everybody knows. Thawing to resume his gait, he casually glances at the clock tower. His walk stiffens, his arms by his side, but after he glances at the clock again, his pace increases, a skip, a leap. Coming to his senses, he begins to sprint, his neck stretched out, his arms swinging wildly.

At last, everyone's on board, and they embark on their journey. Mr. Wickly walks past each member, providing a sheet of instructions. This is no ordinary day and certainly no ordinary school trip. Everyone has a task and, in the strictest sense, a role to play. No stone will be unturned, no detail left to chance. Not today. Not ever. Not with Mr.

Wickly.

Teachers versus students, the ultimate battle of wills and, perhaps, a battle of wits—one moment, one prize, and of course, the prize is conveniently there for one group and one winner only: the teachers.

The students' prize, of course, is to deliciously deny the teachers of their intended goal. But more importantly, it is to continue to live without limits and dwell as they have designed, chosen, and sought for.

Game on.

Mr. Tepper is in a different state of mind, pouring champagne for all the teachers. He smells victory. He wants to taste it, too. Smiling with red cheeks, he wants everyone to see the big picture: This is a crusade of love. Quite sincerely, he misses his students more than they can imagine. And if all goes well, he'll deliver his heartfelt eulogy to their misguided endeavor.

His contagious excitement flutters above the ship. Truly, this is his toast before the students are *toast.* He chuckles and raises his chin, and he lets loose his traditional raspy laugh.

The teachers have, without question, done their homework. Using the coordinates provided, there is only one place, one island, where the students could be, and beyond that, they know their students, their silent needs, and more than anything, their covert schemes. There's no doubt about this place. It fits the bill.

Mr. Wickly, though, is not in a celebratory mood, but even he can't fight the fervor of the moment. Eventually, at Mr. Tepper's insistence, he relents and puts on a party hat, posing without expression for a sentimental photograph.

Snapping pictures, Mr. Tepper's face creeps up, and he lowers the camera. "C'mon, smile. This is our retirement party. You realize what you're comin' home with, right?"

Indeed. The thought streaks across his mind briefly. It disappears, and then it streaks by again. He attempts to suppress it, blinking back the thought. Moments later, it emerges—more clarity, more vigor, sparkling as ever. Then, like a meteor shower, it streaks by in droves, flooding him with emotion irresistibly rising to the surface.

Daydreaming as he is ... *Oh, Wickly, say, "Billion."*

He smiles, smiles, and smiles.

Flash!

MEANTIME ON PLANET NEXT

Huxley looks at the time: 11:30 a.m. He paces his rooftop, anxious.

No need for a reminder; he knows it's the Huxley blackout zone, and he patiently waits for Jed and the Dragon Dale brothers to perform their daily sacred ritual: eating lunch. He's eager to resume the unfinished work left behind, but he knows better than anyone not to interrupt their most precious hour of the day.

Jed's bond with the brothers seems to grow with each noontide meal. They now have an unspoken connection and seem to finish one another's thoughts, particularly where food is concerned.

Huxley stands still. Then he resumes his pace, checking the time once more, checking the skies, checking about, sitting down, standing up ... *Why is time passing so slowly?*

Chester glides in the distance, wings still, no effort, almost lulled; he gently floats and then circles the blue skies—his peaceful oasis.

Huxley sits, his eyes fixed, tranquilized as he watches Chester, enjoying the moment.

Chester suddenly soars higher and breaks, waits a beat, and then tips, beak down, and quickly twirls back. His eyes on Huxley, he flaps with more vigor, more emotion, his pace increasing with each passing second.

Huxley stands. Though he knows what this means, he hopes he's wrong and moves to the edge of the rooftop, impatient for the bird's return.

As Chester nears, Huxley lifts his head, prompting those beaks to provide its message.

"Many pawns, master."

Many? It's a blow. And there's no time to lament. Huxley spirals down the tree in a flash, rushed, breaking branches; he reaches for a liana and then jumps down and runs along the trail. Looking as far as he can, he sees Chandler near the waters.

"Sound the horn!" he yells, waving his arms.

Surprised, she tilts her head up. It takes a moment for her to register his call and its impending doom. But then she realizes, *Horn!* Nodding in panic, she darts up the hill, and when she reaches the pole mounted there, she sounds the siren.

Huxley yells, "Take your positions!" and dashes left, taking a shortcut. After two steps and a jump, he reaches for the rope, swings in an arc, and comes down, bolting forward. He'll meet Jed and the Dragon Dale brothers by the waters, he figures.

They're not there.

A swarm of bodies frantically races by him, their

shoulders and faces rushing past. He continues to look—left, right—then turns and pushes back through the crowd. *Where's Jed?* He runs faster, looks around … *Where are the twins?*

He sees a ramp, jumps six feet in the air, and lands on the sand. Running along the south-side beach, he arcs back, elbowing past onrushing students, yelling, "Have you seen Dragon? Dale?" Heads shake as they blaze past him, and he bolts up the steps and storms through the trees … heading for where he knows they shouldn't be. *They can't be home.*

He's tired, panting, but he keeps sprinting … *Must keep going.* "They had to have heard the horn, unless …"

Upon reaching the final step, he freezes at an unforgettable sight: Jed, Dragon, and Dale lie asleep on the patio sofa, their slumber likely brought on by their hearty meal.

In a tapestry of bliss, like earthly beings having had an unearthly experience, Jed is cuddled with the twins, all lying down, all snoring.

"Jed!" Huxley prompts, stepping up, looking at the brothers, tugging their arms. "There's a ship."

Eyelids snap open, and eyes search while Huxley repeats the message. *Ding-dong*, the words sink in, as does the pathos of the moment: *they're here.*

"Chester says there are many!"

Filled with panic, they sit forward, swapping glances; then, in a heartbeat, they pop up, turn, and storm down, bolting toward the beaches.

Dragon heads east; Dale cuts west with Jed.

"Just place the camochip and start the generator!" Dale shouts, his voice trailing off. "It'll be good enough. I'll start

136

the OC-link."

Dragon keeps running with Huxley close behind. Fully awake now, his footsteps pound, and the recently eaten meal rises to his chest.

Huxley looks to his right, where he expects the ship to arrive, but sees nothing. Not so far. With a boulder of rocks lining the horizon, they won't come into view until they're a mile away.

With a quick burst, Huxley sprints forward and passes Dragon. He yells, "Start the generator!" and detours for the cliff—*Shortcut*—and lifts off, forty feet high ... His feet cycle twice, and then his arms come up, and his toes point down. Holding his breath, he plunges with full force into water. He sinks twenty feet below, touches the ocean floor, and then pushes up. One stroke, then another, and then his legs paddle as he emerges and begins to swim, furiously aiming for the control panel.

A quick glance over his shoulder: *No sign yet.*

Drawing closer, his feet reach the sands below, and he rises and bolts forward, his high-stepping feet splashing water as he looks at the open panel.

Dragon is starved for air, running more than he wants to. Reaching the generator, his arms are limp, his legs barely holding up. He tilts forward in exhaustion and looks on as Huxley tries to place the camochip inside the last panel.

Awaiting Huxley's signal, Dragon watches him frantically working. He then wonders if Dale and Jed have started the OT-link. *They must have.* Pressed for time, he checks over his shoulder and sees the boat. Stunned, he's uncertain about what to do, and he glances over at Huxley, who suddenly looks up and signals with a raised fist that it's done.

Dragon nods, and the generator starts. The camouflage flickers for a moment, and then ... it finds normal.

They wait.

With quiet steps, everyone resumes positions atop trees, behind bushes, inside ditches.

The boat sails on, full steam. It maneuvers past the boulders on a deliberate course, and sure enough, it's aimed for Planet Next.

Imaginations runs free: *Why pass the boulders? What if they saw us? Who could it be? What if they push through the cloak?*

Huxley gently swims back. Everyone's motionless, hidden as they are.

Silence falls, and fear stirs as they watch the boat's approach. In a moment of self-deception, everyone's still hopeful that it's a random ship, an undesigned coincidence. Fingers crossed: *It's nothing.*

Moments later, it draws closer. They can now hear voices warbling in the distance, a few murmurs, and then ... there is a laugh—a raspy laugh. They hear it again, and it sinks deeper. Everyone knows that laugh, that distinct laugh, that annoying laugh: *Mr. Tepper.*

No doubt about it. The teachers are here.

TEACHERS' SHIP

Sounds of jubilation float above the waters as the boat steadily sails to the beat of its own hum. The surrounding music adds its own tempo to the mix, defining a moment pregnant with marvel.

Mr. Wickly stands at the bridge, next to Mr. Farnsworth. Having resumed his businesslike manner, he stares at the horizon. He knows they're close.

"That's strange," Mr. Farnsworth murmurs.

"What?" Mr. Wickly probes, waiting for him to say more.

"Nothin'," he mutters, confused. He looks through his binoculars and does a quick left-center-right, before scanning in a slow arc. "Huh …?"

His curiosity rising, Mr. Wickly wants his finger on the pulse of every matter. He repeats his question: "What? What's happened?"

"I thought. I coulda sworn … I saw it a few minutes ago. Christ, I can't see it anymore."

Mr. Wickly reaches for his binoculars. Then he walks to the bow and gazes about in all directions with them. "Did we pass it?" he asks, turning to look behind him. The ship slows to a gentle drift.

"No, couldn't have."

Mr. Wickly holds the rails and leans over, his eyes searching. Something doesn't feel right.

"This shouldn't be," Mr. Farnsworth says. "The radar signal is also gone."

Mr. Wickly looks straight ahead. He knows his students, and his every instinct tells him, *Look carefully.* Eyes locked, no smile, his demeanor catches the teachers' attention. Raising his hand, he casts an eye over his shoulder and gestures to cut the music.

It stops.

The chatters fade to murmurs, and then there's no audible sound but the smooth glide of the boat along the waters. Like little ducklings, everyone drifts to the side and looks on, with Mr. Wickly leading the way.

His mind ruminates as his eyes rove the skies. Motionless, he continues to listen. It's almost as though he feels something, a presence, but he can't describe it.

It grips him. Without a blink, without a word, his head turns, and he mulls things over for a moment longer. Finally, he whispers, "Hmm?"

"What?" Mrs. Andrews asks.

"Did you hear that?"

"Hear what?"

Mr. Wickly closes his eyes, his mind drifting somewhere. It stays there for a while, and then another breeze rustles through. His lids slit open. "I hear leaves ..."

"What?" Puzzled, Mrs. Andrews tilts her head sideways and focuses. Time passes, but she hears nothing. She attempts again but only hears the surrounding draft. Then she closes her eyes. "I can only hear the water hitting our boat."

Mr. Wickly looks up and gazes about, as confused as he is certain.

Mr. Farnsworth joins them. "Whaddaya want me to do? This is the location. I think we should check a few more miles ahead."

Mr. Wickly doesn't answer. He continues to stare, unsettled. After a moment, he nods, his gaze still pensive.

The boat sails forward five miles, then ten, and after twenty miles, Mr. Farnsworth shakes his head. "There's nothin' but ocean from here on. We should go back."

Not everyone has the stamina to press on. Mr. Wickly does. "Another ten miles!" he shouts over his shoulder, and then he turns his attention back to the water.

The miles fly by, as does the time. Does he want to stop? No. Does he want to relent? Never. But he must do something. Eventually, the ship turns and heads back.

"Take me to the spot you thought you'd seen it," Mr. Wickly requests, still holding hope.

Mr. Farnsworth nods. With glum faces, their eyes downcast, the teachers are quiet. Their earlier excitement has now all but evaporated.

Mr. Wickly stands at the bow, gazing through his binoculars. A mysterious feeling overtakes him as they draw closer to the expected location of the island.

"What do we do now?" Mr. Farnsworth asks. "This is the spot."

"Turn off the engines," Mr. Wickly demands and turns his head to listen again. Other teachers listen as well, curious.

Mr. Wickly bounces his eyes about. He feels so close to victory and even closer to defeat. He mulls the situation, uncertain if he's willing to concede, uncertain if, truly, he has any other choice. *There's always a choice.* Running the debate's soundtrack in his mind, he wonders, *What if the coordinates are off? What if there's no island? A mistake ...? No, that can't be.*

A moment passes as everyone awaits his response, watching him work through the final details. He looks out once again, holding his gaze steady for some time. Finally, he mutters, "Huxley ... X," and shakes his head in disbelief. "Very well ... let's go back."

Everyone sits on the side of the boat, soundless; not a movement is contemplated. They're stunned. At a steady pace, the boat cruises back, along with their dreams.

The sun hovers at its apex without a single cloud, and the water is now as blue as the sky. A nice, cool gust wafts over the teachers' faces, yet nothing feels right. *Where is the island? What do we do now?*

The questions are swirling in their minds when suddenly Mr. Farnsworth looks back and yells, "You might wanna see this!"

All the teachers gather at the bow and look. Not seeing anything, they walk starboard, beside the rails. An incoming ship is sailing some hundred yards away.

It draws closer. They look: it's the police ship.

Surprised, they stand in silence and watch the ship drift by, a serendipitous colliding of fortunes in a reversal of paths.

The police say nothing, though stunned expressions embrace their faces as they observe the decorations and the colorful balloons adorning the teachers' boat.

As they sail by, Mr. Wickly looks left and darts an evil eye at Mr. Tepper, piercing him with a knowing gaze. Mr. Tepper yields to his stare, his tongue frozen. He can't recall what he's done wrong. Like a man on death row suddenly forgetting his last words, his lapse of memory is disastrously timed. Then Mr. Tepper remembers. Trying to stay calm, he lifts a hand and gently removes his party hat.

Chief Ross elbows his way through his officers. He stares at the teachers' vessel, sees that it is empty of students, and shoots a perplexed gaze at Mr. Wickly. The chief raises an arm, but then he stops himself from waving.

Mr. Wickly nods. He can't muster an expression and does nothing more.

Moments later, the police ship is in the rearview, and a few teachers huddle, murmuring undecipherable words.

Mr. Wickly finally glances over. Their hushed voices continue and crescendo: "That's perfect!"

What's perfect?

For certain, they now have Mr. Wickly's attention and, more importantly, his interest. He steps closer, and their huddle opens and swallows him inside.

As the whispers continue, Mr. Wickly grumbles. Their heads tilt further in; they are immersed in something … Their murmurs press on.

Finally, Mr. Wickly's head lifts up, and he shouts, "Turn the ship! Turn the ship! Follow them!" He points.

Raising his hand, Mr. Farnsworth looks back and nods. *Got it!*

With no other surrounding vessels, the ship makes an arc and sails full steam ahead in what's now a two-boat race.

"They'll lead us to them," Mr. Wickly says, smiling.

Mr. Farnsworth is unsure if he wants to comment on some of the obvious differences, but he does so anyway. "You realize their boat is the one holdin' the guns?"

Mr. Wickly nods. "You realize this boat is the one holding the teachers? Just follow."

On the police boat, the chief eventually comes to the stern for a view of the teachers' ship. Shaking his head, he mouths something they can't hear. The only certainty: it wasn't something merry to their ears.

Their boat picks up pace, as does the teachers', curiously cruising in exactly the same direction, to the same coordinates as they had an hour before, and though the teachers know the result, they follow, hopeful of a different conclusion. At last, both ships arrive at the same precise location.

The police are baffled. As they stand frozen, their eyes stare at the empty space as though there should be something there.

It doesn't go unnoticed by Mr. Wickly, who shifts his head to listen, his attention focused. Then he notes something, and his head tilts up. "Did you hear that?"

"Hear what?" Mrs. Andrews asks, confused again.

Mr. Wickly closes his eyes and listens … "Birds."

A second later, he opens his lids and claps his eyes on the sky. He sees nothing. Unsettled by the discrepancy, he stares, turning his head left and then right. "Strange ... very strange."

Mrs. Andrews listens carefully. "Sorry ... can't hear it." The police boat slows, and its officers huddle at the bridge. They appear to be in an animated discussion about something.

As the teachers' ship draws closer, closing the gap, Mr. Wickly walks to the bow to meet Chief Ross, who has come to the stern for a friendly chat.

"We're still working on the same team ... I hope?" Mr. Wickly asks.

"Team? You mean the students. Yes, of course, though we're here for another matter altogether. And you?"

Mr. Wickly stares, scanning the chief to determine his intentions. Then he frees a smile. "Oh ... the teachers are bored. It's a beautiful sunny day." Shrug. "We have the boat till four."

After a muted moment of analysis with an undertow of mutual suspicion, the chief nods and then turns back. They resume their journey, circling aimlessly for some thirty minutes, after which, they sail back, navigating toward shore.

This wasn't the ending they were expecting—far from it. No one says a word. No one makes eye contact. Dejected, no one wants to because no one really can.

It has been a strange, strange day, indeed.

POLICE STATION
MEETING ROOM

The office is quiet. Everyone sits at the table, staring aimlessly, feeling low.

Three days remain until the deadline, and over one billion is on the line. Yesterday's near victory is tomorrow's certain loss.

Chief Ross begins the deliberations.

"Do we have any other leads?"

"None."

"What about Huxley X? Does he have any inherited properties from his natural parents?"

Officer Higgins looks at his page. "Nope. They were quite young; they actually didn't own a home."

"Really? Tell me more."

"Parents, both teachers, worked at the same school Huxley attended. They died in a fire. It's reported that Huxley was responsible. A case of a magic trick gone wrong ... School burned down."

Everyone mulls this over. No one says a word.

Chief Ross finally breaks the silence. "Well, not much has changed, has it? Another school, another mess, another fire for everyone to put out, though, this time, he's acknowledging responsibility upfront. It's starting to make sense. This kid has a beef with parents and teachers."

After a pensive moment, Officer Higgins gruffly asks, "So, what's left to check?"

"All trails still lead back to Mr. Jules. He's the only adult," Officer Angelos replies. "We've visited every property, his homes, his cottage, and this mysterious island that doesn't exist."

Another pause lingers, weighing on her last words. "We double-checked the island's coordinates," Officer Jefferson chimes in. "Unless it sunk under the waters or fell off the map, I don't have any explanation for this."

"Well, the water levels have certainly risen from the recent storms," Officer Higgins confirms. "But enough to sink an island? It doesn't make sense."

"There's one way to know." Officer Angelos nods.

"What's that?" Chief Ross turns to look at her, curious.

"Intelligence satellites." After a moment, she adds, "They'd give us up-to-the-minute images."

Chief Ross sits back and lets out a long breath, thinking. He knows she's right; the idea is good. He just doesn't know how to reject it. Satellite clearance means federal agents, and in practical terms, you can't use their intel and reserve a billion-dollar donation exclusively for your own use. Right now, he's not in the mood to share.

"Interesting. Somethin' to think about," he finally answers, hoping to never touch the subject again.

Shaking his head, Officer Higgins asks, "Why don't we use Mr. Mubanga's services—Satellend?" Then he shuffles through his papers, rushed, remembering something, searching as though he's stumbled on an important finding. "His sons ... Dragon and Dale, are part of the missing students," he says, looking up. "He owns a private remote-sensing satellite company. He's the one who offered the two hundred million."

Gazing back at his notes, he taps his sheet. "Startin' last week, the service was made free for the Florida region ... He's already read our minds."

The chief mulls this in silence. He shrugs. The idea is worth a look, and more importantly, it's free. What does he have to lose?

Another plan is gnawing at him, though, and he can't let it go. After a minute, he looks up. "It's not such a bad suggestion," he says, tapping his finger on the table. "But there's somethin' else I wanna try first."

There's an easier way to seek answers. He knows it. He lets loose a relaxing smile and nods. *It's good.* The idea is as simple as it is sensible, with the best part being, of course, that he thought of it.

PLANET NEXT
DAY FIFTY-EIGHT

It's been two days since the last visitor and the island's closest call. While Huxley feels the walls closing in, he's relieved of worrying about one front. Phase III of his plan, the cloaking device, is now completed.

Though this critical phase has passed, weighing on his mind are his remaining projects, yet to be unveiled. But, alas, this requires a few pieces to fall into place and a few more to fall out. He's waiting for a sign; he's just not sure what, but he knows with certainty that when he sees it, he'll know.

The island has evolved, ardently, steadily, laboriously, to reach its potential. It's now autonomous, with sustainable food, clean water and energy, and a code of living. A culture has also developed: respect, hard work, cohesion of purpose, feelings of solidarity, and a sense of anything and everything they didn't have while living at home.

Although the students have agreed to a six-month term, Chandler has had a change of heart and has reassured Huxley that when everyone sees things as she does, they won't want to leave.

Of course, there's plenty of time; yet time is an illusion—an illusion of form, an illusion of the sun, an illusion that moves deceptively from time to time.

The time right now: 9:00 p.m.

Huxley's tired, as he should be. Tonight he sleeps early. One more sweep for Chester, and they'll be done for the evening.

Huxley waits, lying down, looking at the stars. Somehow they seem farther away, less glittery, more reclusive. He doesn't care. Exhausted, his eyelids heavy, he fights to keep them open, but they're equally stubborn and fight harder to close. One flick, open. Two flicks, open. Then three flicks, flutters, and another flick … he's gone.

Time passes, and so does the night.

Eyes finally unlock—*what happened?* In terror, he pops up, sweating, and though it felt like he slept for only a moment, he knows from the surrounding sunlight that it was much longer. Chester is perched at the window, looking on.

"Many pawns, master."

Stunned, Huxley looks at the time: 8:45 a.m. Panic sets in, and he runs to the window. There's a ship arriving.

Bursting out of his tree house, Huxley hustles down to the ground, jumping the last leg. He races through the jungle, hopping a rock, then another, passing trees, logs, and fallen branches, winding his way down to the beach, bolting faster, in disbelief that he slept.

Noting the people already in position, he stops, hides behind a tree, and peeks out.

Jed, Dragon, and Dale are in view, ready. The camouflage is on. Jed nods, raises a finger as if to say, *Keep calm, everything's under control*, and smiles.

The ship sails closer, unconcerned. It's rather large. No sound, no movement, and despite the cloak, everyone's reflexively hunkered down.

Voices can be heard from the ship. *What are they saying?* No one can identify what, why, or who they are.

Mysteriously, it draws near and then stops. No ship has ever drifted this close before.

Though he's curious to look, Huxley denies the temptation and stands still. A distant voice murmurs a few indecipherable words. Huxley listens. Confused, he stretches his neck and draws an attentive ear. *Spanish?*

A surprised Jed looks up and then turns in recognition. "Jose ...?"

"Mr. Jed ... is that you? Where are you?"

Jed signals a twirling hand. The optical camouflage is turned off, and stepping closer, he sees a stunned Jose standing at the side of the bow, looking down.

"How did you do that?" Jose looks about, surprised to suddenly see the island.

"Ahh ... a long story." Jed nods. "Whaddaya doin' here?"

Unable to snap his mind away from the illusion, Jose stares longer, eyes roving, and then, finally, he answers, "I was just passing through, goin' on vacation, and thought to stop by and let you know, the police came around yesterday."

"Oh really, what did they want?"

"Nothing, just fishin' ... like before. Since our ships are listed to dock next to one another, they asked about your island. You know ... if I knew where it was." He waits a beat and tosses in, "I didn't tell 'em anything."

"Thanks a bunch." Jed nods and notes something of interest and immediately cuts to, "That's a big vessel to travel with ... alone."

Jose looks behind him. "Oh, no, I always vacation with my family." He motions to them to come forward, nodding, letting them know it's okay.

A moment later, a few heads pop over the taffrail, and then a few more. Jose keeps waving, and they keep arriving in tides, and just as it seems to end, several more heads emerge above the rest ... and then more.

Huxley's jaw drops in shock. One by one, some three hundred people crowd toward the taffrail, heads leaning over and faces overlooking shoulders. At last, the people smile and wave as the echoes of "Hola!" ring from the ship and over the water.

In disbelief, Huxley whispers, "That's a big family." When his dread fades to gloom, he asks, "Are you sure the police didn't follow you?"

Jose looks puzzled, as though the thought hadn't crossed his mind, and then he confirms it. "Good question."

Lovely.

Jose raises his palm as if to say, *Wait*, and disappears from view. A minute passes as he peers about, and then he returns. "Don't worry. They didn't follow."

Huxley looks to Dragon and Dale to see if they're as surprised as he is and, no doubt, as sure of their demise.

The moment is as naïve as it is cataclysmic.

Oblivious, Jose nods to Jed as if he wants to tell him something; he turns, bends down, and lifts a cooler bag. "We hafta go, but I brought you a gift. Again, it's not Texan, but this one is Cuban," he offers and lowers it to Jed, whose arms are raised in jubilation.

"Thanks, Jose. Appreciate you stoppin' by."

"Is there anything else you guys need?" Jose asks. "I pass this way often."

Everyone swaps looks, shaking their heads in answer. Huxley, though, has something in mind. Uncertain, he pulls Jed aside and asks him in a loud whisper, "I'm feeling less comfortable with his visits. Can we trust him?"

"Who ...? Them?" Jed says in a hushed voice, dismissing the question. "Look, even if you paid 'em a hundred thousand dollars, they'd never speak about this."

Huxley stares at him, needing confirmation.

"I promise."

Seconds pass as Huxley mulls this over. Then he turns back and nods. "Mr. Jose, if it's no trouble, I'd like for you to mail something from the mainland."

"Sure ... anything you like."

Huxley lifts a polite finger. "It'll just be a moment." Walking away, he disappears into the woods and returns to his tree house. He quickly looks for his sheets of paper and some envelopes, and then he jots down a few notes.

He's done. From his dreamlike smile, it would appear he already knew what he wanted to write and, of course, what not to.

Meanwhile, Jed keeps the ship company, chatting with Jose and his family, enjoying the banter as always.

At last, Huxley returns with some envelopes. The notes are lifted up to the ship with a long wooden stick, and Jose takes them.

"Thank you for this." Huxley nods. After they exchange goodbyes and waves, Jed gives Jose a thumbs-up, and the ship sets sail and coasts away.

A few minutes pass as they watch it drift into the horizon. Huxley's uncertain about what to make of what just happened. The fact of the matter is, everyone on the ship saw the students, they saw the cloak, they know where the students live, and now there's a reward. He turns to Jed and repeats his question, "You sure?"

"Positive."

Despite the reassurance, Huxley's doubts linger. How can they not? Stirred with suspicion, Huxley finally finds words for his angst. Locking eyes on the skyline, he says, "I hope you're right, Jed. I truly do. Knowing these parents, their wealth, their patterns, their motif … a hundred thousand dollars may, indeed, be what we're up against."

POLICE HEADQUARTERS
THINK TANK MEETING

Forty-eight hours remain: no students, no Jed, no island, and no clue where to look. It doesn't look good.

But nobody dares tell Chief Ross. This is a battle he must fight and win.

Mr. Mubanga's company, Satellend, recently provided, at no cost, satellite images. The police, focused on the surrounding waters, have filtered through enough data to view the desired region.

Looking at the images in disbelief, it's not what they were expecting.

"How can an island just disappear?" the chief says.

"It's hurricane season. Water levels are higher."

"For heaven's sake, if that's the case, they're all dead."

"Or moved somewhere else," Officer Higgins adds.

"Where?"

Officer Jefferson cuts in. "Should we at least consider deploying an underwater search team just to be sure?"

The chief mulls things over, uncertain about what to do and what choices he has left. He looks at his notes, almost as though he's attempting to do the math once more. Perhaps staring again will spark an idea.

The officers all gaze at each other in silence, waiting for his response, when suddenly the door opens. It's Officer Angelos. "Chief, we just received mail. You'll definitely wanna see this. It's for you. There's no return address, just a name at the top: Huxley X."

It takes a moment for her words to sink in. Heads turn in sync, surprised. Standing, the chief reaches for the letter, rushed and excited, and tears the side of the envelope and pulls out the note.

Still amazed, he looks up at everyone with a sense of relief. At last, they have a new lead. They've been waiting for a break. Here it is. He unfolds the page, and after a sharp once-over, he reads:

Dear Chief,

We hope this letter finds you well and finds you searching to no avail. Seeing that we donated our previous efforts to our parents, families, and teachers, we didn't want to overlook the most sacred institutions of this land: the law.

We know, and know well, that your badge stands for justice, that it stands for respect, that it stands for fatherly duty, and it is with sincere regard for that badge that my uncle Jed proudly wears it every Halloween with its companion attire.

More than anyone, you understand what it is to be a

man of the people, to be a man of the constitution,
and to be a man who upholds the maxim "to serve
and protect" the innocent, the blameless, and the
kindred of this land.

For this reason, we ask: Please serve. Please protect.
We're innocent. We know that. And, by now, you
know that, too.

While we admire your committed talents and
professional mastery at hide and seek, you won't find
us. Nor should you want to.

Please send regards to our families and a kind word
to let them know we're well, we're happy, and we're
not coming home.

Sincerely and quite candidly,

X ... on behalf of the united citizens of Planet Next

The chief stares at the page even after he's finished
reading it. Then his eyes drift up, though his mind is still
lost somewhere in its words.

Everyone's thinking. Every sentence is a clue. He
knows that better than anyone. Muted, the officers mull
things over together.

The chief turns the envelope and looks closely at the
postmark, observing its date. "This was mailed a few days
ago," he mutters. "It was also mailed from Florida."

Eyes wolflike, he senses a clue. Yes, even the things
they want you to see are hints. He stares up as though he's
searching the vaults of his mind. He understands too well
that he must trust his instincts, the instincts of a battle-

hardened police officer with a nose for solving crime. He sees facts in that invisible abyss where the legends of his ilk are born.

He turns to the other officers, looks at each one, and finally nods. "They're not on an island, nor near any body of water. Dammit, nobody would go to an island during a hurricane." It's clear to him now.

"But, sir ... Mr. Jules's island is the only place we haven't checked."

"Yes. And it doesn't exist. It's a brilliant diversion. That's what they want us to chase. Trust me—they're on the mainland, where this letter was mailed. And they know we're searchin' for them. They're watchin' us."

He looks up at the four corners of the room; the other officers reflexively gaze up, uncertain what they're searching for.

With a face of steel, he gazes back down and says, "Every criminal makes a misstep somewhere. Search every house, park, and green space we've already been to. They've seen us. This boy, Huxley X, has just made his first mistake." Shaking his head, he whispers, "Thanks a billion."

MEANWHILE, AT MADISON SCHOOL

Mr. Wickly stares at the ceiling, lost in space, uttering the same phrase: "For every weakness, there's a challenge to reveal it." *Oh, Wickly, think ... how to expose these mites?*

If only he knew. His mind drifts deeper now, into another realm, and he hovers there for a while, still baffled.

The teachers have scoured all possible sources: social media, yearbook photos, daily chats with parents, friends, and neighbors. There's not a single clue.

The room is quiet as everyone works diligently, and everyone will work late. Why? Because Mr. Wickly wants them to.

"We've gone over this a hundred times," Mr. Farnsworth laments. "All paths link back to Huxley X. And, go figure, he's the one guy we know nothin' about."

Mr. Tepper thinks for a moment before turning to Mr. Wickly. "How do you know him, again?"

Floating in his thoughts somewhere, Mr. Wickly takes a mental respite, stares for a moment, and then answers, "I told you ... He registered earlier this summer."

"But I thought you said his uncle came alone to register him."

The door screeches. A distracted Mrs. Andrews walks in and looks up, holding the mail. She flips through an assortment of customary envelopes, and suddenly her eyes stumble on a letter with familiar writing.

She freezes, staring at the cover, knowing what it implies. It takes a full three seconds for the information to travel from her eyes to her mind, bouncing between cells, bouncing between a few more, fearing Mr. Wickly's scorn, before finally sending a reply: "THIS IS IT!"

Hopping in glory, she throws up her arm as though holding the winning lottery ticket.

Immediately, teachers huddle around her, looking on, before Mr. Wickly steps up and reaches out with two fingers and snatches the letter from her hands. The huddle swiftly moves to surround him.

He looks at both sides of the letter: no name, no return address, but the handwriting is strangely familiar. He swiftly reaches for a paper knife, and like a surgeon demonstrating his craft, he opens the envelope with precision. Everyone gathers closer, some looking over his shoulder, others jostling beside him. Mrs. Andrews's head pushes right up against his, jutting past Mr. Farnsworth's.

Mr. Wickly unfolds the letter.

He stares at it. It's blank.

An odd moment ... Mr. Wickly turns the page and glances at both sides. It's not signed. It's not dated. It's not addressed to anyone. Is he seeing right? Yes, he is. Indeed, there's no message, just a white page of ... nothing.

Everyone's quiet. They know every blank word is an invitation to their eyes. *Invitation to what?* Mr. Tepper wonders. *A challenge? To failure?*

With the letter in hand, Mr. Wickly walks to the window. No need to check; he knows this page has the fingerprints of Huxley X. Gazing outside, he thinks for a moment as the teachers murmur behind him.

"What's it supposed to mean?" Mrs. Andrews asks.

Shaking his head, Mr. Farnsworth is having a psychologist's lament. Eyes glued to nowhere, he mulls this over. "It doesn't make much sense, does it?" he grumbles, attempting to grasp the logic. "Though the psychology of nothin' is still somethin'," he reasons, quite amused at his creative conclusion.

"They're teasing us," Mrs. Andrews quips.

Their sounds linger while Mr. Wickly stares out the window, still in thought. After a moment, he draws the letter to his face and takes a deep breath, smelling carefully.

160

Sweet as it is, he does it again. Then he looks up, closes his eyes, and ponders, imagining himself elsewhere. He reopens his eyes, smiles, and takes another sniff, allowing the scent to dwell longer.

His smile widens. Staring at the horizon, he whispers, "For every weakness, there's a challenge to reveal it. Thank you, Mr. X ... Thank you for trying to be so clever."

MAINLAND PROPOSAL
MADISON SCHOOL AUDITORIUM

Twenty-four hours to deadline. The police have searched all possible leads on land and have run in circles. With no solutions, they've arrived, quite frankly, at the same conclusion; ditto for the teachers.

Conducting his own search, Mr. Wickly presses on, and after purchasing a small boat, he independently hunts all islands, private or not, within fifty miles of shore. This much, he knows: the students are close to the water and surrounded by trees. No doubt about it. He's smelled it.

After a phone call to the chief ... a discussion, a proposal, back-and-forth negotiations, then counter-offers, some concessions, a few withdrawals ... at last, in principle, they shake hands. It's done. They have a deal. Both police and teachers will meet tonight with the parents to seek an extension. What's more, they'll work together, as each party claims to have privileged information the other wishes to possess.

Though directionless, they can both breathe a sigh of relief. There will be time, and everything will surely be made right. These precious children will be returned to their parents.

The auditorium is full, and once again, it's standing room only. Anticipation has built. Everyone's as excited as they're afraid. It's time to begin.

The chief and Mr. Wickly take turns with their slide presentations, presenting the facts, their thoughts, their research, their hard work, their diligence, and of course, their Christly love for their kids.

From the cell phones left behind by their children, they have a slideshow of photos before their disappearance: the last party, hints of their plans, pictures of Huxley, pictures of Jed. In sequence, every culprit is revealed.

Hoping their concerns will rain down in a flood of logic, they remind them and then remind them again of the uniqueness of their case: there is no kidnapping; there is no ransom; this is not a case of lost or missing children. This was a voluntary act. Public interest may be exactly what they desire, attention-seeking as they are, and community involvement will, most certainly, make matters worse, adding fuel to the children's already blazing ambition to provoke authority.

So far, so good—it makes sense. Standing at the altar of wisdom, they wait for their nods before they press on. They argue it takes time to digest a lump of doubt into atoms of trust. And like well-seasoned attorneys making their concluding arguments to rows of suits and dresses, with all the boxes checked, the chief and Mr. Wickly each make their plea for more time: more time to discover new tracks, more time to unlock new doors, more time to consolidate intelligence from diverse origins, and, assuredly, more time for the children to send letters providing additional clues. Sealed with love, this much is clear: their children, with certainty, will be found if the time is provided.

The auditorium is silent; no one says a word. Parents gaze about and swap glances, curious to see each other's reaction to the new proposal. Everyone's teeming with energy, but no one's ready to uncork its force. Each member looks to the neighboring seat to initiate that first domino.

Mr. Wickly looks to Chief Ross and says nothing; they gaze back at the audience, waiting for some reaction. Their optimistic half-smiles hint at their belief they've already won. *That's a wrap, folks.* No response is a good omen and, perhaps, a sign of consent. Still, they wait for it to be confirmed in words.

And here it comes. Mr. Collins stands up, straight-backed, broad-shouldered, ready to speak and surrender a few thoughts. No microphone; none is needed. As before, his formidable voice echoes through the halls unassisted.

"Thank you, Principal Wickly ... Chief," he says, nodding in turn at both. "I know others share this sentiment: We all appreciate your hard work."

The chief and Mr. Wickly nod back. With expressionless faces, they quarantine their mental sighs of relief inside and listen.

Mr. Collins continues. "Over the past few weeks, the parents also took the liberty to meet several times alone. And I'm happy to say we have raised another five hundred million from the parents' generous donations to a total now of one and a half-billion dollars."

Breathless, Mr. Wickly and Chief Ross look at each other and resist a smile. They can already feel the reward of their collaborative effort. Muted, they stand; muted, they watch, resisting the allure to daydream about those words, gulping down their saliva.

"However ..." Mr. Collins says, pausing to capture everyone's focus. Then he repeats, "However." That mentioned word doesn't go unnoticed. Nobody has to tell Mr. Wickly, an English graduate from the finest universities throughout the United Kingdom; he knows, and knows all too well, any sentence that begins with "however" is a sorcerous means to a hideous end.

Mr. Collins gazes about and echoes the word again, raising a wagging finger this time, and finding the absolute attention he seeks, he finally finishes: "The plan will go as scheduled. We've arranged for the press conference tomorrow."

Hideous, indeed.

Mr. Collins stands up, determined, focused, and stubborn. With no desire to parry, he turns and heads up the auditorium with a businesslike manner: no smile, chin up, his gaze locked on the exit.

The message is clear: the police, the teachers, and Principal Wickly swung and missed. All the parents rise, some casually, some more measured, but most pop out of their chairs and follow.

Failure dominates the moment. The chief and Mr. Wickly stand speechless, too stunned to respond, too confused to protest, wondering, *What just happened?* Mr. Wickly's jaw hangs low, and the presentation pointer drops from his hand. He suddenly feels weak.

"Son of a gun ..." Chief Ross whispers, unable to complete the sentence.

A few minutes later, thawing from shock, in silent order, the police officers and teachers leave successively: no waves, no goodbyes, no arranged times to meet again. It's back to square one for both groups, with many more competitors now on that square.

PRESS CONFERENCE

Night gives way to day, which, in due course, waves in the noontide hour.

The media is present. They've been clued to the important incoming announcement.

Mr. Collins marches in and stands at the podium with twelve worried parents behind him. He shuffles through his papers, glossing over their message, but then he stops to stare at something. He looks over his shoulder at Mr. Mubanga, lifts his sheet, and points at it. "How do you pronounce this name?"

Mr. Mubanga puts his glasses on and leans forward, staring quietly. He reveals a frown and sounds out, "X ..." but he struggles to complete the word. He looks again more closely, trying to whisper the syllables, and then says, "Your guess is as good as mine."

Mr. Collins looks back at the page and decides not to make an attempt. After a headshake, he steps forward and adjusts the microphone.

As he gazes forward, he's signaled to begin in ten seconds. Looking at the television cameras and the flash of photographers circling in front, he sees the countdown with a silent show of fingers—three, two, one—and he begins his address.

"Good afternoon, everyone. My name is Greg Collins, and I speak as the voice of the parents at the Madison School for the Gifted ... some of whom are with me tonight. Our message is to the citizens of our state, our country, the supporting friends and family, and all the parents across our land.

"Like most parents, on the morning of the first day of school, we began the day like the start of any school year: with hope and with anticipation. Our children had left home a little earlier that morning; otherwise, it was the same as in any other academic year.

"Unfortunately, this was anything but a typical school day. At 9:30 a.m., the parents were informed by the teachers, the principal, and the various authorities that our children, a total of 751 students, had collectively elected not to attend class and had left a note that they'd chosen to leave their homes, their families, and begin a new life elsewhere at some unknown destination.

"After consultation with the police, we were reassured there was no evidence of an imminent risk of danger, and as such, we were content to allow law enforcement and other collaborative associates take the necessary measures to return our children home.

"More than sixty days have now passed. It is with regret that I stand here before you to declare that despite their best efforts, our expectations have not been met, and our every faith of heart has been countered with a stronger measure of failure."

Stopping to clear his throat, Mr. Collins looks back at the camera. Finally, he resumes. "Our children are our treasures; they are the bearers of our hopes, the promise of our future, and they are, in many ways, the fulfillment of our dreams.

"Since the day they disappeared, our life has met no rest, our thoughts have known no peace, and our grief has known no boundaries. If they are watching, we want them to know: we love you, we miss you; you're in our hearts, and we want you to come home."

Mr. Collins pauses and removes his glasses to wipe his suddenly damp eyes. Then he turns sideways, pointing to a prepared poster on his right.

"It is our understanding that this scheme was initiated and launched by one of the school's students, widely known as Huxley X." With his moral pitchfork raised, he points. "This is a photograph of him shortly before the students' disappearance. The necklace he's wearing belongs to my deceased wife. It's one of the few treasures my family has from her memory."

Turning back to face the camera, he presses on. "With no avenues to explore and with no alternative means for a solution, the parents at the Madison School have decided to join hands and pool our efforts to put forward a reward of one and a half billion dollars for any individual, group, or organization that can return our children home safely.

"In the coming days, we will provide additional information, as well as pictures, names, and bios of each of our children, and we'll do our best to answer the many questions you may have.

"Thank you ... and God bless."

FALL

ENEMY NUMBER ONE
IDENTIFIED:

HUXLEY X

PLANET NEXT
DAY SIXTY-ONE

A new planet, a new civilization, a new way of life, and, indeed, something never dreamt of before. Like a maturing tree, stretching higher, spanning wider, more verdant, more vibrant, it yearns to course to its potential. The citizens of Planet Next, as they commonly call themselves, usher in a fresh vision, a fresh hope, driven by moxie and the credo to live as if it's your last day but prepare to live as though it's your first day of forever.

With the recent visits they've had in nearby waters, they know that the risks and benefits of both possibilities exist in parallel universes, as do life and death.

They don't care. Though the summer is over, it's still warm. Students swim in the waters, inside the cloak, within the heart of the pi.

Are they having a good time? How can they not be? Repeat after Jed: "Be chill ... or be that radiant straw that breaks the camel's back." That's right. Watch Jed, follow his lead, and keep it real. A Jules Rule, no doubt, and they're learning. This is youth.

On the other side of progress, recording a running tally of student participation for their planetary vision, it's now one hundred percent. Is someone actually keeping track? There sure is. And she likes what she sees on the scorecard.

Driven by an invisible force—as well as one very visible source, Chandler—they march forward, building their dream: a charter of human rights, an animal charter of freedoms, sustainable development, a judicial court system, and a planetary tribunal.

"A penitentiary," Huxley chimes in, looking at Chandler, drawing her attention.

"What about it?"

"These glorious plans of yours, well, they need a yin for their yang, don't you agree?"

She sits back and thinks, hoping to refute the idea. She knows she can't, but she searches her mind, intuitively knowing that a clever response might do. "Perhaps, then, you'd like to build it?"

"Perhaps, then, I will," he says to her raised brows.

Chandler clearly wasn't expecting that response. "Well, maybe just start with one cell ... baby steps," she pleads, still stunned at Huxley's newfound compliance with her wishes.

He nods. "One, it is."

She stares at him suspiciously. "In that case, we'll need a judge ... We'll also need one for marriages, I guess. I'd prefer it be a different judge than for criminal charges."

"That's definitely Jed's department."

On that marital note, he turns and marches off to tour

171

the island like the head of an army preparing for battle. Indeed, a war is coming, and like any responsible supreme commander, he must think of the protection of his people and land.

"We'll need searchlights surrounding the island," he tells Jaxston, who seems unsure. The idea seems new, but really, it's not. Huxley plotted and shared the design with him before their arrival, and its cargo container is still on the south side of the island.

"But I like the stars without the lights," Jaxston protests, hinting at the source of his angst.

"I do, too," Huxley says, smiling. "But without the lights, we may not have the stars for much longer."

He points above the central waters. "The lights must be able to search the island, the perimeters, inside and out."

Today is a workday, and as they walk to the north side of the island, they realize their largest undertaking is nearing its conclusion. The Dragon Dale brothers lead a team of three hundred people to put the finishing touches on the renewable resources project: solar panels, windmills, and hydroelectric power from the nearby waters.

"Once this is done, we'll have enough energy for a permanent camouflage." Dale nods. "We'll practically be gone from this planet."

"Splendid." Huxley smiles. "Our *own* planet …"

"By the way, when will we finally work on Project X?"

Dragon overhears the operative word and listens attentively for the response.

Huxley gazes at the waters where Project X lies. He knows that soon its vision and unprecedented scope must be unveiled. "It's a little early, but we're not too far. We need to be completely cloaked before we can even consider it."

On the island's south side, two hundred students collect food: pears, apples, oranges, bananas, cherries, peaches, walnuts, and hazelnuts. The trees were there before their arrival. However, the potatoes, tomatoes, cucumbers, herbs, garlic, and onions were planted earlier in the summer. And inserted into the list last month were strawberries, raspberries, eggplants, zucchini, spinach, kale, peas, beans, honeydew, beets, carrots, and green peppers.

Dinnertime is here. The bell chimes, echoing from the speakers, near and far, to the east, the west, the north, the south. All the students stroll in.

Eating together for dinner is a sacred obligation, one that's led by Jed. A single line of rectangular tables, side by side, in chained sequence, rolls for some three hundred yards through the hills, valleys, and surrounding meadows, disappearing into the dips of the vales, seating exactly 752—the students plus Jed.

The seating arrangement is random, with one exception: Jed sits at the head. Everyone else sits wherever they desire.

Like a charismatic showman, Jed stands, holding a microphone. Dinnertime always begins with one of his speeches. Tonight he makes a toast. Sensing an imminent battle, this is his Churchill moment. Raising his glass of orange juice, he nods and begins his oration. "Young men and women of the planet next door, tonight we're celebrating our two-month anniversary together: a time of pleasure, a time of innovation, a time of historic milestones, and, for a few ... a time of pubertal milestones.

"Please give yourselves a round of applause." He nods and points to the boys beside him, gesturing at their collective achievement and, most certainly, their newly sprouted mustaches. "Jules Rule: praise given for praise earned."

They smile, raising their arms in embarrassment and waving away the humor.

"But we're not alone," Jed resumes. "No, we're not. As Chandler will attest, we've had nondiscriminatory immigration—the best kind. We're the first planet to draft a charter of rights and freedoms for birds."

Everyone claps, and a few people whistle. Jed lifts an arm to acknowledge their ovation and then carries on. "We've accomplished more in two months than most developed nations do in one year, accomplished more in one week than other countries do in a decade, and with a bird's-eye view, we've accomplished more in one day than past generations have in a lifetime."

Everyone cheers and raises their glasses, and Jed calls out, "To Planet Next!"

Voices echo, "To Planet Next!"

Dinnertime begins. It is truly a feast for the eyes. And, perhaps, it's also the last of its kind—the feast before the war. A set of new rules are to be introduced in the morning.

Galvanized, rejuvenated, and in high spirits, the Planet Next citizens celebrate, knowing that fresh preparations will be underway for an undertaking to secure their ongoing freedom at the turn of the next sunrise.

Cheers.

MEYERSVILLE DOCKS

In the coming days, the parents organize, assemble, and put forward pictures, stories, and biographies of each student in an orderly succession, hoping that endearing familiarity will arouse a greater interest and, perhaps, more people will vie to claim the reward.

Intriguing thought. Sounds fair, and it works. Furthermore, it's now the buzz of the town.

As for the reward, which is beyond the boundaries of imagination, this is the highest amount of any prize, be it a contest, lottery, or ransom, anyone has seen. Not only does it capture the nation's attention, but slowly, like an earthquake, its gentle rumble reaches and stirs a vibratory force in faraway places.

Ancillary to the people's interest is the media's attention, which adds not only fuel but limitless range to the fire.

As promised, greater details for the rules also emerge. While it was already known that a return of the students is a requirement, what wasn't known is the collateral condition: returning Mr. Collins's wife's necklace. No doubt, this is an attempt to besmirch the infamous Huxley X—now the villainous magician who masterminded their children's disappearance.

For their part, the police motor on with their investigation, not dismayed by the additional competition to their quest. "We're ahead of the curve," the chief reassures his staff. "We have information they don't have and won't find."

The teachers at Madison School, however, aren't as united. Far from collaborating with the police, Principal Wickly, disillusioned, has lost faith in continuing to work with his teachers.

Drawn by a premonition, he knows where to search. He's not interested in exploring erroneous leads, places, or other miscalculated hunches. The youth are at sea somewhere, and he will find them, *alone*. He works best when he works without distractions, *alone*. And, of course, the reward will now be awarded to him and him *alone*.

It's nighttime, and the ocean is quiet. Mr. Wickly sits on the dock, viewing the water, hope not having left him. It's serene. His thoughts circle the possible choices for his search, like flipping through pages of a curious book. He glances at an idea, winces, and then flips through the pages again, at times burning through a chapter and then stopping to carefully understand another. At the moment, he's reached an impasse, and he stares at the problem like it's a mathematical equation craving to be solved.

Not much has changed ... still searching for X.

He asks himself question after question, attempting to

solve this enigma, crossing out, reattempting, rewriting the question, trying again. He's only certain of one conclusion: the teenage years are evolution's blunder.

Be that as it may, there must be an explanation for all this. *How can they hide in the ocean? Where would they go? Perhaps they're traveling by boat from land to land.* While the idea amuses him, he knows ... *751 students, unstable circumstances, unreliable food resources ... nope, not possible.* He shuffles away the idea.

When are teens most likely to be seen? He does a headshake. *Well, that's simple ... when they're most annoying: at night, when people want to sleep.*

The waters are calm, the air is peaceful, and the sounds, or lack thereof, are beautifully unmusical, other than the ocean waves' mystic charm. Then, like a spark of inspiration, or more precisely, a spark of his own genius, he lifts his head to look at the skies. *Huh?* A feeling of bliss overwhelms him. He has an idea ... and it's brilliant. Alas, the only thing to champion a Wickly is, well, Mr. Wickly himself.

He glances at his watch: 9:15 p.m., perhaps too soon for the party hour to begin, but just the right time to set sail.

They'll be where the waters are unsettled. The wolf may be calm during the day, but its howl will betray its den at night. He smiles, looks at his motorboat. The vessel was purchased last week. It's the fastest model. Its colors: ocean inspired. Was it expensive? It definitely wasn't on sale. But he now wonders if he may only need it for just one more night. Still, he's relieved. Mr. Wickly knows what must be done and, most importantly, where he's erred in his search.

He treads toward his boat with his customary dignified

steps, but he feels the irresistible urge to move faster. Breaking into a sprint, he races to his craft, where in a sequence of practiced steps, he unties the vessel from the docks. Then he switches the engine on, drifts forward, and turns the boat, and finally, he gently rides out from the harbor. He's on his way, and what's more, he's picking up speed, still floating in the ocean of his thoughts.

Where to go?

Needless to say, that's the brilliance. He smiles again. The sounds will let him know. *Listen for the night howl and their sounds of joy.*

Driven by a sixth sense, the vibe of victory fills his being as he courses the water for one hour, guided by his sense of perception, of intuition—merging to a marvelous tapestry of faith.

As he sails eastward, leisurely and in a straight line, confident as he is, he knows their annoying sounds will undoubtedly arrive. He stands, his eyes pointed to the heavens, confident as ever.

Waiting, expectant, even before the sound, he notes a peculiar sight. Under the bright moonlight, he gazes at something in the skies that holds his attention: a bird, or perhaps, more precisely, a falcon ... No, no, that's not right; it's a falcon-parrot hybrid. Yes, he finally remembers from the pictures and their reports.

It's black, it has checkered wings, and it's large. Indeed, this is the one.

He smiles, his eyes tracking his target. "Lead me to your master," he whispers. "What should I call you? Oh, yes ... Mr. Chester."

In an unintended meeting of the eyes, the boat doesn't

escape Chester's attention, and suddenly he turns and flaps off, shifting direction, winding, accelerating, not looking back, flying away.

"You won't evade me," Mr. Wickly says, and he increases his speed, locking eyes on the bird's wings.

After soaring east, west, and higher, Chester then makes an abrupt course change, reversing direction, flapping northward. Not to be outdone, Mr. Wickly looks over his shoulder, glances left and then right, keeping pace, turning the boat, but then he loses sight of his target for one instant. *Where did it go?* Vanished—like witchcraft: no bird, just darkness, nothing gracing the skies. After making three circles with the boat, Mr. Wickly turns and stares, and then he does another round to be sure, gazing first at the eastward skies, then southward, and then at the remaining horizons. There's nothing there.

Listen. Closing his eyes, he sharpens his ears for the students' sounds. He knows they must be close. *It's 10:30 p.m. They're just warming up.* A moment passes in his mind, and for the first time, all senses have escaped him. He hears nothing, feels nothing, and sees nothing … Nothing, that is, but the empty sound of dark water.

All expression vanishes from his face. *Alone*, he rides. *Alone*, he listens. *Alone*, he thinks and spins and spins again for another look, another take, rechecking the horizons, keeping calm—no surrender, no abandon, full commitment—before he realizes, quite indisputably, this is no mistake.

How can this be? It can't be. It shouldn't be.

But it is.

And just as he started, Mr. Wickly is now simply *alone*.

PLANET NEXT
VISION

It's 6:00 a.m. Huxley's awake, and he stares at the ceiling. He's too tired to sit up, too indifferent to roll over, so time marches forward, wandering to 7:00 a.m. Lulled by the tranquility, he listens to the birds sing, but not Chester, who flies down and sits beside his ear, nudging him to rise, not to be lazy.

Finally, Huxley stands, stretches out his arms, and bathes in the sunshine. Enjoying its warmth, he admires the calm waters and knows it's just an illusion.

They're coming. They already have. And they'll do so again.

Turning sideways, he looks at Chester. Quite persistently, the bird tried to wake him last night, but Huxley was too worn, too achy, after doing hard labor he didn't enjoy, and had visited that charming comatose state.

Now that he has awakened to his morning reality, it's time to set his plans in motion. Yesterday evening, they'd already started with new guidelines: early curfews, noise restrictions, and lights out after 9 p.m.

Tonight they'll commence their vigilant twenty-four-hour surveillance. In successive shifts, everyone will have a turn to work security and contribute to protecting their ongoing vision: Planet Next.

The vision that began as a spark is now moved by a palpable force, a palpable will, every member advancing its cause, promoting its values, refusing to pry their grip from its transformative potential.

Its possibilities are unlimited, its capacity unexplored, its reach unexploited, and its scope uncharted, and the students, having seen the first rays of its range, having felt the first glimmering of its warmth, begin documenting their stay with a spectrum of videos, images, paintings, and diaries. They know, with a jarring reminder, that they need to savor the moment: the old civilization seeks their eventual arrival.

"The searchlights are ready!" Jaxston shouts from below, waving at Huxley.

Meeting his gaze with a smile, Huxley nods as he stands at his window. "Splendid. I'll be down to join you soon."

As he turns to leave, Huxley notes he has a visitor: the Cuban kite. He's tempted to take a closer look, and after a brief pause, he glances over to make sure Chandler is asleep.

Indeed, sensing a fortuitous possibility, he quietly steps closer and whispers to Chester, "Shall we get a better view?"

Chester flies over to Huxley's shoulder, where he looks on and says nothing. As they inch closer, the Cuban kite looks back with a mysterious gaze and then freezes, holding its stare. A heartbeat later, it flies away.

After watching it wend its way across the sky, Huxley glances back at Chester. "Considering their history, can you blame them for being scared?"

"Can you blame Chester for being hungry?" a voice crackles behind them. Huxley turns. It's Chandler.

"I didn't think you were awake?"

"I didn't think you'd approach the Cuban kite after the agreement we all had."

"Yes, *your* agreement; you're quite right."

"Can you blame Chester?" she repeats. Both Chester and Huxley are amused at her sudden spell of fondness.

After a nod, she says, "Chester is a predator of small birds."

"Yes, but not of the Cuban kite variety; you're forgetting he's also part parrot."

"You're forgettin' he has instincts other than just playin' *Ches*."

"Correct," Huxley says, looking over his shoulder. "See, you have an outspoken supporter." And on that note … "Chester?"

"Aye, master?"

"Shall we play a game of *Ches*?"

Flapping with excitement, the bird knows what that means. "With pleasure."

Staring into Chester's eyes, Huxley asks, "What must a bishop bring to help its king?"

Chester flies off. Huxley waves goodbye to Chandler and swiftly disappears from his tree house.

Heading toward the water, he passes some early risers

182

and then has an interval of solitude to enjoy nature: the gushing waterfalls, the meandering stream, and the trees whose rebellion of colors charm the moment.

He waits at the ocean, and Chester finally arrives, descending slowly to his shoulder. "And what must a bishop bring to help its king?"

"Allies, master."

"Well done, Chester," Huxley says, awaiting his sought-for confirmation.

Several minutes pass as he silently stares at the jungle, with him speaking to Chester while looking at the sun and the water and the gold shimmers on the horizon. He enjoys the moment; it's as gripping as it is soothing.

Then Huxley hears a faint sound crop up behind him. He turns and can now discern footsteps, growing louder and louder. At last, Jed, Dragon, and Dale emerge from the trees.

Arriving closer, they nod, and Dragon says, "Chester said you wanted to meet."

"That's right."

"Sure. What is it?" Dale asks.

With a nod, Huxley confirms, "I think it's time."

No one speaks. Dragon looks at Dale, and they both glance at Jed, who nods back. Everyone swaps looks in a three-way ping-pong, not wanting to break point, until, finally, Huxley steps forward and says, "I retrieved the scuba gear last night from the cargo. We're ready for Project X. Now we'll never be surprised again."

Dragon smiles, as does Dale. Arms are raised to a high five above and then arc down to slam below.

The smiling twins have been waiting for this moment a

long time. Frankly, it's something they've wanted to do their entire lives.

Huxley nods to let them know it's now for real.

MUBANGA RESIDENCE

The camera crew gears up while Mr. Lusala Mubanga looks in the mirror, flanked by his assistant and makeup artist; they adjust his attire and glamorize his face in preparation for tonight's show.

A dab, a little color, some glow, some moisture, and he looks left, right, left again, and stops. He's set. He likes what he sees.

At the suggestion of Mr. Collins, the owner of Collins Wave Television, they'll have a nightly program with in-depth views of each student, their parents, their siblings, and their lives before their departure.

Seeing that most of these students have exceptional talents, as well as some of their parents having extraordinary lifestyles and backgrounds, Mr. Collins believes the show will captivate the audience, which, in turn, will spur further discussion and widespread interest in returning the children to their homes. Will it work? Maybe. The upside: huge. The idea: definitely worth a shot.

Mr. Mubanga, a creative and financial leader, has multiple technology companies that provide internet services, wireless devices, observational and communication satellite networks, and services for smart homes. He's a self-made billionaire and, by all accounts, a fascinating man, as are his sons, Dragon and Dale, two of the school's most gifted students. It's a good place to start.

Born in Tanzania, Dragon and Dale moved to Florida when they were just three months old. They like football, which is always a good entry point. Where academics can't sell, football certainly can. Never underestimate the power of marketing.

"We'll begin in ten minutes!" a voice shouts.

Mr. Mubanga buttons his suit, pulls it straight, and looks at his wife, who has come down to stand beside him. She's ready.

He turns and smiles, and she slides an arm around his, clasping hands. Together they walk to the couch and then turn and nod to the cameraman. United they stand—one, two, three—united they sit—one, two, three—and united they lean back, gazing at the cameras, waiting, tilting up their concerned faces.

Dragon and Dale are their only children, and with no other siblings, the parents will be the show. Preparation and legwork have already been done, and being the attentive parents they are, they want no detail to be missed, no good stories to be left out. And so, they've spent the last few days speaking to their nanny and discovering their sons' favorite foods, favorite hobbies, favorite books, favorite music, their friends, their daily routines, and the many acts of goodly deeds they've evidently done.

In their thorough research, there were videos to be browsed, photographs to be seen, many of which they were viewing for the first time, and, most certainly, stories worth retelling.

Dragon and Dale are, indeed, sons to be proud of. Their nanny, Maria Marin, was flown in. She was released from the Mubanga household two years ago after their sons turned fourteen. The boys were too old, too mature, and it was, perhaps, no longer cost-effective to have someone who had nurtured them since birth to remain on the payroll.

In a bid to make their sons independent, she'd also been forbidden from making contact with them. But today is a day to remember the good times, and Ms. Marin is standing behind the camera crew, nodding, smiling, giving the parents a reassuring wave, letting them know everything will be all right.

Another hand beside the camera is raised, counting down, and words are silently mouthed, *And ready in five, four, three, two, one.* The cameraman points.

They're on.

"My name is Esther Mubanga, and this is my husband, Lusala." No smiles, no expressions, their tone is serious. Details of the day of their sons' disappearance are discussed.

"It's a call no parent ever hopes to get," she says in a trembling voice, fighting back her emotions. The host comforts her, allowing her space to share her experience unfiltered and without pressure, and eventually her story emerges.

When: "We were on summer vacation when we received that phone call."

How: "We really don't know how this could've happened. Our last moments together were so beautiful, teleconferencing every week."

Why: "Well, of course it's Huxley X! They were happy children."

Its impact: "In a word, devastating."

"Sons, it's time to come home," Mr. Mubanga pleads, looking into the camera. "Your mother deserves better."

Dragon and Dale aren't ordinary kids. Technological geniuses by any measure, they built their own computer at age five, designed an industrial robot by age seven, submitted their first patent at age nine, and are now owners of over thirty patents. And oh, yes, they also play football—defensive end—and are avid watchers of it, too.

"They were best friends since birth," Mrs. Mubanga says, shaking her head, pausing, brimming with passion, struggling to find the right words. "The brothers did everything together: they played together, ate together, built together, roomed together, and owned every invention of theirs, well … together."

Brilliant as they are, Mr. Mubanga nods at each of their listed achievements. He's moved by her story and interjects, "Many of my company's innovations were born at home, from them, right here."

After twenty minutes of heartfelt disclosure, Mrs. Mubanga provides a tour of their thirty-thousand-square-foot home, showing the rooms where many of their sons' creations were born and the room her sons shared and, along the way, recounting inspiring stories of them in each room—none of which are her stories. Ms. Marin walks behind the camera, nodding, encouraging Mrs.

Mubanga to continue.

It's a beautiful moment.

And even more beautiful is the dramatic ending. Mr. Mubanga's eyes well with tears, waxing sentimental, and he whispers, "Daddy loves you ..." After a beat, he echoes, "Daddy loves you," the words wheezing from his lips as he puts his head down and cries.

The telecast, which airs later that evening, is decorated with music, baby photographs, and toddler videos, in a heart-warming, tear-jerking, one-hour show. Slipping into a familiar punchline, it closes with a few chosen words about Huxley X. Sly, wild, and of crazed mind. Make no mistake—this story has a villain.

Well received and well viewed, it's more than loved by the people. Satellend stock is up ten percent. The verdict is in: rich, poor, young, and old, everyone wants Dragon and Dale to come home. They want them to come now, and everyone wants to see it happen soon, so they're united once again with their loving parents in their storybook home.

The only thing people look forward to more than a good show is, naturally, the sequel to the drama. That, conveniently, will be aired tomorrow night, and every night after, starting at 8:00 p.m.

But one thing is for sure. No one can stop talking about Huxley X ... that rebellious, unruly student you don't want your children to be friends with. Clearly, he's a cult leader of sorts, preying on the blameless, the naïve, and the broken; he's that baiter who ultimately leads his followers into that abyss, the inextricable amalgam of chaos and darkness.

Who knows what he may have done to them by now? Pray, just pray. And may the good lord help the pure, the innocent, and the parents of the Madison School students overcome this evil-minded plotter.

Amen.

ATLANTIC
OCEAN FLOOR

Relaxed, weightless, and floating, the three friends, Huxley, Dragon, and Dale, continue working in sequence, oblivious of time, oblivious of the world above, mindful of only one thing: their task at hand.

A fish swims by and nudges Huxley softly. He looks up, and there are a hundred more. Suddenly fleeing, they are gone in a flash.

The coral, the plants, the jellyfish, the sea fans, everything is bright, and everything's a delight to one's eyes, even the worms. In charming style, everyone drifts in slow motion, particularly Dragon.

Location: the seabed.

Depth: one hundred feet.

The feeling: calm as ever.

The waters are bright blue at the surface but much darker underneath. They won't complain, though. Sunlight reaches to about six hundred feet, so it's dim but still nice.

It's quite opportune, actually, for the ocean bed to rise near their island.

The average depth of the ocean: 10, 955 feet.

They're lucky.

Scuba gear on, they work in tandem while Jed sits above in the dive boat, situated three hundred feet from the island. He keeps track of time, tugging on their ropes, letting them know: no one can stay down for more than fifteen minutes. It's a Jules Rule, perhaps, but it also keeps them alive, so they follow it.

It's a beautiful day to be outside, enjoying the Atlantic. The sun shines, no wind, not a single cloud. There's nothing but ocean and Planet Next in view. Jed looks up and squints at the sun and then glances at his shadow. Naturally, now sitting away from the island, he surveys the surrounding waters with concern.

Indeed, Mr. Wickly has been drifting by daily. Something strange seems to have happened to him, and that has the students confused. It appears he's had some type of spiritual revival and rides his boat with eyes closed, smelling the air, in a trance of sorts, as though he's tapping the door of a psychic link.

With sunglasses on, Jed checks his watch: Huxley's time is up. He tugs on the rope.

Dale drifts down to relieve him. *Pass the baton; keep it going.* There's work to be done.

The ocean floor is the holder of the secrets above. Wars have been won and lost unveiling secrets and private matters on the ocean floor.

Since the 1800s, transatlantic cables have been laid down to connect the planet, at first sending telegraphs and then paving the way for the fiber-optic cables in the 1960s. In a series of measures, the planting of these cables continued for some six hundred thousand miles, connecting nation to nation, continent to continent, circling the earth more than twenty times in an endless maze of tracks.

The undersea cables transmit anything and everything on the internet, and over time, satellites were included to help with the transmission. However, the heavy lifting is still done in the ocean below and not in the skies above, with these three-inch cables carrying more than ninety-nine percent of internet activity.

Surprisingly, the cable locations are made public so that shipping can avoid inadvertent damage. This, of course, comes at a cost: with the right tools and the right knowledge, you can tap that cable, and you've got everything you need to know about what's happening anyplace, anywhere, to anyone, through cameras, accounts, and anything that can be accessed virtually on the net.

It's quite common for nations and agents to wiretap the cables—a compromise of cybersecurity, they call it—but, usually, these labors of spies have submarines, and they journey to great lengths not to be spotted.

Though in the heart of the Atlantic, Jed's island is near such cables—easy access, the seabed rises, it's private, it's secluded, no interruptions. You just need the right people, and ...

Dragon surfaces. "It's done."

Dale pops up next to him and takes a deep breath. "We're in."

Swimming unhurriedly, they sweep their arms out twice and reach the boat. Huxley and Jed lean over and pull the brothers onto the deck.

Standing up, Dale removes his regulator, mask, and tank, with water dripping everywhere. Dragon is already stripped of his equipment. He's wearing his dive suit and holding a small cable. He connects the cable to a small device and turns it on.

Huxley presses the power button on the computer. Dale joins in, as does Jed, and the four surround the screen as Huxley connects the computer to the device.

A moment passes as Huxley types in codes. He waits ... then types in another one. The screen goes dark. Everyone leans in and watches ... It flickers ... and then their anticipated moment arrives.

"It works!" Dale confirms, pumping his fist.

He's excited, as is Dragon, but not more than Huxley, who seals all emotions up. Arriving at this critical juncture, Huxley knows: Phase IV of his plan is finally completed. *Three more to go.*

He quickly searches, entering site after site, bathed in sunshine. As they're lulled by the power of connection, darkness suddenly hovers over them as though the sun has vanished behind a cloud and its rays have been replaced with shadow.

In a flash of surprise, their heads lift up. They're shocked as a large boat rolls in gently behind them.

Scared and swapping blank expressions, they look on, waiting, unsure about what they've encountered. Then a head pops over the rails.

"Hello."

Everyone lets out a big gasp of relief.

"Jose ... you scared us." Jed sighs.

"I thought I might see you guys passing by this part of the ocean," Jose says, smiling.

Moments later, five hundred heads jut out over the rails. The visitors wave as chants of "Hola!" descend.

Overwhelmed by the sight, Huxley's and the others' jaws unhinge. Huxley exchanges looks with the twins. Truly, he can't remember this many people being on Jose's boat the last time. "Is it my imagination, or has your family expanded since we last saw you?"

Jose chuckles. "We went to my sister's wedding. This is her in-laws' family, too."

Fighting his surprise, Huxley is uncertain about what to say, and quite frankly, he's uncertain what to think. He says nothing and watches in amazement at the smiling people, who are still waving.

"Well, it's great to see you all," Jed says, nodding.

"By the way, I mailed those letters," Jose mentions, looking at Huxley.

"Thank you." Huxley lifts an appreciative hand. "That's very kind of you. I hope it wasn't any trouble."

"None. Is there anything else you need? Anything?"

It's a kind offer. It seems sincere. After an exchange of looks and a few shrugs, everyone agrees. Everyone seems good. "No, I think we're fine," Huxley confirms.

Jose then bounces a look over his shoulder, seemingly alarmed. "Just so you know ... there's another ship comin' this way, some ten miles behind us."

Everyone nods. "Thanks for the heads up."

Huxley shoots a glance at Dragon. "Let's go back. We can always resume later."

"Agreed."

"We'll be off, then." Jose waves. "Bye, guys. Bye, Dragon. Bye, Dale."

"Bye," they all say, waving back.

The ship drifts away and is soon swallowed by the horizon, and as they watch it disappear, Huxley murmurs, "Terrific. Now there are five hundred of them who know where we are."

Those words reach Jed's ear. "Don't worry," he says.

"I'm trying not to."

"Look," Jed says, turning to Huxley, poised to make a point. "Even if you paid 'em two hundred thousand dollars, they'd never say a word. I know. Don't sweat it. Okay."

Huxley gobbles the thought in his mind and allows the comment to pass unchallenged. His face conveys a thousand words of doubt he won't express. Finally, he nods noncommittally. What choice does he have?

Dragon and Dale continue to stare dead ahead. They're confused, both silent, trying to put *something* to words but not quite certain what it is they heard that didn't feel right. Their minds search, pausing, playing forward, then rewinding the soundtrack, and finally—it hits them. "Wait a minute," Dale pipes up, looking at Dragon. "How did Jose know our names?"

POLICE STATION
DAY EIGHTY

Time: 8:00 p.m.

Everyone huddles together, sitting, eyes locked on the television. There's important work to be done.

"Turn up the volume!" Officer Jefferson shouts.

"Chief, come on! It's startin'!" yells another, waving an arm.

Everyone leans in. It's the fourth straight week of *Planet Next Victims*; the name of the show was adopted, of course, from the parents' lips as well as the content shared in the students' letters. As for the program, it's a hit! News stations, social media, people on the streets, everyone wants to talk about the students and, most certainly, Huxley X.

The chief arrives with popcorn. "Remember, we're doin' research. Take notes. Look for clues inside their home that they didn't share before. Take hints from everythin' they say. They may reveal somethin' new." It is, indeed, the power of show business.

Officer Jefferson nods, and then he picks up a pumpkin seed and cracks it between his teeth, chewing rapidly, intensely focused.

The opening music starts. The chief sits back, pops a kernel between his lips. One chew; it's tasty. Then he pulls up a handful and stuffs it in his mouth ... a few chews, and he washes it down with a soda. The show begins.

Tonight's parents: Mr. and Mrs. Jansen.

The victim: Jaxston Jansen.

Talent: musical genius.

Favorite music: heavy metal.

Favorite band: Hell's Peeps.

Favorite person: Jesus Christ.

He's of Dutch and South African descent—a prodigy from birth, a virtuoso at school, an expert at all dance and music. An array of Jaxston's videos, songs, and performances are played, punctuated by stories of his childhood.

His talents are certainly not a matter of chance: hired instructors, music psychologists, more instructors, parental involvement—practice, practice, practice—definitely a team effort, twenty-four hours a day, his diet, his sleep, his rest, everything fitted, everything measured, everything leading him to a limitless world of greatness.

"This is good," the chief cuts in, pointing, pulling up another handful of popcorn.

Officer Jefferson nods, too involved in the show to look over, picking up another pumpkin seed.

After a musical interlude, the video cuts to an interview from his childhood where Jaxston talks about his future: "I wanna be a pilot when I grow up."

"How old is he here?" Officer Angelos asks.

"They said twelve," Officer Higgins says.

"That's just three years ago." The words linger in her mind.

The chief turns and mulls this over. It's a good question. He's surprised he didn't think of it first.

At last, the camera zooms in. Here it comes, the anxious look of his father. You can see only his face now—every detail, every expression, every wrinkle. He doesn't look good.

Then, with concern in his voice, he pleads with Jaxston: "Come home. There's still time to catch up with practice."

The perpetuator—tune out if you've heard this before—Huxley X.

Having finished his popcorn, the chief now starts with the pumpkin seeds from Jefferson's side of the table, digging in.

"I like that gun," he chimes in, splitting a seed, making good on his promise of investigative research.

"Where?" says Officer Higgins.

"Behind him ... on the wall." He points.

"Oh, yeah."

Everyone nods. After a minute, the closing music starts, and the end credits roll with a brief public message about the reward. And with its impressive high ratings, tonight's program will also stream online.

The chief switches off the television and then turns and looks at the officers, ready for business. He dusts off his hands. "So, whadda we got?"

Officer Higgins draws his chair forward, looks at his

blank page of notes, and shakes his head. "I didn't see anythin' new. Same as what they told us before."

Silent shrugs pop up here and there around the room. Then Officer Jefferson chimes in: "He did mention he liked being a pilot so he could pass above islands. That was his dream ... to live on an island."

No one says anything. No one is sure what to say. It is a curious comment, though, one that others have certainly noted as well.

"But ... we already investigated that," the chief says, "and we also checked the satellite images."

Everyone silently debates if it's worth discussing again.

"Yes, but ..." Officer Angelos tilts her head down, her eyes scanning notes marked with a highlighter ... Then she shuffles a few papers and begins to leaf through them, searching for something.

Having found the page, she resumes. "But ..." She pauses again, turning to her laptop. "There is something about these satellite images that I can't figure out."

Confused faces creep up as everyone listens for her to make her point.

"I've gone over these images a hundred times." She points, her eyes darting back and forth between the computer screen and her corresponding notes.

"Yes, over here. Look. You see no island. But check carefully. Every day between 11:00 a.m. and noon, beside where we'd expect to see it, directly over the open waters, right here, there is a cloud of smoke."

Everyone leans in; indeed, she's correct. Waves of smoke drift by at that hour.

Officer Angelos shrugs. "I just can't figure out where

it's coming from. There is no land or islands nearby. There are no ships. And there are no signs of life to explain this sudden appearance of smoke at that specific hour EVERY SINGLE DAY."

Everyone draws forward to review it again. She shows image after image confirming her findings.

"A heatwave ... maybe ... water vapor," the chief mumbles, searching his mind. "No, that can't be ... The pattern doesn't fit."

"The pattern," Officer Jefferson replies, digging in, "is definitely something burnin'."

Officer Angelos flips through more images. She seems more rushed to make her point. "It's like there's some kinda ritual at that hour, occurring quite predictably every day."

"Huh?" The chief raises his head in curious wonder. He knows this pattern; it feels familiar, like he's seen it before, though, right now, he can't put his finger on it. He steps away, pacing, thinking. Then he shakes his head and gives up. "Well, I guess we could take a look again ... perhaps stop by at that specific time. But ..."

"But what?" Officer Jefferson says, interested to know what the chief is debating, wondering if there's another explanation to validate this.

"It seems right in theory, but is it right in practice?"

Baffled, everyone gazes at him, awaiting his explanation.

With mature experience under his belt, it seems the chief is letting Officer Angelos know that while everyone is entitled to an opinion, hers is just wrong. "We have to be wise with our time," he says, feeling the surge of excitement of his own conviction. "There is one item of Mr. Jules we still haven't discovered."

"What's that?" she wonders.

"His yacht ... it's been missing since they left." He nods in satisfaction. "That's where they're living."

"But, sir," Officer Angelos politely interjects, "they'll need food. This isn't just one or two people. You can't have some seven hundred people live on a yacht forever."

"And they don't. They stop and go ... stop and go." He gestures and throws in, "I want every yacht within a hundred-mile radius to be checked. The yacht could be painted. It could be disguised. But we're not leaving anythin' to chance. Find that yacht, and you'll find those kids."

"That's incredible!" Officer Higgins whispers, losing his voice.

As one would expect, with such precise deductive reasoning, who could argue with the logic?

Case closed.

PLANET NEXT
PROJECT X

The watchtower is now built. At last, there's someone to guard, someone to protect: the island, its citizens, every hour of the day. Ships pass daily, some alone, some in sequence, and sometimes too many ships to count, but, interestingly, many carry national flags. On Planet Next, everyone's confused. *The waters weren't like this before. Why so busy? What's up with the flags?*

Thankfully, the ocean in this region is vast, with no nearby land or islands. There's just a boulder of rocks in the distance, prompting ships to alter course; consequently, the likelihood of a random collision remains low.

With the recent ocean traffic, the voyage out into the water to access the internet connection has been on hold.

"We can try and loop it back to the island," Dragon says, "but to do it right requires time." And, obviously, time is something they're challenged to find, owing to the passing ships.

Despite the risks, Huxley has a hunch there's pertinent information they need to discover, and soon. What are the authorities planning? Why are ships visiting nearby waters? What's tempted them to this side of the ocean?

As they attempt to tie together the flurry of cues, everyone feels something is not right. None of this makes sense.

It's dinnertime. At the table, questions consume their conversation. In sequence, they chime in their thoughts.

"Maybe it's a celebration?" Jaxston asks. "Many of the boats are filled with youths."

"Mardi gras," someone tosses in.

"Carnival!" shouts another.

"Nope to both." Dragon waves the suggestions off. "Those happen in the winter."

"Environmental disaster."

"Do environment disasters bring people to the water?"

"Unless they're cleaning the water," Chandler claims.

"Perhaps a local disaster?"

"Can't be. There are ships from every country."

"Maybe they're sending relief efforts?" Dale wonders.

"Nope," Jed chirps. "They've been partying,"

"How about a pandemic?"

"Would they be on a ship if it was a pandemic?"

"Good point."

"A sporting event, then?"

"In November?"

Baffled, Coco says, "It's weird, but it's like how traffic clears every night just before eight and stays that way for an hour."

In their seesaw discussion, Chandler finally cuts to

Huxley. "What do you think?" Voices fade and heads turn as everyone watches him nibble on his meal. He's purposefully quiet.

At last, he opens up. "I'm almost afraid to guess. But I do know one thing ..." He stalls midsentence to think and then swallows his words.

"What?" they all say, curious now.

"One way or the other, we'll find out tonight."

Jed and the Dragon Dale brothers understand what he means. They swap glances. Chandler is confused, but Huxley nods to reassure her; she'll find out soon.

After some conventional chitchat, the plan is set. They need to know, need to untangle this unexplainable mystery. Tonight they'll venture into the ocean in an attempt to unravel the genesis for the recent commotion.

An hour passes. The time: 7:50 p.m., everyone's ready. It's been almost ten minutes with no signs of passing ships, the last one being a five-hundred-foot yacht. Chester also wings by to chime in, "No pawns, master."

Coco sits in the tower. The signal is raised, and Huxley, Jed, Chandler, Jaxston, and the Dragon Dale brothers brave the waters in a boat, with Coco keeping a close eye.

After they arrive at their desired location, efficient and in a rush, it takes fifteen minutes to set up and reconnect to the World Wide Web—every site, every email, every account, every camera, and, ultimately, to the inner channels and web of every home, particularly in the state of Florida. This is the first time they've had an opportunity to see, play, and explore since their earlier connection. Truly, it's a meddler's dream.

They all huddle around Dragon as he enters code after code. Finally, tapping the last key, he says, "We're in," and he reaches out to adjust the screen.

"Where should we go?" Dale asks, turning to Huxley. "We can enter anywhere so long as it has a computer, a video camera, and an internet connection—provided they're on."

"Let's start with the news," Huxley replies, worried, shaking his head, hoping his suspicions aren't true.

Dragon and Dale seem surprised at the mundane request. *What?* They swap looks. *The news?* It's not the start they were hoping to unleash with their newfound powers. Most certainly, they were optimistic about exploiting its full reach and are visibly disappointed.

Dale nods. "You mean, *news*, as in we look inside presidential homes and heads of state around the world, right?"

"Or a look inside the backstage of news stations?" Dragon adds. "To know what's really happening behind the scenes."

"I wanna go right inside that yacht that passed by," Jed says in admiration, turning back as if imagining it's still there.

Huxley shakes his head. "No, just the plain news; there's got to be a reason for all these flags."

"Okay, sure … if you wish." A dejected Dragon hesitantly nods and sluggishly begins to type in the web address. A few seconds pass as they wait to connect to the international news page.

The site finally flashes up, and Dragon begins to scroll down. Suddenly his hand slows as some familiar faces roll up.

Everyone's shocked. Their jaws drop.

Top caption: "Watch Live: Planet Next Victims."

The title: "Nations Vie to Capture Huxley X."

The pictures below: a split image of Huxley X and Chandler, with Chandler's father's thumbnail photo in the corner.

Bottom banner: "1.5 Billion-Dollar Award. See award rules. See nations enlisted."

Caption below: "See past episodes."

A list of links is provided for each of the victim's names and corresponding episodes over the last month.

Dragon and Dale chime together, "Whaaaaa ...?" Their surprise ruptures as they read their own names.

Everyone's frozen in disbelief, not permitting their eyes to blink, scanning every word. Then Jed approaches within a foot of the screen, clinging to the hope of seeing things differently if he moves closer. After a minute, he draws in even more, still hopeful. He's denied once again. "I can't believe this."

Everyone's lost in the abysses of their minds.

Huxley's shocked, and his eyes are locked on the screen. It's simply inconceivable. *How could this have happened?* This isn't what he'd intended. His motive, unknown to anyone but Jed and soon to be unveiled, was always justice. He never imagined inviting the world to this stage.

Shaking his head, Dale clicks on the contest link for rules and details, and a new screen pops open. They read.

No one speaks. The page leads to another … more bios, more rules, more of the parents' concerns.

Dragon and Dale are absorbed with fear and a dose of excitement. They're not sure what to feel. Their goal was never to create a new vision or a new planet. It was simply to escape the one they'd been living in. In the process, they found something they weren't seeking: a connection, a sense of belonging. And more than that, they found a role model they never believed existed: Jed.

Chandler looks on with passion. She smiles. This is an opportunity—the global platform she'd always sought to deliver her transformative message. At long last, after spending her life chasing a new world, the new world has come chasing her. But she wonders: *Why is Huxley taking all the credit?*

Sitting down, Jaxston's hope begins to wane as he scans each line. He's starting to remember his old life: the drills, the practices, the lessons, his parents. He stops reading. It'd always been his dream to live on an island, and before that, to live in a tree house. Some dreams fall short of expectations, some of glory, some of even being intrinsically worthy. Not this one. Not by a mile. While he was indifferent at first, he bought into the plan, the hope, the dream—the vision of Planet Next. He puts his head down in trepidation, remembering a life he never wanted.

Standing beside him, Jed reads and reads again. As he stares with rapt attention, his pulse rises in the rush of realization. He'd always envisioned that the project would have a global impact and even prophesized its glory. He helped pen the first letter, shared his personal island, shared in the vision, purchased the supplies, and was a coconspirator at every step of the plan. At last, everything has come to fruition just as he'd imagined, and he revels in the attention ... with just one notable problem: he can't find his name written, not one mention anywhere. He draws even closer now ... then draws back. He's upset. How could this have happened? This wasn't the ending he was expecting when he designed the fireworks at his house. More than anything, he wants to belong, he wants to be mentioned. And yes, he wants to be blamed. His coming-of-age story was to come with fanfare, the type he enjoyed only in one place, on the surfboard, in the water, with a wave of excitement surging above. But, contrary to his hopes, he's somehow, unexplainably, all but excluded from the narrative and the blame.

Tuning out the surrounding world, he tunes in to the sound in his own mind, volume turned up. "I can't believe it!" he repeats, shouting this time, and doesn't want to elaborate further.

Their worlds rocked, everyone sits back. Chandler grins, Jed frowns, Jaxston is pale, the Dragon Dale brothers' faces are cheerless, and Huxley offers no expression. None.

Everyone is mute, lost in a myriad of their own thoughts. No one cares to share. Not right now.

"This is everythin' we wanted," Chandler finally says. "We got the world's attention."

No one responds. Not even an attempt.

"It's wonderful, isn't it?" she adds, looking around for support, smiling dreamily. A feeling of triumph graces her words.

Nobody offers her eye contact.

Silence lingers.

Then, his eyes glazed, Dragon murmurs, "One and a half ..." and Dale continues the thought, "billion ..." and they both chime in, "dollars," while staring off into the distance.

Huxley gently looks down at his necklace. He unclasps the ring and slowly takes it off. He places it on his palm and attempts to hand it to Chandler.

She closes his fist. "You made a promise. Our job is not done yet." She softly pushes his arm away.

Huxley stares at his hand. Yes, true, that was his promise. But can he keep it now?

Jaxston looks zoned out, like he didn't hear a word Chandler said. "How long until the world finds us ...? Before the dream is over?"

"We're living on borrowed time," Dragon says, his head tilted as he looks up at the sky with Dale. The brothers watch the stars, the moon and gaze around, perhaps searching for the satellites they know are up there.

As Jed sits, a frown sets in. His eyes are fixed on the horizon. A moment passes, and he blurts out, "It's not fair," refusing to dive back to the world of positivity he knows, still not wanting to elaborate further.

Conventional wisdom would seem to suggest, as is the case with any crisis, that "this, too, shall pass," but Huxley wonders, *Will it?*

Chandler scans the perplexed faces about her, and attempting to cheer the mood, she has a suggestion: "They mentioned they'll air a show on my life tonight. Who'd like to watch it?"

Everyone swaps glances, not once, but twice. No one

dares to answer the question.

No one.

PLANET NEXT
VICTIMS

It's nighttime. The waters are calm. The sky is dark. Everyone watches the horizon as though they can see something on the black and fearful skyline.

Their emotions are anchored; the mood doesn't want to change. It needs to be what it is for however long it wants it to be. And they let it be.

Chandler digs in and wishes to see *Planet Next Victims*. It's the show about her; why let it pass? Circumventing the surrounding sentiment, she leans forward and streams the video online.

The show has just started. Everyone's head gradually turns, indifferent, their attention drifting in and out.

Most of its details, they already know, but a few, they didn't, and surprisingly, Chandler seems more interesting on television than they'd ever given her credit for.

She was born two months premature, during a tsunami in Southeast Asia, where her mother, Canadian by birth, had been volunteering for a service project. As Chandler had once called herself, she is the product of an environmental disaster. She always knew she was earmarked for the earth. Regrettably, her mother didn't survive the tragedy. Chandler had never seen nor met her mother, though she carried her vision and her familial talents.

Huxley leans forward, more curious. Something is missing. He waits for it, but it never arrives. Oddly enough, the show never mentions that her parents had been separated at the time of her mother's passing.

Mr. and Mrs. Collins were as different as fire and ice. A business tycoon with multiple corporations, many of which are on the watch list of companies harming the environment with global emission, he was the adversary not only of Chandler's mother but also of Chandler's uncompromised interests. The father–daughter dynamic ultimately transitioned into a polarized relationship, with Chandler eager to pursue her mother's legacy.

But tonight's show is remarkably about unity. It's about a father's undying love for his daughter. It's about a husband who lost his wife—the pain, the suffering he's endured. Simply put, he cannot afford another loss at the hands of fate and criminal minds like Huxley X. Most certainly, he would be willing to give it all up, every penny of it, for his daughter's safe return.

Chandler is overwhelmed with emotion. She's quiet, her eyes now suddenly moist. It's a touching moment. Mysteriously, she doesn't see the oddity Huxley does.

The show then strangely segues into a mini-infomercial about his companies and its various services before shifting

213

once again to Mr. Collins, the husband, the father.

Huxley's more interested now. His attention misses nothing. His ears are fixed on Mr. Collins's voice, and his eyes study his expression as his mind deciphers his message. He's not easily swayed. Every instinct tells him something's not right. While instinct is not an exact science, it is to him. And he knows when to trust it.

He stands up to watch, all in, more focused than anyone, and that captures the attention of Jaxston and the Dragon Dale brothers, whose heads turn in sequence.

Huxley's curiosity has them excited. Has he seen something they've missed?

Jed finally comes around, and he's interested, too; the bitterness has faded, and he wants to be happy again, really happy, and he wonders what has Huxley so psyched.

The show nears its end, and predictably, Mr. Collins reminds Chandler, "Daddy loves you ... more than you can imagine. Please, Chandler, if you're watchin' ... come home to Daddy. I can't go on like this much longer. I just can't."

Staring at the screen with unblinking fascination, Huxley waves at Dragon and Dale without turning his head.

They stagger up next to him as he watches, confused by his cryptic response.

When the final credits roll, Huxley, following a hunch, says, "We need to tap his computer right now."

"You realize this broadcast was taped earlier," Dale says.

"I do." Huxley nods. "But the people of interest may connect right after the show."

"People of interest?" Dale repeats, looking at Dragon,

uncertain what Huxley means.

"Yes," Huxley says, more convinced now. His gaze lingers on the screen for a while before he turns slowly and nods. *People of interest.*

PEOPLE OF INTEREST

Time: 9:00 p.m. They're in. The Collins residence is host to a bevy of gateways: security cameras that link online, multiple computers, two of which are on, and several phone lines, all of which are virtual. It's a hacker's dream: more technology, more virtual, and, of course, more entry points for an unmitigated and comprehensive live broadcast.

The time required for Dragon and Dale to deliver the anticipated experience: three minutes.

"Let's take a look at what we've got," Dragon says, nodding and high-fiving his brother.

Then he begins his directorial debut by linking the microphone and cameras. He checks the angle: high, low, aerial, eye level ... He checks the sound: pitch, volume, quality ... Then he checks the image: resolution, color, and, of course, exposure. At times, he provides a split-screen display, and at other moments, the camera rolls seamlessly from one room to the next.

Dragon's fingers type endlessly, commanding instructions, working their magic. "And ... action!"

It's the kitchen. It's quiet ... an invention of dreams: shiny marble floors, swirling large island, two fridges, cream-colored cabinets, modern appliances, incandescent lighting, and the design—a revolution to the eyes.

Chandler elbows in, curious to catch a glimpse. Like flashbacks of a forgotten life, she begins to remember her old home. Her eyes track every detail. It's large, it's beautiful, and she doesn't miss it. Her father is still in his suit and appears docile. They all huddle to watch him pour a cup of coffee. He adds milk, no sugar, and stirs once. He stops and then stirs again. Finally, he taps his spoon dry and lifts his cup—the scent, *It's nice*, a sip, *It's hot*, and closing his eyes ... gulp ... and a beat later, a sigh of pleasure.

Everyone looks at Huxley; he nods, hinting, *Just wait*.

Mr. Collins lifts his mug for another round. This time, his experience is more drawn out—his sigh more dramatic.

Dragon shoots a pessimistic eye at Huxley, and they swap glances—neither says a word. Dale's head tilts past Dragon; he wants in on the swap of glances. He's thinking the same thing as his brother.

Then Mr. Collins's phone rings, and their eyes snap back to the screen. Dragon changes the angles and tunes in as Mr. Collins accepts the call. Dragon links in ... they're listening live.

"Hello, Lusala," says Mr. Collins.

"How are you doin', Greg?"

Dragon and Dale immediately lock stares, and Dale says, "Is that ...?"

"Dad …? Why is he talkin' to him?" Dragon wonders, looking back at the screen.

"I didn't think they knew each other," Chandler says, leaning in.

"They don't!" the brothers answer.

Everyone huddles closer to listen to the conversation.

"Sure, Greg, give me a moment. Let me sit at my computer, and we'll do a conference call."

Mr. Collins hangs up. He seems perked up, the early tears now gone. And sure enough, his demeanor is more upbeat, more vibrant, and his feet move with excitement as he trots to his computer.

"A conference call …?" Dragon finally says, still lost.

Waiting for the anticipated video chat, Huxley looks at Chandler, and in sequence, they exchange glances with Jaxston, Jed, and the Dragon Dale brothers. No one has any idea what has caused this friendship of fathers.

Mr. Collins accepts the invite, types in his ID and password, hits enter, hits accept … and he's in.

The screen waits for the other members to come on—a blink—Mr. Mubanga logs in, and moments later, up flashes Mr. Lee, Mr. Clarkson, and, at last, Mr. Lon Jansen.

"Father …?" Jaxston blurts out, his eyes locked on the screen, his jaw low. He can't believe it.

"Greg, that was wonderful tonight," Mr. Jansen says.

"Fantastic," Mr. Lee agrees. "And this is just the beginning. We have more than seven hundred students to do shows on."

They chuckle out of sequence but with unified motive.

"The ratings will go through the roof after this," Mr. Mubanga adds.

Mr. Clarkson chimes in, "Aren't our kids beautiful?"

"They sure are." Mr. Collins nods. "Another week, and there's no stoppin' this. They'll make us richer than any of our businesses."

Everyone laughs.

Mr. Mubanga's grin lingers, and he shakes his head. "Thank heavens I was able to sabotage the satellite images early on to give 'em time to put up the cloaks. I gotta hand it to my boys. I never lost faith that they'd do it."

Gobsmacked, Dragon looks over his shoulder at everyone. No words can make it out of his mouth.

"But," Mr. Mubanga carries on with a hint of reservation, "I'm still a little worried."

"How so?" Mr. Collins wonders.

"With so many people involved, they may actually find them."

"I have to agree," Mr. Jansen says.

"Me too," concurs Mr. Clarkson.

Mr. Mubanga presses on. "There are many boats around where they are. What if there's an accidental collision?"

Emerging to reality, Huxley looks at Chandler, shocked. Everyone swaps knowing looks at this unforeseen tale, speechless.

"He's right," Mr. Jansen says. "There's no way we can risk one and a half-billion dollars."

"Don't worry; you're all anxious about nothin'," Mr. Collins says. "Like I've said before, you won't lose a penny. One of my companies, Lagunaz, is keeping an eye on this. Their ship is within a mile, from early mornin' till midnight. If there is any doubt, they'll go in."

Huh? Jed leans forward, pale in disbelief, curious to

know how they've missed it.

"What if they spot them?" Mr. Mubanga responds, answering Jed's thoughts.

"Guys, guys ... relax. They can't. They're cloaked, just like their island." Mr. Collins laughs. "That's the beauty of this whole thing. Once this show is over, we'll have another series about their time there. We've set up video cameras all over. You gotta see the footage. It's a gift that keeps givin'."

Shaking his head, Mr. Mubanga warns, "Cameras can be spotted. That's risky."

"Not these. I've got drones disguised as birds. Not just any birds, but ones that are almost extinct. Trust me. My daughter is a humanitarian nutso; if she sees these sweet little things, she won't let anyone near them. She'll give those birds unlimited access to anythin' they want."

Chandler gasps in shock. "I ... can't ... believe ... this."

"Wait till you see the reel of this Huxley kid waterskiing with sharks. We got enough material for three more seasons."

Mr. Collins pauses, smiling at his thoughts, and then carries on. "The only thing we hafta be certain of is to edit out all their climate change endeavors and all that humanitarian mumbo jumbo. Lon, I'm sure your utility company wouldn't want that kinda press. Same for you, Lusala. You, too, Paul."

"Hell, no!" a voice shouts with a chuckle.

"Well, let's do what we have to," Mr. Jansen says, "but let's also see to it that no one gets hurt."

Mr. Collins nods. "Our men have been told not to shoot, and if they do, that Jed guy is the first to go."

They burst out laughing. Jed turns white.

"It might actually help the ratings," someone doles out in a guffaw.

"WHAT!" Jed yells and pops up, his face finally flushed with color.

Mr. Collins shrugs. "His coming-of-age story will circle to a coming-of-death ending. He's arrived ... and gone." They let loose belly laughs.

Chandler grunts, unable to make another sound. Jed, though, puts words to everyone's thoughts. He shouts a string of curses, one quite pleasing to his soul, and then shouts something else, something much longer and even more pleasing to everyone else. Then he tosses in, "I'm gonna make those dimwits pay!"

"Hopefully, nothing bad happens to the kids," Mr. Collins says. "But, Lusala, I have to ask. These kids can be defiant, and terrible things sometimes happen when they're as rebellious as we know they can be. You're the only parent who has two copies of one child. Can you part with one of them if required?"

Everyone joins in on the banter.

Mr. Mubanga muses. No response. Not yet, anyway.

Dragon and Dale look at each other.

"What? Why is he even thinkin' about this?" Dale shouts.

Mr. Mubanga's thoughts linger as he mulls the question. Finally, he says, "Maybe Dragon ..."

"Wait a MINUTE!" Dragon yells.

"No ... maybe Dale." He reverses.

"WHAT THE ...?!" Dale yells.

"I don't know." He finally decides. "This one is tough."

The laughter of the People of Interest drone on as do their inappropriate jokes and comments.

"We'll televise a coming home party," Mr. Collins says. "And by the way, Lusala, thanks for arrangin' the smart home for my house. It's wonderful. I've never felt safer and more at ease."

"Me too," the other members echo as they each nod back.

Huxley turns the screen off and looks to his friends. Some apples fall far from the tree. They're all as quiet as they are upset. No one speaks. Silence grips the moment.

"We can't let them do this," Huxley finally says, eying every member in the group.

Anchored to frustration, his emotions are raw. He knows how dangerous that can be. Still, it's in him to fight. Alas, for the first time, he has no strategy, no designs, and no phases of a plan. And he knows better than anyone how dangerous that can be.

With emotions stirred, they all watch Huxley. Is this an insurmountable impasse? Perhaps. But what are they to do? No one imagined they'd be fighting an invisible enemy. For the first time, they're not in control, not leading the future. And just maybe, they never were. The idea feels strange. The sense of doom that beats in their hearts feels even stranger.

Calculations swirl in their minds. How could this have happened? Where did they go wrong? They were to be a step ahead of the curve. *Not true.* They were to be the guardians of change. *Not quite.* They were to be the champions of hope. *Not now.* They were to be the custodians of its promised land. *Not ever.* And they were to be the ones to hold a pen and script a hero's quest. *Well, not exactly.*

Like eyes within a book, a firsthand witness to every written chapter, perhaps, their onlookers weren't holding the pen—but they were the judge and jury to each and every narrative.

Lids open, no blink, their thoughts flick through the successive chapters of their journey. It's clear. No question about it. Looking back with a bird's-eye view, at last, they're starting to see the secret eyes in their story they'd missed.

Ten minutes glide on in a faraway gaze. The waters are calm. The only light now is from the moon. They know there's a ship out there, watching them, and birds on the island that will observe them even closer on their return.

Conscious of what they know, nobody wants to go back to the isle. These waters in between are the only place they feel safe.

More time passes in contemplation. "We should probably pack up and leave Planet Next," Jed says, defeated, his soul crushed. "It's probably best for all."

"I don't wanna go back," Dale says. "Ever."

"Why do we need *them?*" Dragon asks. "We got everythin' we need right here: our friends, the people who care for us … the family that guides us. We got Jed." He points.

"Thanks, Dragon." Jed nods. "But you'll probably need real adults to take care of you. That's not what I am."

"Whaddaya mean? You're a five-time surfing champion. You have a multimillion-dollar swimwear underwear line. Your surfing Vibeboard ... that's genius."

"It's true," Dale says and stands up for support, nodding at the suggestion and waiting for Jed to agree.

Gesturing his appreciation, Jed is overwhelmed. "Guys, I dunno what to say. I'm touched. But I'm really not all that. Okay, maybe the surfing part. Yeah, I was really good." He frees a half-smile at the memory of his youth. "As for the rest, the underwear line only sold with elderly people who didn't want to wear diapers." Not wanting to explain further, he shrugs. "The market just wasn't ready for it. It was a little head of its time, I guess. As for the surfing Vibeboard, it took off on water, but it couldn't handle waves, so that's not really surfing, is it? We had to recall it."

Everyone's quiet, looking on.

"Everythin' that I have," Jed goes on, his head hanging low, "is because of my parents, and that's what you guys need ... real grownups."

After a moment of reflection, Dale steps forward and says, "Whatever you wanna call yourself, it won't change what we think. You taught us more than our parents did our whole lives. You gave us your time. You shared everything you had with us. To me, to us ... you're still the best." After a pause, responding to his sentiment, he leans forward and hugs Jed, as does Dragon.

There's a circle of smiles as Jaxston also joins the embrace, launching a tour of joy.

Huxley nods, happy. "I agree," and he steps past the brothers to give Jed a hug. "I'm the testament to what a great uncle, a great parent, and a great role model you are," he says over his shoulder before releasing his embrace.

"Where's Chandler?" Jaxston wonders.

Everyone looks about, and they note Chandler had stepped away and is now lingering alone in the back of the boat.

"Chandler?" Huxley calls out.

Her gaze has drifted to the horizon. She says nothing as she turns, her eyes damp. She wipes them dry. "Humanitarian nutso?" she gripes. "Is that what everyone thinks of me?"

They all shake their heads. "No, no, no ..." Dragon and Dale chime in sequence.

"You don't hafta lie," she mutters. "I know how you all feel."

Sadness marks the moment and dominates the mood. Chandler had always been a port in the storm, that powerhouse of strength and imagination. They haven't seen her cry before. This is a first. There are as surprised as they are concerned.

"You're the best thing that's happened to this place," Dragon says, his voice soft with sincerity. "Because of you, we all have a vision. We have hope. None of this woulda had any meaning if it wasn't for you."

Dale steps forward to calm her as well. Suddenly he almost trips, and something pops out of his pocket.

Chandler looks down and sees a colorful wrapper under the moonlight. "Wait, are those bacon chips?" She glances up at both Dragon and Dale.

Silence pervades. Dale's fall is tragically untimely. The package is bright, its cover unmistakably labeled. Truly, he's not sure what to say, but the moment demands an explanation. Parting lips that don't lie, Dale shrugs. "It's ... *Texan?*"

WINTER

EPISODE 101:
PLANET NEXT VICTIMS

WILL THE PERSON RESPONSIBLE
PLEASE STAND UP?

PLANET NEXT
WATCH

Months pass, nothing happens. The parents are content with the status quo. The show must go on. With the passage of time, everyone on Planet Next becomes disillusioned watching the surrounding waters stir chaotically with vessels. But akin to a tree of hope, its roots anchored to a wondrous dream, nobody wants to unclasp their grips from the unbreakable branches of its limitless promise. What else can the tree do? It grows.

At night, when the waters are calm, a few citizens venture out to watch episodes of *Planet Next Victims* and hear the recent narrative on the most-wanted teen: Huxley X.

Fair or not, someone has to take the fall. While his enemies aren't certain which pixie dust powers this rechargeable rebel, they're certain on one element: his day of reckoning is near. Together, the ringleaders have made a plea for Huxley's arrest.

Is it doable? *It doesn't matter.* They'll try.

But he's a minor. *Who cares?*

Huxley shakes his head. *Not happening.*

To make matters interesting, more parents, along with some well-wishing groups, have increased the ante, and the reward now sits at an even two billion dollars.

Not that anyone should be counting; still, they are.

Further to that, Mr. Wickly has announced that Huxley will be expelled from school upon his return, and as a proactive measure, every school in the district has joined forces to ensure Huxley will never be admitted to a school in their region.

Is Huxley worried? How can he not be? Yet why does he look so calm? How can he be so indifferent? Beneath that composed exterior, there must be some emotion, no? Hurt, anger, fear …? Well, if it's there, he's certainly not letting on. Does he have the support of his friends? You bet. And for now, that's all that matters.

In disbelief, the Dragon Dale brothers watch the telecast, their thoughts muted, and that's fine. Alas, while the Planet Next citizens have concerns, nobody knows what to do or when they must leave.

Much to their surprise, they've now passed their agreed-upon six-month stay. Oddly enough, no one complains. Everyone agrees: Why tinker with happy?

Then, of course, there is the other matter: those curious birds, Collins's drones, which drift amongst them. Every day, they watch them fly, knowing what they represent, knowing what they must ignore, knowing they must put on a fine act lest they betray any knowledge of their purpose.

But, clearly, every good show deserves another. As

such, every evening, the Dragon Dale brothers venture out with Jed … and fish. Or so it seems.

You can't catch a ghost with a net, and you can't see a cloaked ship with your eyes. The only way to defeat an invisible enemy is to make it visible. And there is a way.

They know unlimited information is available from the underwater cable—Mr. Collins's emails, video chats, and uploaded receipts—and it doesn't take long for them to uncover the whereabouts of the contracted company, Lagunaz, and tap their servers.

With ease, they key in to the ship's virtual devices to see and hear what's happening in the rooms and on its screens and know where it's navigating.

"That would put them at three o'clock … next to the boulders," Dale says. "Don't look."

After another episode of *Planet Next Victims* is concluded, Huxley angrily paces, muttering to himself while resisting taking a look at the hired ship, "We can't let them win."

Though the odds are stacked against him, he doesn't care. Not everyone has the will to fight, but Huxley does. And he wants his friends to fight, too. But how?

"We're not meant to win. Not this one." Dale shrugs.

"There's not much we can do," Chandler adds. "They have another ten episodes scheduled. After that, they'll be coming for us."

"People's view of Planet Next is already tainted," Dragon chimes in. "Can't change that."

"But … what if we could?" Huxley says, pacing faster, not wanting to give up. He wants, dare it be known, to win.

Jed lifts his chin, curious. "Whaddaya mean?"

Gazing out at the horizon, Huxley collects his thoughts and reviews his options. They line up in a menu of disaster. But he wonders ... "What if there was a way we could change how people view Planet Next?"

"How ...?" Chandler asks.

His eyes arc left, then back, debating, mulling things over in silence, contemplating the risks. He can't let failure win. Not today. Not ever.

Turning back, Huxley motions for his friends to huddle, and drifting in, they sling arms over shoulders in a circle, linking together. With their heads down, Huxley grumbles something, and then he whispers something else; there are a few mumbled exchanges and headshakes, after which, rumbles of discontent rise in a rapid-fire exchange of views. The buzzes drone on, people groan, and then, at last, Dale caps it off with, "Done!"

Satisfied now, they all look up and release closed-lip smiles. There's agreement. Finally.

A circle of nods goes around. No need for further words. With silent conviction, they sail back to the island and begin to prepare.

In the coming days, everyone is awakened to the approaching challenge, but no one gathers. Instead, a chain of intelligence travels from ear to ear. When a person is clear of the drones, the message is whispered ... and then passed on. The citizens are informed: there's a battle, a score to settle. And here is the plan.

Working covertly, everyone's on the same page,

echoing a call to stand together: 751 students with one goal.

"Nets."

They need to put up nets. The gymnasts amongst them will put on an aerial show tonight, including silks, straps, trapeze, and trampoline. They will require a large perimeter. While the nets provide safety, more importantly, they carefully block off an area from the intruding drones.

"We'll keep them to the outside," Huxley says, promising the citizens their privacy for a covert meeting of the minds.

Come nighttime, everyone passes through the nets for the planned event. Interesting birds hover outside, jostling for a view.

Spotlights come on, and Coco rises above, swings on the trapeze, and signals thumbs up. It's time. The aerial show must go on so the parents don't suspect an ulterior motive. And of course, they always love a good performance.

The show occurs nightly for the next week. And while the citizens receive their privacy within this boundary of safety, they all know this may not be enough. And, truly, it's not. In good time and with calculated steps, new measures need to be taken.

One evening, standing on his rooftop, alone and away from watchful eyes, Huxley waits until it's dark and then calls out, "Chester?"

"Aye, master."

"Shall we play a game of *Ches*?"

Chester flies circles around Huxley before declaring, "With pleasure."

Huxley nods. "What must we do to protect the rook?"

With delight, Chester responds, "Everything."

"Indeed. Please visit the foreign birds and give them our love."

Chester rises, circles once more, and soars off, flapping around the island. In stealth mode, he flies ...

He sees it. He tracks it. He wants it. He's happy. One down.

In truth, he's been hoping for this day since those peculiar birds arrived, and now he's been provided an opportunity to deliver their due and to display his falcon-like hunting instincts. Nothing escapes his vision or his justice.

With the meddling birds now relieved of duty, the visiting eyes are finally shut.

The next evening, Dragon, Dale, and Jed drift out into the water to watch *Planet Next Victims*. Looking at the ocean, they note the water has been oddly calmer the last couple of days and the surrounding ships have seemingly vanished. *Strange.*

Moments later, Huxley, Jaxston, and Chandler join them on a motorboat. They have plans tonight, but first, program on. They all tune in to find out.

Tonight's victim: Coco Lee.

Age: fifteen.

Ethnic origin: South Korean.

Born in Florida, she's not only an academic whiz but a world-class gymnast and a trapeze artist. This would have been her last semester at Madison before pursuing gymnastics full time. In a summer of sadness, she was ill prepared to say goodbye.

Her father, one of the wealthiest men in the world and the fifth-greatest contributor of prize money, will be interviewed in his home with his wife.

Everyone watches the show deliver its predictable platitudes, waiting for its dramatic finish.

Then, in methodical sequence, after the program, they tune in to listen to the parents' nightly chats, laughs, banter, and, of course, unfiltered discussions about their cryptic plans.

"The waters around their island were becoming too busy," Mr. Collins says. "To pull some of the ships away, we had people blast rumors of sightings near Samoa and South Africa."

Mr. Mubanga nods. "That's perfect."

"It's full international participation," Mr. Jansen says with a smile.

"The ratings have skyrocketed off the charts!" Mr. Collins affirms. "But we had to pull back our drones for a few days. That stupid falcon thinks they're food."

After their usual chitchat about the need to draw out the show as much as possible, they conclude their discussion, waving goodbye until tomorrow.

"Isn't that kind of them?" They won't let anyone find us," Huxley says. "We live another day."

"It's like they're working on our side now—they just don't know it," Jed says with a grin.

The team is ready, their plan set in stone. Everyone knows what happens next, but they wait for Huxley to make it official. After a beat, Huxley turns to Dragon and says, "Fire away."

And with that, Dragon enters code after code, spoofing the IP address so its location can't be traced. At last, he looks at everyone and nods. "The video is uploaded ... The world can see it now."

"And see us." Chandler smiles.

"Shall we watch it?" Dale asks.

Everyone nods and huddles around the screen. Dale presses play, and they watch the opening credits fade in and out. Then music plays.

"Welcome to Planet Next," Jaxston greets while hiking in the forest with a camera trailing behind.

Touring the island, he points at the different sights, various wonders, gazing back every so often.

"While it started as a planet for us—a planet for teens—we don't discriminate." He smiles.

The camera switches to Chandler. "You may think there are no rules here. There are many, but they're the right ones, the ones that matter, the ones that build inclusivity, not exclusivity, the ones that build community, not tear it apart."

Huxley watches with interest. Earlier in the day, a video had been crafted. Jaxston and Chandler had stitched together various images the students had taken during their stay, adding some extra footage in the morning. They wanted to tell their story, their version—a depiction not directed or designed by their parents, teachers, or the police.

Going off script, Jaxston and Chandler also decide to pay tribute to the founding person of this life-changing, fate-altering decision, the auspicious Huxley X.

The video shows footage of him guiding, extending a brotherly hand, and, as always, presenting a few of his magic tricks and charms.

As Chandler explains ... no, they are not victims—no pied piper, no honied lies—they were not preyed upon, and they were not misled into a web of fantasy. Huxley is their friend, someone they care for, a person of merit, and for all intents and purposes, they intend to stand by his side, regardless of the consequences.

Chandler discusses the promises Huxley agreed to, promises of a better world. And more importantly, he kept them: reusable energy, sustainable farms, drafting and defending the vision of human rights for all, and, most certainly, the *unhuman* ones, too.

In a montage of images, they show where they live, how they live, the tree houses, their sense of community, their dinnertimes together, their sources for food, choices of leisure, and, above all, every member's contribution to the betterment of a new civilization.

Dragon and Dale pay tribute to the forgotten hero of their land: Jed Jules. The man they consider their adopted uncle; the man who taught them, and everyone who wandered in, the Jules Rules; they marvel at his creative mind, his lessons in music history, and praise the exemplary mentor who expresses his kindness with actions, not words, and offers his friendship in a way most people don't: sharing his home, meals, time, and wisdom with them every moment of every day.

As the video fades out, music plays, and the credits roll, Huxley and his crew watch, understanding that now there's no turning back.

By the next evening, one billion people have viewed the posted video. The site crashes, as do the hopes of the band of people who crafted its excitement.

But something else has erupted, and the inhabitants of Planet Next know it. There's no hiding now. The cannons have fired. The skies are lit up. A war has begun.

ATLANTIC OCEAN

The midnight hour strikes. The hope lives. The bell chimes. Mr. Wickly looks at the clock tower: it's time.

Blame them. Resent them. But the scorecard shows one tally: he hasn't found them. Mr. Wickly has his own war to win, and he knows: that, if at first you don't succeed, well, just try a little later. Yes, the later the hour, the likelier it is he'll discover these unruly teens.

His moonlight escapade awaits. Indeed, it's a full moon, and he expects the wolf to howl from the dead of night till the crack of dawn.

Excited, he turns on the boat and its lights, and then he's off.

This must be methodically executed, the Wickly way.

He will show them who's boss, and of course, who's not. Drawn by a premonition and his fifty-point plan, written nowhere but in his mind, Mr. Wickly sets sail on a familiar course.

Speedometer: check.

Fuel: check.

Navigational coordinates: check.

His scheme, every detail examined to perfection: check.

And, undoubtedly, know your enemy: double-check.

He races at full speed, rehearsing his plan in his mind: *Slow within one mile and wait. Listen for it. Wait for it. Follow it. It'll lead you to the pack.*

With a look of delight, he thinks, *It's truly a remarkable plan.* Drawing a picture of glory in his mind, he smiles. He glances at his bag: inside are a gun and handcuffs. But, alas, even Mr. Wickly knows he won't need them. He places them under his seat.

More powerful than a firearm, more terrifying than any untamed weapon, and more respected than any display of brute force, he has what he knows to be the teacher's magic wand: a ruler.

Lost in fantasy, he lifts it, feels its power, and rubs its sharp edges. Then he closes his eyes; he knows he will *rule* once again.

Times may have changed, but not for Mr. Wickly. With a ruler, he will command. With a ruler, he will direct. And with a ruler, the students *will* obey.

As he fixes his gaze on the clear skies, he knows that destiny will lend a helping hand. There is a gentle breeze as he heads northeast, and his boat floats with purpose, bouncing with each wave.

With the fateful hour drawing close at hand, he reviews his tasks: walk in, raise your voice, gather the herd, raise your voice again, expect a challenge, raise the ruler, threaten suspension, threaten their future, threaten parental involvement, and raise the ruler again, higher this time.

They must have a ship. Indeed, they must. Once aboard, he'll call Mr. Collins, call the parents, call the media, meet at the docks—*Isn't it beautiful? There's a winner!*

Oh, Wickly, it's too good to be true, and yet ... it is.

He laughs, laughs, and laughs. Mr. Wickly can no longer contain his wild emotions, live and unfiltered.

Time passes as he continues, and he checks his current location, distance, coordinates. He's near.

The boat slows now. Lights off, engine off, his boat drifts to halt. This is the spot.

He looks at his watch: 1:00 a.m.

There are no sounds. Confused, he looks around. *Odd.*

Time moves along: 2:00 a.m.

There's not even a murmur.

Mr. Wickly waits. He stares at the skies and sees nothing. In a mental redo of the math—*Not to worry. It will come.*

He waits: 3:00 a.m. No sounds. The skies are clear. He's worried now.

Another hour passes, and Mr. Wickly's eyelids are heavy as he watches the night sky, battling hard to keep awake; a second passes, and then ... he's asleep.

His eyelids flick open. There's a hint of light, and it's annoyingly urging him to rise. It's the break of dawn.

As he stares at the skies, one eye gently closes, but he sees something peculiar with the other eye ... a bird.

He lifts that eyebrow as he focuses his sight, and in his half-awake state, he attempts to grasp ... It's black. It's checkered ... He pops up: it's Chester.

Suddenly discovering his energy, his eyes narrow, and after a beat, he hurries to turn on the ignition.

You won't escape me this time.

Chester turns and flaps away, quickly, strongly, fleeing without resistance. But equal to the task, Mr. Wickly chases, his eyes fixed on his target, the boat's velocity set to maximum, closing the gap.

Chester shifts left-right-left. Then he makes a U-turn and eagerly flaps eastward.

The engine roars with purpose. "You're mine," Mr. Wickly whispers, keeping pace, smiling, the air blowing his hair in all directions.

And just as before, Chester wends his way higher, circling before cutting right.

Mr. Wickly grins, and then in a blink ... the bird is gone.

Stunned, his eyes widen, his jaw hangs low. *What just happened?* Before, he believed this to be a trick of the night sky, like a twinkle of stars. Now it's daytime, and he's not sure what to call this illusion of the eye. This time, though, he does know what to do. With an air of defiance—at full throttle—Mr. Wickly tracks the trajectory of Chester's direction and keeps sailing.

"I can't believe ... it," he mumbles in frustration, and then suddenly—*BANG!*—he believes ... he's actually flying. The boat hits a rock, and Mr. Wickly looks back, his body suspended in air; he's thinking something, something fearful ... as he watches his boat behind him, along with his bag, his map, his jacket—floating—and right at this moment, his tie is suspended annoyingly in front of his face, blocking his view. And then … SPLASH!

He tumbles in the water, once, twice, and the third time is truly the charm, though he doesn't yet know it. He's too busy cursing.

However, once he bitterly stands up in the shallow waters, and once he finishes grumbling about his suit being wet, and once he madly clears his nostrils of the salty water that has taken residence deep within their pits, he looks up, still wiping the water from his arms, still cursing, and … *Oh, my. What have we here?*

Indeed, he stops, shocked into silence. It's a sight to behold. It's … it's … paradise … His lips fall still.

The trees are thick as a bridge, the flowers are lit with a dazzling blaze of punchy colors, and the lush vegetation is a vivid green … He's never seen green so green before; he's never known bark so brown. Truly, he's never seen … anything like this at all.

Staring with wonder, his mouth open, his eyes refusing to blink, his head slowly drifts to the left. There is a curious sign: PLANET ᴨEXT.

It would seem that an introduction is in order: his genius has just met luck. He stares. Too amazed to even smile, he feels pleasure, he feels glory, and it all feels strangely familiar … He feels … just like a principal again.

With measured gait—and a delightful one—he walks to shore and treads on the beautiful golden sand glistening from the sun's reflection. The noise of the waves, more noticeable now, is as peaceful as it is white.

It's quiet. It's early. Everyone's asleep.

He treads into the jungle, carefully, calmly admiring this marvel with every step. As he meanders into the heart of the forest, dense with trees, he discerns tree houses above, dotting the background, though he's not yet certain what they truly are.

"What in God's name is this …?" he says like the opening line of a principal's prayer. And while he's not one to pass judgment on the air his students breathe, this place has more oxygen than he'd ever wished for his unruly teens.

Then, he spots something in the hills. "Waterfalls …" The word rolls off his lips, coated with bliss. Gripped by its splendor, he slows to clap eyes on the rainbow levitating over its mist. One hundred percent, this must be a sign. How can he not feel lucky?

Drawing closer, he stops to view the mansions in the sky; each seems like a stunning example from the history of architecture, and together they provide a geographic mosaic of the planet.

A cool breeze drifts in, and he can now hear the rustling of the leaves and sees them moving above. A few flutter beside him, and he smiles. A wave of satisfaction ripples sweetly through his mind. And then another one surges forward even sweeter. It's a teaching moment, no doubt: never second-guess a Wickly.

In a storm of wonder, he resumes his journey along a trail, admiring the beauty, each step a measured twenty-five inches, most certainly from the years of practice at boarding school. Suddenly he steps on something, something unusual, and quite clearly, he hears a *snap!*

That didn't sound right.

No, it did not. Like a deer in headlights, he freezes. Oh, he knows: something's about to happen.

ONE MINUTE PRIOR: HUXLEY'S TREE HOUSE

In a battle of bird versus master, Chester sits on Huxley's chest. His repeated calls and nudges have been deliberately unanswered. Now Chester takes a more proactive measure to wake him up: pulling his hair.

The message is clear. Huxley opens his eyes. Chester flies over to the window ledge.

"One pawn, master."

"It's okay. We have the camouflage permanently. We'll be fine, not to worry."

Chester looks to the jungle, and suddenly, like thunder, there rushes in a scream: "BLOOOODY HEEEELLL!"

Huxley freezes, his ears surrendering to the scream. He knows this voice. The specific words uttered don't miss the mark, either, nor does it miss the attention of every member sleeping on Planet Next.

In a flash, he quickly runs up the steps to his rooftop to get a glimpse of what's happening, and Chester flies over to perch on his shoulder.

On the roof, Huxley stares across the trail and sees nothing. *Where did the sounds come from? It must be here, somewhere.* He looks higher, but he just sees barks, vines, branches, and leaves.

That doesn't seem right. Is he confused? Yes, but he's certain of what he heard. He's searching inch by inch of this panoramic view when, from the corner of his eye, he sees something swinging. He turns. "Oh, yes … the net trap."

Then he looks closer: suspended fifty feet in the air, a figure sits in a net and swings—left-right-left-right—like a perfectly weighted pendulum, hanging by a rope.

244

Target confirmed. He leans closer and stares with delightful interest, and though it's oscillating, the gentleman's eyes seem quite firmly fixed on his.

Ah, what a lovely sight. There really isn't much Huxley can do; nevertheless, the moment requires a response, so he lifts an arm and gently waves back, his smile casting dimples.

It's an interesting exchange, and they both realize it.

Welcome to Planet Next.

WICKLY RISING

Indeed, that is Principal Wickly fifty feet in the air, looking hotly through the net, hurling curses. He yells until he hears the echo. He seems upset.

Huxley walks along the trail and arrives at a score of students rushing in droves, all awakened, some rubbing their eyes, others in nightwear. It's still early.

Coco Lee was on duty last night and is first to arrive. She glances up. "Sorry, Huxley. I fell asleep."

"That's quite all right." Huxley nods, surrounded by the students drifting in.

They all gaze above with curious eyes.

"This fell out from his net." Coco lifts up her palm.

Huxley looks closer—*Interesting*—then closer still. Truly, he's not sure what to think. "Is that a ruler?"

She shakes her head anxiously. "I dunno what to do. He threatened suspension. He threatened to talk to my parents … he even threatened my future if we don't set him free right now."

"Marvelous," Huxley says, smiling. No surprises there. He glances up and waits until Mr. Wickly meets his gaze. "My apologies if the net is uncomfortable. We'll be taking you somewhere, shall we say ... your quarters. But I'm afraid you have been trespassing, and while we don't advocate shooting intruders, there are still a few Jules Rules we'd like you to become acquainted with."

Everyone silently looks on, stunned at the sight, stunned that Mr. Wickly actually found a way through, still unsure of its implications.

Then Huxley, calm and poised, looks at his shoulder and calls out, "Chester?"

"Aye, master."

"Shall we play a game of *Ches*?"

"With pleasure."

Huxley removes a pair of handcuffs from his pocket and looks up at Mr. Wickly. Then he commands Chester, "Checkered and measured, far from unfettered, dark and light pieces move until life ceases. What must be done when treason is what pleases?"

Chester takes the handcuffs in his beak and soars above, wending left ... wending right, and then he circles the net, drawing closer and closer with each round; finally, rising higher, he tilts down and drops the handcuffs in Mr. Wickly's lap before flying away, twirling, descending, and resting once again on Huxley's shoulder.

With Chester's work completed, Huxley tilts his head up and looks Wickly squarely in the eyes. He nods as if to say, *You know what to do.*

Looking back at the other students who still frightened, Huxley offers a reassuring smile. He's delighted, of course, though he has substantially overestimated Mr. Wickly, and he secretly wonders: *What took you so long?*

Phase V of Huxley's plan: completed.

POLICE BOAT

At 9:45 a.m., all officers are on deck. Chief Ross arrives to find a row of uniforms awaiting his advent. After an unproductive search, the chief has relented to the officers' repeated requests for another look for the island. Alas, with no further leads, they now seek to discover, and perhaps understand, the trail of smoke detected by the satellites in the middle of the ocean.

In a businesslike manner, the chief marches past his officers and onto the boat. Excited, he is not. The results are clear. It's a worthless pursuit, but this will be a teachable moment for them all. Time is precious, and it's in short supply. The award is now open to all nations, and as an extension to the rules, international seekers can work individually or in teams. As such, the show will be aired globally, stirred by the widespread fervor for its outcome.

Sitting in the boat, they watch the commercial for tonight's show, and as usual, it's delivered with dramatic force.

The victim: Zümra Demir.

Age: fourteen.

Talent: mathematical genius.

She's of Turkish descent and moved to Florida when she was six years old. The chief nods. It seems interesting. He's already curious. The advertisement ends with a comforting reminder of the award. How can he forget? Two billion dollars is more than the gross national product of some nations. The foreign seekers, not able to search on land, have attempted to search on water. Rumor has also spread that Jed's yacht is missing, and despite the police's best efforts, it hasn't been found. In an endless discussion on radio shows and televised debates, the oceans are the most suspected site for their search. As such, every day, every hour, the seas are busy, and this morning is no exception.

Cruising at a steady pace, the police boat crosses from territorial to international waters, and suddenly it hits a wave of national flags, appearing on boats like a multicolored rainbow of hopeful contestants.

The officers lean over to view several boats with a different emblem. They are filled with students and the flags of Huxley X. Today there's just enough wind gusting through to stretch their flags fully open.

Amusing. They say nothing. But it's obvious. Hero or villain, love him or hate him—everyone's drink is stirred by Huxley X.

In a mingling of defiance and hope, the civilians, on seeing the police boat's approach, cross their arms above their heads—a figurative X—to convey their support for

Huxley X.

That's art! Indeed, an imaginative bunch they seem to be. Relaxing their arms, they pipe up a chant about their hero and tease the officers to sing along—if they're so inclined. Their voice of rebellion looms large, but on closer inspection, there is a voice for something else.

"I think they're seeking immigration to Planet Next," Officer Jefferson says, watching the students cheer, as their boat passes.

"They're not American," the chief says, shaking his head.

"That one is." Officer Higgins points as he steers the police boat, with Officer Angelos standing beside him; she assists with navigation today, confirming the coordinates.

Chief Ross steps to the back, opens the cooler, and searches through the various sodas and food. With the increased attention, the moment calls for a drink, and finding his cola, he opens the can.

Passing boats flicker by like a gallery of dreamlike images. With his shades on, he nods to some, waves to a few, and gives a thumbs-up to one. Then he takes a sip and raises his head. The wind blows his hair. It's refreshing. He feels important.

It's a beautiful, sunny day, and he's already forgetting his earlier frustration for having agreed to this trip.

The exhilaration of the speed causes his veins to expand. As the boat cuts through wave after wave, bumping and rising with each one, he lifts his chin, narrows his eyes, takes a deep breath, and remembers: he's the chief.

After another ten minutes, the boat's rumble descends

to a lower octave. He looks up; he knows what that means. He sees Officer Angelos pointing, and seconds later, the rumble lowers another octave. They're close.

Will the chief please step forward? He hears that call in his mind every time, a call that only a chief knows and recognizes—a call to duty. Chief Ross comes forward to take command of the situation. He raises his belt and rings his thumbs around his waistband, the cardinal sign to move aside, boys and girls—the man of the world has just stepped in.

At last, the boat wanes to a stop.

With the engine off, they wait.

Chief Ross stands at the bow, holding the rails, waiting for something. He takes another sip and nods. "What time is it now?"

"It's still 10:59, sir."

After a moment, Officer Angelos adds, "The heat source always comes at exactly 11:00 a.m. ... from that direction."

"Of course," the chief confirms, squinting at the horizon.

A few minutes pass, but nothing happens. They all look around, but still ... nothing.

"This doesn't make sense," Officer Angelos says, panicked, reexamining her satellite images, stumped by the incongruence.

"Let me stop you right there," Chief Ross says with a corrective headshake. "This is the first lesson every officer has to learn in the police force, and sometimes we just have to learn it the hard way: the difference between practice and reality, the difference between knowledge and application, the difference between an intuitive hunch and an investigative lead—"

"Look," Officer Jefferson interjects, pointing. "Over there. There's smoke."

Everyone's head snaps up, tracking the direction, and sure enough, up in the sky, like a magical cloud arising from its mystic wonderland, there is a cascade of coiled clouds, streaming, rolling to the heavens, from absolutely … nowhere.

"Son of a gun," the chief whispers in disbelief.

Everyone is confused, uncertain what this implies.

"Should we go closer?" Officer Angelos requests. "What is that?"

The chief raises his brows, smelling something. Twirling his lips, he closes his eyes and imagines himself somewhere above that mist. He knows that smell. He waits for the answer to come, trusting that it will. All his investigative senses are flooded to ecstasy, and all his investigative powers are alive with bliss. Floating in his ocean of thoughts, he's deeply drawn into the detective chasm every chief knows and every chief must battle, and battle again until he wins.

Everyone looks at him, awaiting his next words.

At last, like a slow-motion reel, his eyelids lift open. His eyes glazed, his pupils dilated, he stares but says nothing.

Silence lingers like the last minute of death.

He hoarsely mutters, "I'm … hungry," and clears his throat, its gulp noisily traveling down like a wave.

After a moment, he looks about. Then he turns, shoots a tense eye at the back, and rushes straight toward the cooler.

"I can't think when I'm starved." He opens the lid and shuffles through the contents, digging for the bottom before finding his meatloaf sandwich. At last, he removes the wrapper, sits, takes a bite, and closes his eyes. He's calm.

Everyone watches.

"I'm hungry, too," Officer Higgins says, and he bolts forward, joining in, browsing through the cooler.

Moments later, a bite, a chew, a smile, and they look back, and then suddenly—*What happened?*

No one can believe it. "The smoke is gone," Officer Angelos says with surprise.

"None of this makes sense!" Officer Jefferson adds, tilting sideways, trying to bind the logic to what he just witnessed.

The chief stands and glances around. Indeed, something peculiar has just happened. He takes another bite and chews.

"What do we do now, Chief?" Officer Jefferson says. "What do we do?"

PLANET NEXT
FIVE MINUTES PRIOR

Huxley leaves his tree house dressed to kill: tuxedo, bow tie, cape, and, of course, Chester chiming in, "With pleasure," while sitting on his shoulder. They're both wearing a necklace.

Huxley comes down the spiral staircase, steps onto the suspension bridge, and arcs around the island, making his way to its northeast end.

He passes by Jed's home and sees them cooking in clear view. How can he miss it? He tilts his head forward, gives those Huxley eyes. They know what he's thinking. *Must you? Not this day.* They quickly turn off the grill and join him. Indeed, this is not just any moment, and he needs their assistance.

Nearing the end of his trek, he sees in the distance a congregation of students awaiting his arrival. He stops and leans on the rope handles to watch. Everyone's buzzing with energy. Having the school principal as a captive might have something to do with this, particularly when that principal happens to be Mr. Wickly.

Nodding, he looks at Chester, and then they resume their route toward the tree house marked "Cell House X."

It's striking to one's eyes—the largest tree house on the island—and though it sits ten feet about ground, it requires four trees to anchor it. Huxley designed its elaborate details, and Jed and the Dragon Dale brothers helped him build it. It was vacant until this morning. No one was expecting a prisoner. Huxley, though, seems pleased it finally has one. Quite truly, he's been waiting for it.

Voices hush at his arrival. He signals the outside guards, letting them know he's fine to be alone. Then he looks over at Chester, who flies above the cell and sits on its roof.

Jed and the twins also arrive, and they direct the spectators away with friendly gestures.

The crowd disperses, and when Huxley is alone, he opens the door and steps inside … Then he stops. Situated at the center of the compound is Mr. Wickly. He's surrounded by seven concentric squares of cell bars, and like a grid, sliding doors are punctuated everywhere. The structure is a maze of cell bars, and it's roofed like a cage.

Huxley stands and observes his subject. *Interesting.* He stares through the seven rows of cell bars, and finding a path through a narrow sliver, his gaze meets Mr. Wickly's. The principal stands stoically, his chin up, prepared, expecting Huxley's arrival.

256

No keys. Huxley slides the first bar door open, steps inside, and the door automatically slides back and locks. He stops to watch Mr. Wickly. The principal doesn't flinch, and neither does Huxley. Then Huxley quickly steps forward and does the same action for the second, third, and fourth cell bars, waiting for each door to close behind him in sequence. On the fifth one, he opens it and steps inside, and like a labyrinth, he walks around the corner before entering through a cell door to the sixth square. Then he stops.

A perplexed Mr. Wickly bounces his eyes around at this unusual nexus of cell bars. He's unsure where Huxley may go next.

Huxley then walks around with confident steps until he's directly in front of Mr. Wickly, separated only by one row of bars.

They stare at one another, neither making a sound. Each waits for the other to make the first move. It seems, for a moment, that the silence will last forever, but then … it ruptures.

"Mr. … Wickly," Huxley says, staring with purpose.

Silence resumes.

"Huxley … Xanahanabarlatow," Mr. Wickly responds.

"Remarkable pronunciation; you haven't lost your touch." Huxley smiles.

"Pity, it seems you haven't lost yours. Still wearing tuxedos to the beach, I see."

"Indeed," Huxley says, calmly breaking his gaze.

"It must get hot when you play with fire," Mr. Wickly says flatly, bearing no expression.

Huxley steps forward, faces him, and waits a beat. "You

mean like this?" Fire gently comes out of Huxley's sleeves, and he holds it lightly in his hands.

A surprised Mr. Wickly steps back, watching the flames' glow. This is unexpected, but he feels something else, something peculiar: for the first time, he's unprepared to respond.

Huxley spreads his arms. "I do this quite comfortably, knowing there is nothing but lumber and trees around us. Do you want to know why?"

"Not particularly," Mr. Wickly chirps. "But if you must share."

Making a fist, Huxley puts out the fire. "It's a simple triangle: oxygen, fuel, heat. Cut off the oxygen, and the fire can't start; limit the fuel, and the fire will cease; absorb its heat, and the fire will fade."

His lesson complete, Huxley restarts the fire, this time holding it higher. Mr. Wickly steps back, disturbed.

"The control is simple," Huxley continues, "until someone changes the equation." He waits a moment and adds, "I'm never afraid of a fire that I control."

Then he puts out the flames, walks around to the north side of the room, slides open the cell door, and enters Mr. Wickly's cell.

The door gently glides behind him and locks. Now there's nothing between them, and they trade unfiltered stares.

Huxley stands silently, unafraid. Even-tempered, he looks at the bars above, past them, and out beyond the open roof. There's a refreshing breeze that drifts through.

"I thought you'd enjoy the view."

"Seems like we're both enjoying it now, doesn't it?"

Mr. Wickly says sarcastically. Yes, it certainly would appear they're both locked in the cell.

"Perspective, of course, is everything," Huxley says, tilting his head sideways. "Like the perspective of having a seven-year-old take the blame for his parents' death. I'm sure you haven't forgotten that."

Silence descends and stays there for a while.

"I don't know what you're talking about," Mr. Wickly finally says. "I was not even at the school when it happened."

"No, you weren't. Apparently, I wasn't the only magician there that day."

Mr. Wickly stares at Huxley, quiet.

"I know what you did," Huxley murmurs, but he adds nothing more.

Mr. Wickly's eyes dart back and forth. He appears on edge, though he's trying to look calm.

At last, he looks away and says, "Oh, yes, I thought it was a little strange when your uncle registered you under his last name and then called just a week before school and made the switch. Although, come to think of it, I didn't know any other Huxleys, so I should've probably suspected mischief just by the name. Well, at least he was generous in his donation."

"Yes, he was. Some habits die hard—good or bad." Huxley waits a moment and then tosses in, "I know of your bribes ... and the illegal activities. I read my parents' letters. It was quite an inadvertent discovery I made a year ago, reopening their belongings, reopening my wounds. I didn't know what to think of it at first, but I wanted to review all the incriminating evidence ... all the evidence that was apparently against me."

Mr. Wickly stares coldly at Huxley.

"Strange," Huxley continues, "the police never quite understood why my parents were in a classroom alone."

"I can think of a few reasons," Mr. Wickly cuts in. "They were unruly, like you."

"Yes, and I can think of a few more." Huxley nods. "It's bizarre; they also couldn't figure out who some of the visitors were that day—an unsolved mystery, as they called it. I guess it didn't matter; they already had their story. They had a seven-year-old boy who was playing with fire."

Mr. Wickly's face remains blank as he suffocates all emotions.

"On second look, truly, a magic of the cameras, there's one peculiar lady wearing a Knightlord ring. I'm sure you're familiar with that award."

"Our school had many distinguished parents," Mr. Wickly breaks in.

Huxley shakes his head. "It's remarkable that a lady wearing a Knightlord ring would visit but you weren't in the building at the same time to greet her. I can only imagine the superlatives in that chatter."

"I agree. It would be … indescribably stupendous." Mr. Wickly says, raising his chin.

"Yes, it probably would … except, quite curiously, of the women who had won this award, only three were alive at that time; two were over eighty, certainly not the woman seen, and the other, interestingly, had moved to Australia and hadn't visited London for over ten years. And, of course, none of them ever wore their rings. With a name like Knightlord, can you blame them?"

Mr. Wickly stands tensely, not daring to drop his eyes.

"Incidentally, of the seven living male winners, they all wore the ring on the right hand; you're the only one who wears it on the left. Would you care to venture a guess as to which hand the ring was on?"

Mr. Wickly's tongue goes numb.

Huxley pulls open the cell door to leave. He holds it open to make another point, but then he changes his mind and releases his grip, stepping away. Suddenly Mr. Wickly leaps forward and slides past before the cell door closes.

Standing behind the bars, he stares through them and smiles. "Your tricks betrayed you once again. Does that *ring* familiar?"

Huxley calmly watches him walk to the east side of the cell. Mr. Wickly looks back and waves and then continues to the next cell door, but it's locked. He glances over his shoulder, shocked, still tugging on the door.

Huxley casually draws open the door on the south side of his cell and works through another row. Then he paces around until he's face to face with Mr. Wickly. Opening the cell door, he joins the principal once again.

Mr. Wickly is confused. After the door closes behind Huxley, Mr. Wickly checks, but he can't open it. Examining the door, he's unsure how it locks or unlocks.

"My tricks don't betray me," Huxley says, "when they're not tampered with. Does that *ring* familiar?"

Mr. Wickly lightly paces around the four sides of their enclosure and pulls on the cell bars, but they're all locked; he is baffled as to how Huxley opens and closes them with ease while he can't. He gently tugs the cell door again and looks up and down, still uncertain.

Huxley continues. "The mysterious woman visited the classroom where my parents were during the lunch hour."

"Your imagination is as wild as your magic. Please," Mr. Wickly mutters in a disgusted tone.

"The hallway cameras show her peeking inside the room for a moment, saying something, while her hand curiously fiddles with the lock. It seems quite harmless. But then, of course, some thirty minutes later, she casually walks by and closes the door.

"You have an inventive mind." Mr. Wickly grumbles.

"It's quite remarkable it was never noted. Ah, yes, the fire was just a mishap of a seven-year-old boy's magic. And there, of course, was the craft of the second magician. It's the oldest trick in the book."

Huxley raises his left hand and plays with a gold coin, rolling it between his knuckles. "If I distract you with my left hand, you don't notice …" Huxley lifts his right hand, drawing Mr. Wickly's attention, and waits. "The cell door on the right just opened."

Mr. Wickly turns, surprised, unsure how it happened. It doesn't matter. He swiftly steps past that open door, snaps it shut, and walks straight to the next door: it's closed. He checks all four sides. He's locked in. Again.

Huxley follows Mr. Wickly and opens a parallel cell door, then another in front, and stands across from him behind the cell bars. He stares at Mr. Wickly, awaiting his response.

"You're forgetting you still caused the fire," Mr. Wickly reminds him.

"You're forgetting you asked all the students to leave their props behind the day before their presentations."

"Your imagination …" Mr. Wickly says, frustrated.

"Your transgression," Huxley retorts, feeling the stab of its memory. Gripping the cell bars, he begins to push, and the four sides slide, getting closer and closer.

Mr. Wickly looks about, surprised, suddenly feeling claustrophobic.

"Have you gone MAD?!" he yells, angry, gazing about as the bars grow even closer.

Huxley says nothing, encased in his anger … Then suddenly he stops. Mr. Wickly clears his throat in relief. After a tense moment of exchanged stares, Huxley flaps his cape open and turns around. Pulling cell door after cell door open, he walks swiftly to the exit.

Mr. Wickly tries to follow him. He can't. The cell door is locked. "Open this!" he shouts, watching Huxley close the last door. Infuriated, he paces back and forth, venting, knowing his threats will not break Huxley's resolve.

Stepping outside, Huxley rushes to the suspension bridge. His emotions awakened, he sees Jed, Dragon, and Dale in the distance, but he does not respond.

On returning to his tree house, he stands and stares at the water. Though it's calm, he is not. All the students have gathered near the shore, as if an apocalypse has happened.

While the stormy weather may have passed, Mr. Wickly is here, and everyone knows, that's more or less the same season. Its haunting memory is starting to come back to them now: the flash floods, the rip currents, the windstorms, and who can forget the tornadoes.

Despite the raw emotion, Huxley knows everything is going according to plan. His guest has arrived, his dwelling has been built, his stay confirmed, and according to plan, he will be served as all guests should: with unexpected offerings.

THE WORLD VERSUS PLANET NEXT

In an endless game of reciprocating videos, the battle of narrative-makers wages on, cascading to an entertainment rumble. Episodes of *Planet Next Victims* arise nightly, only to be rebutted by recordings of *Citizens of Planet Next*.

Inspired by *their* vision, other videos soon emerge from people, groups, and communities around the world, seeking immigration, pleading to become denizens of Planet Next.

But first, they must find the missing students, and they intend to. Over the ensuing weeks, ships of migrant teens appear, attempting to make good on that promise. News stories and other media coverage also show them drifting through various oceans, yearning for a new life.

Shrouded in mystery, the *Citizens of Planet Next* videos are analyzed by scientists worldwide: the hills, the landscape, the trees, the animals, the habitat all provide a host of hints on possible locations. With an amalgam of the world as its vista, it's a riddle even for Mother Nature to unravel.

Observing the trees, some speculate that they are in South American waters, others wonder if they are close to the African mainland, while still others are certain, because of the flowers, that they are on one of the Galápagos Islands. Each armed with a surplus of evidence, they all believe they're right.

In a seesaw battle, ships converge on suspected sites, until, of course, another location is presumed—new evidence, a new revelation—and, like a flock of sheep, they move and vie with each other to seek that undiscovered land.

Planet Next is not only a battle for the world but, for many, a battle for a new world. Today's destination has ships drifting in the waters of Australia, New Guinea, and New Zealand.

In the last episode, Chandler included clips with the owlet-nightjar flying elusively in the background, certain that it'd be spotted and knowing that the sought-for zoologists would chime in on their native land.

"I told you it'd work," she says, smiling, noting the vacant surrounding waters.

"It's so cool to use their tricks against them." Dragon nods.

"Yeah … except they like it when we do," Dale mutters with a headshake.

Indeed, oddly enough, the participating parents welcome the additional attention drawn to the contest by the *Citizens of Planet Next* episodes.

After a detailed investigation, this much is clear: at least fifty parents are involved in this scheme, if not more. *Nobody gets hurt. The kids learn a lesson. We get rich.*

It all seems too easy. That is, of course, if everything unfolds according to their plans.

It's 8:00 p.m. The waters are calm. Dale and Dragon have, at last, linked the underwater cables to Jed's yacht. Sitting in a new motorboat, they do another leisure spin and sail in. No stunts today, though they have a few planned for tomorrow.

"Nice boat, mate," Huxley remarks as they drift closer, staring at their curious vessel. It's shiny, it's flashy, and it belongs to someone else.

"Mr. Wickly has good taste," Dragon announces. "Give the man credit." He smiles and high-fives his brother.

It's definitely a boat that amuses, leaving the twins with some wonderful aftereffects: cries of laughter, an addiction to happiness, and an uncontrollable urge to fly.

Dale steps up onto the platform after his brother. They're ready to begin. A hundred students wait inside the yacht's indoor theater. They're excited. They'll be watching the evening broadcast together.

Tonight's victim: Matilda Moreno.

Age: seventeen.

Talent: languages. She's a gifted polyglot who speaks twenty-seven languages fluently—each with its native accent.

She's of Argentinean and Icelandic descent and moved to California when she was ten years old before moving to Florida at the age of thirteen.

Everyone claps and cheers when her name is

mentioned, with competing arms reaching out to pat her shoulder.

Childhood videos are shown of her carrying on a conversation with seven different people in seven different languages, with a seamless transition from one to person to the next, language to language, conversation to conversation, never interrupted, never stalled to search for a word.

Following the show, everyone departs, remembering not to speak of the event on Planet Next lest the spy drones reappear.

Members walk off the yacht with straight faces, no smiles, speaking, of course, about the supposed video games they played on the yacht.

Once the last citizen has left the boat, Huxley nods to Dragon and Dale, and they covertly log in to the nightly online chat already in progress. Their work is not done.

"Greg, this has to end. There are now thousands of ships. Our satellite images show them all pointed toward Florida," Mr. Mubanga warns.

"That's not possible!"

"Check the news. Someone spotted your Cuban kite. I didn't believe it, but sure enough, it's on the last video, in the background."

"We can't afford a mistake," Mr. Jenson chirps. "They're already scouting the satellite images of the oceans from last year. If they suspect those waters, it's only a matter of time before it's discovered."

"On a separate note," Mr. Clarkson says, "your daughter's climate change efforts aren't helpin'. There are already lobbyists protesting outside my company parking lot."

"Mine, too," Mr. Lee agrees.

There's an exchange of worried looks; nobody wants to say it, but somebody has to.

"Very well ... we end it tomorrow." Mr. Collins shakes his head. "I'll call my men first thing in the mornin'. They'll be captured and brought home."

"That won't be enough," Mr. Mubanga responds.

Surprised, everyone hangs on his words. Indeed, as with all contests, there are winners and losers, and then there are the intangibles. It's not sufficient to win the battle; they must win the war. They have to be victorious in the struggle of optics.

"We need to change the narrative of their stay," Mr. Mubanga finally adds.

Stern faces and nodding heads confirm Mr. Mubanga's statement. "They need to see polluted waters. They need to see chaos. They need to see students fighting, not getting along. People need to see the importance of our children coming home and being free from that Huxley X."

Silence stirs; nobody adds any further comment. Their path is clear.

"You know what needs to be done," Mr. Clarkson affirms.

"I do ... and don't you worry." Mr. Collins nods. "I'm on it ASAP."

With their conversation concluded, Huxley turns off the computer and steps away, turning to his friends. Stunned faces stare at him from across the room. They're shocked at the realization that one way or another, they'll be leaving Planet Next. Their time has run out. Their mission has reached its terminal point. No further episodes, no further plans, no further dreams. It ends here.

They sit on the couch, no one saying a word; silence clutches the moment, as do their fears—a full-throttle disaster of the imagination.

"Well, we all knew this day would come," Chandler says in sad tones, "and, I guess, we all know what we're supposed to do now."

They do, but nobody wanted to believe it would actually come this soon. Some hoped the day would never come. A practical thought? Not likely. Impossible? Certainly not. But today it's reality.

They sit in denial, not ready to say goodbye to each other or to Planet Next. They all look to Huxley to make the final call. He doesn't want to, but he knows he must. He waits, stretching the moment as long as he can, but, at last, he reluctantly turns to Jaxston. "Do you have the final video?"

Jaxston nods and, with a heavy heart, gently pulls the data card from his pocket.

They're prepared. Everyone knows the plan. And everyone understands their task for the coming apocalypse. With a chain of nods, everyone swaps glances and then rises. This is it. Take your hats off and make a bow.

It's time to say an ode to Planet Next.

CELL HOUSE X

Rising like a musical orchestra, with every instrument adding its unique sound to a beautiful symphony, every member of Planet Next is informed of the coming calamity, and they, too, know what to do.

However, one item is still outstanding: Huxley's plan for Mr. Wickly has not progressed as he wished. Their daily meeting has not produced the confession he seeks, the admission he knows Mr. Wickly must provide. But there's one last measure he hasn't yet attempted. Alas, he realizes that if it doesn't work, he'll be out of options. He's also hopeful that if done right, it can't fail.

This task has to wait until the twilight hours, until Mr. Wickly has reached exhaustion, confusion, and he can be caught off guard. No small task, considering the subject.

Huxley waits till the dead of night, when his own eyelids are heavy. Feeling their weight, he knows it's now time.

Prepared, he gives a command to Chester, and they

leave the tree house to the bird's chime of, "With pleasure."

They set off, both wearing necklaces, and march to Cell House X, listening to the chirping of crickets along the way.

The time: 3:00 a.m.

Holding a lantern, Huxley walks up the steps, looks at Chester, and nods. At this, the bird flies to the rooftop.

Then Huxley walks in. It's dark. He holds the lantern up and slowly swings it side to side. The room feels empty. He looks closer, leans in, and then sees Mr. Wickly lying down, sleeping.

Opening the doors, Huxley pulls cell bar after cell bar aside and walks a path to Mr. Wickly's cell; the bars automatically close behind him.

The clinks and clanks chime in sequence until, at last, they wake him up. Finally, Huxley arrives, standing in front of his prisoner. Mr. Wickly gazes up, half-awake. He's tuckered out and not in the mood to talk. Truly, this is as good a time as any.

"I just have one question," Huxley asks, putting down the lantern.

Mr. Wickly sits in silence and looks away.

"Where did you find the fuel? You know, for this." He lights a fire with his hands, and now he can see the details of Mr. Wickly's face, the wrinkles and the eyes that squint against the light.

"I don't know what you're talking about," Mr. Wickly says, annoyed. "It was your mistake. Answer your own question."

"But you're more intelligent. I want to know yours," Huxley says with amusement.

"Well, hard to disagree with that logic, of course. But, really, you should've known flammables are not allowed inside the school. I didn't do anything."

"Indeed," Huxley says. "And how did you know the magic trick would be done when my parents would be locked in the room. They wanted to see my performance. That was very astute, breaking the lock."

Mr. Wickly turns to stare at him. "I told you. Your parents locked themselves up. You play with locks enough times, they will break. Don't blame me."

"I see."

"Please leave," Mr. Wickly says. "When the police arrive, and at some point, they will, you'll have a lot of explaining to do. You have no evidence, just a ring. Kidnapping carries a high charge, even as a minor. You'll spend many years thinking about your regrets."

"Oh, but I have proof," Huxley retorts.

Mr. Wickly stares at Huxley and slowly rises, his expression tense, his tongue silenced.

"If the police arrive," Huxley warns, "we'll just turn them away. They have no jurisdiction here. Do you want to know why?"

Mr. Wickly lifts an eyebrow. "Oh, please, do tell."

"The island we're on is technically British territory. You won't even have to be extradited to England. We're already here."

"Lies," Mr. Wickly grumbles.

"Well, I'll allow you to explain that to the British navy. Their ships are quite the marvel. I'm sure they'll be delighted to accommodate one more."

"More lies!" Mr. Wickly says, louder this time. "You'll

regret this."

"Thank you, but I have already buried my regrets. You'll have plenty of time to think about where to put yours."

"Preposterous!" Mr. Wickly yells.

Huxley just stares. Finally, he turns and, opening door after door, walks in a straight line. Then he turns, pulls open a few more, and then reaches the last one.

Mr. Wickly shouts, "Come back!"

Huxley ignores him and strides straight out.

"COME BACK!" Mr. Wickly roars, and he waits there, standing, hopeful of a return. There's none. Finally, his face crumbles, and he slides down and sits on the floor, leaning back against the bars. Feeling an explosion of emotions, he grasps his head with open palms. "Regrets …?" he mutters to himself. "Plenty. Oh, how I wish … I'd killed him, too. I had the chance. I should've soaked his whole costume in butane … and not just his sleeves."

The moon sits at its apex, flushing the trees with its light. Huxley treads back through the jungle and doesn't stop to look back. The air is cool, and his emotions have been awakened by the memory of his parents. With agitated steps, he returns to his tree house.

He knows, like all good magicians, that the proof of any illusion comes in the third act, and true to plan, the promise is tendered before its deliverance.

Huxley's parents died from carbon monoxide poisoning, not from a broken lock or a locked door. It was surmised that they simply closed the door to prevent the smoke from getting in and protect themselves from any explosion. Mr. Wickly's admission, along with the video surveillance of the lady with the Knightlord ring, should be sufficient proof. But Huxley wants more. He wants a full admission. And every third act needs a good ally.

He paces back and forth in his room, anxious, and then he suddenly turns to the window to wait for his ally.

Some minutes later, the sun begins its ascent, and gold streaks light the skyline. Huxley wonders if this will be his golden moment.

Then, finally, from the corner of his eye, he sees Chester flying above. The bird circles the tree house before descending and sitting on Huxley's shoulder. It calms Huxley. He removes the necklace from Chester's neck. Then he repeats his earlier question: "What must we seize from a lying king?"

"Record the fights that sting," Chester replies.

Huxley stares at the necklace he holds in his hand and its hidden recording device. "Indeed." He looks up at the horizon, deep in thought.

Then he remembers a karmic memory; though it's not a pleasant one, it does fit the moment. Raising his chin, he whispers, "For every weakness, there's a challenge to reveal it."

Nobody has to tell him. He knows. Phase VI of his plan: completed.

Mr. Wickly sits in his cell; he can't sleep. The moon glides above him, its glow shining on his Knightlord ring— a taunting reminder of his fate. He looks above, past the bars, beyond the trees, and finding the moon, he's too grim to appreciate its fullness.

Then his eyes catch something they hadn't noted before. *Interesting little thing. What have we here?* Above him, he sees the screws that hold the bars in place. He glances at his ring and its crossed emblem, and then he shoots an eye back at the metal fasteners.

Standing up, he looks at the screws a little longer, more curious now, and then reaches up, extending his arm, pushing forward his ring … and a second later, it pops into a groove. Though the room is dark, his eyes light up. Shades of red adorn his face. Gently he turns his hand, and in an unexpected twist of fate, he feels the screw twist as well.

In disbelief, he stops to smile. A nice breeze touches his face, gracing the moment. He knows all too well what this means. It was always an inevitable conclusion.

Indeed, it's time for Wickly to rise.

SPRING

LAST (SCHEDULED) DAY OF SCHOOL

THE WORLD SEEKS HUXLEY X

OCEAN OF POSSIBILITIES

With his tree of hope yielding its ultimate fruit, sleep finally finds Huxley; though it's only for a few hours, it's the most peaceful slumber he's ever had.

Come morning, high-strung, he rolls over and is met by a winsome face.

"Good morning, Chester."

"Good morning, master."

It's actually a great morning; if only it wasn't their last one. Standing up, he takes a deep breath. The air is crisp. Slowly he works his way up to the rooftop and takes a final glance at the daytime horizon.

Chester joins him and sits on his shoulder, and they both watch: blue oceans, clear skies, and nothing else. It's as beautiful as it is sad. Huxley's eyes finally let go of the view. The day has just begun, and if everything goes according to plan, it will be a long one.

Staring to the north, he sees Coco directing a few members to the yacht. Other citizens hustle to gather their final mementos. Chandler is talking to Jaxston, providing some instructions, and Jed and the Dragon Dale brothers are making their way to the shore, laughing about something, hunched over and holding their bellies.

Everyone is ready. The plans have been set in motion. They know what needs to be done. Indeed, some tasks have already been completed.

Meanwhile, on the mainland, Mr. Collins wakes up feeling rested and more invigorated than normal. It's a glorious morning for him, too. The sun is shining, and strangely, it seems brighter than he usually remembers it.

He looks at his alarm clock: it's off. He looks at other power sources: The power is out. He checks his phone: no service. Curiously, though, there's a message on his phone: "Help is on its way."

It would appear that was the last message before his phone stopped working. *But that doesn't make sense.* His senses are right. He stares at his phone, trying to dial again and again. It doesn't work.

He checks his email just to confirm … and it won't connect, either. He calls out to the artificial intelligence control to open his balcony door. For some reason, it won't answer. He yells his command this time and tries to manually open the panel. It's tough luck once again.

It's quite remarkable, all of this, and if he weren't in such a wonderful mood from last night, he might be upset right now. The home automation setup with its accompanying cell phone and internet connections are all services he's received from Mr. Mubanga's company. He wants to call Lusala to make sense of this occurrence, but how?

Then, he stares at the balcony door edges, curious, studying: above, below, the lock. He shakes his head and steps away, deciding to tread down the stairway. Why spoil the moment? He won't. He's hungry.

Arriving at the first floor, he glances at the kitchen, but something else tickles his mind, and he can't let it slide. In random order, he begins to check every door. They're all locked. *How can this be? Oh, well, it must be another day of dealing with a virtually secure home.* And so he walks to the kitchen and prepares to meet his breakfast.

After a glance, he knows it will be a cold one this morning: bread, jam, and butter. He's not satisfied, but what can he do? Nothing. He patiently makes his sandwich, gets a beverage, and then sits. *Help is on its way.* A bite, a chew, and then he taps his fingers on the counter before sipping his lemonade. A beat later, he looks at his watch and takes another sip. *Something doesn't feel right.* Of course, this could be his imagination. He knows better than anyone how inventive it can be. He nibbles again, chewing faster, frowning, mulling—his impatience swelling. *It's probably nothing.*

Ten minutes later, in the Mubanga home, Lusala wakes up and he's puzzled. His smart home's program voice is atypically quiet. *No good morning, no how are you, no music ... What's going on?*

Moments later, Mr. Jansen, Mr. Lee, and Mr. Clarkson also wake up in their respective homes. Normally, they're early risers, but not today. After sitting up, a yawn, a stretch, a glance, they each note their alarms ... Surprised, they have a curious experience—a Collins experience.

This is odd. The power ... is it off?

They each wonder, *Who should they call?* They can't. But after a quick check. *Oh, right, help is on its way.* It appears they all have the same ally as Mr. Collins. Yes, they do.

Meanwhile, at his home, Mr. Mubanga seems confused. *How can this happen?* It's his company after all, and he can't ever remember such an occurrence or such an alert. *Who sent this message?* He shrugs it off, walking to the window, whistling a mellow tune. Looking at the skies, his eyes reflexively search for the Satteland satellites he can't see, and he wonders: *System failure? Impossible. A hacker? Nah, be realistic. Inside job? C'mon.* That's unimaginable too. From a practical point of view, no one has the capacity to pull off such a heist except for ... *Hang on a SECOND!* His lips fall silent. He suddenly turns pale. Then, he stares at the ocean in the horizon. His eyes rove, lulled by the possibilities of his sons' talents and their creative minds. *Uh-oh!* Uh-oh, indeed. Emerging to certainty—yes, he has. "GOOD LORD!"

Fifty miles away, at his residence, the manager at Lagunaz, Mr. Iggy Lagoy, is hoping to sleep in this morning. It's his day off. But he's called repeatedly by his employees, and finally, lifting his head from the pillow, he answers.

"Sir, you gotta come in," a voice mumbles.

In an attempt to stay awake, Mr. Lagoy rubs his eyes and listens to the urgent matter that can't wait, and after a mental debate, there really is no choice. He shakes his head. "Gimme thirty minutes."

Unhappy, unshaven, and uncombed, he gets dressed, cursing the day, cursing his staff, then cursing just because he wants to. He drives off and arrives as promised. He storms in, prepared to unleash his fury on the bearer of any further bad news and, quite frankly, anyone who asks a question—good or bad.

"What's goin' on?" he asks, his voice whipping sharply.

"See for yourself, boss."

Mr. Lagoy still doesn't believe it. With hurried steps, he moves to the bridge of the ship, its command center. He gazes about, looks at the screens, the power status, the bridge communications, electronic chart display, radar screens, steering gear controls, control panels. A few lights flicker. It doesn't look good.

Worried now, he pushes buttons and turns knobs. Rushed, agitated, he inspects everything and then checks the various measurements: engine RPMs, wind, echo sounder, air pressure.

Everything's malfunctioning.

Shaking his head, he storms out, and the captain and several crewmen follow him down the stairway and toward the lower compartment at the rear of the vessel.

Walking toe to toe with Mr. Lagoy, the captain tries to explain his understanding of the findings. Mr. Lagoy doesn't care. He likes solvers, not complainers. Mind you, he had other plans for today. Then, as he opens the door, he stands frozen, his jaw low. He can't believe it: the captain is right.

"Holy … smokes! What the heck happened here?" he says, still trying to add words to express his surprise. Considering the view, it's not easy.

He grumbles under his breath and stares in shock for a bit longer. Then he rushes in to examine what his eyes can't believe. Parts of the engine and equipment are missing, and so are the components of their cloaking device.

In a turn of events, Jed and the Dragon Dale brothers followed their boat last night. It was time to add a parting gift for the time spent watching their stay.

In disbelief, he stutters, "W-we needa let them know," and then he storms out of the compartment and furiously sprints up the steps.

Upon reaching his office, he calls Mr. Collins. No answer. He calls again … Same result. He calls three more times, rushed, restless. Finally, shaking his head, he leaves a message.

An hour passes, but there's no news. He calls again, frustrated, and delivers another message. Nothing seems to be going his way today. After some time, he sends a text, followed by an email. He's not leaving anything to chance.

Several hours pass. Nothing happens.

In the Collins home, wearing his suit now, Mr. Collins paces back and forth. He stops, glances at his watch, and

then paces again before another round of checks:
Cell phone: not working.
His internet: no access.
His doors: not opening.
His windows: locked.
It's noon. He's frustrated. Debating his options, he lifts a chair and wonders whether or not to break the window, but then affection for the Italian Renaissance-style panes prevents him. *What to do?* Mulling things over, he's cranky, and that, too, outdistances all sentiments. He motions, stops himself, motions once more, and then stops himself again. Too dazzling, too elegant ... He can't do it.

At the docks, Mr. Lagoy sits, confused. All attempts to contact Mr. Collins have received no response. Anxious, he calls again, angry now, and begins to leave another voicemail.

A crewman scurries into the room. "Boss!"

Mr. Lagoy signals for him to be quiet as he finishes his message to Mr. Collins. After he hangs up, he darts his eyes at the crewman and says, "What?"

"You hafta see this."

"See what?"

"Come on," the crewman pleads, and he waves Mr. Lagoy forward.

Leading him to another room, the crewman tries to explain, talking fast, stumbling to report, speaking in riddles, but after catching his breath, he decides it'd be best to show what he can't describe.

The other crewmen arrive, and everyone huddles around a large screen, gazing intensely at it. The opening credits fade in and out for this known sequel.

"It's *Citizens of Planet Next*," the crewman tells Mr. Lagoy.

Indeed, the show is playing at an odd time. The soundtrack plays, and a video montage follows. It's succeeded by footage of each of the citizens saying their goodbyes, sharing their affection, paying tribute to their unearthly home. Each voice chimes in to a nostalgic chorus of:

"We'll miss you."

"We love you, Planet Next."

"Life will never be the same."

"We learned here how to live together."

"There will never be another place like this."

An outpouring of emotion, honor, and homage flows in a montage of images, videos, and words from the multitude of its citizens, along with their experiences and untold stories.

For the world, Planet Next has a simple message: "We're coming back." And this is accompanied by the following notice: "Further details to be provided later about our arrival."

Back at Mr. Collins's residence, there's no further progress. His emotional temperature rising, he fidgets, looks once again at the cell phone message, "Help is on its way," and wonders … *When?*

Impatiently, he stands at the doorframe, examining its features. *How can it be opened? Manually … screws, drills, hammer? Nope, it can't be done. Well, certainly not easily.* Then he hears something, and he lifts his chin and listens … There's a hum, then a clatter, and then a rumble. He stands back. It's coming from the door. He waits, and suddenly—*boom!*—the door is knocked down.

Startled, he ducks, terror clutching his face. Discovering his equilibrium, he glances up at a flood of light blinding his eyes. He sees something and waits. As the cloud of dust clears, he sees a figure step into the doorway. The person is tall, middle-aged, and angry: it's Mr. Mubanga. Trailing behind him are Mr. Jansen, Mr. Clarkson, and Mr. Lee, all with identical expressions of concern. They definitely recognize the confused look on Mr. Collins's face.

They nod. Mr. Mubanga doesn't even know where to begin. How to explain it? Shaking his head, he can't. "Greg, come. Let's go. You won't believe this."

WORLD AT ITS SHORES

The camouflage is still raised; it's now 6:45 p.m. They were planning to leave by now—but they're stuck. It's been raining for a few hours, and fog thickens the skies. *Where is the water?* Huxley can't see it. He stands on his rooftop and waits. At last, the mist lifts. The sky is gray, and a red streak lights the skyline. He views the horizon as though a glorious sunset is about to arrive, unaware that the event has already passed.

But the weather is not the reason for their delay. Eminent analysts tirelessly scoured through historical satellite images from a year ago and noted a peculiar occurrence: an island in the Atlantic hosting a hub of activities. As they followed its course through time, they saw it suddenly disappear and reappear before disappearing for good—all without a reasonable explanation.

Huxley knows visiting ships, already near their Florida waters, will arrive soon to inspect the area. He also knows what that means.

Plan B.

Below, he sees the Planet Next citizens curbing their activities, watching the seas. They know the time is near.

Fifteen minutes later, there are no clouds, but it's darker. Finally, the destined moment arrives. Turning in a complete circle, Huxley sees ships arriving, lined up in a two-mile radius, from different continents, different nations, all gathered, all waiting, looking at a vast ocean of nothing.

Huxley nods. There is no way out, and the impossibility excites him. He looks through his binoculars and sees the police, but not the British navy. Contacted earlier, they were provided coordinates in the ocean five miles from the island. Even with a reward at stake, they're late.

What to do with Wickly? Huxley views the ocean again and sees a curious sight in the distance, several miles away. It's Mr. Lagoy and the captain beside him, shouting about something, likely debating how to get past the vying ships.

Then, in sequence, his eyes cut to a series of ships with people on board, fists raised, arms crossed in an X. Grounded in solidarity, they're pledging their support.

Understanding the implications, the Planet Next citizens stand near shore, their eyes fixed above, and on meeting Huxley's gaze, in unison, they lift their arms up, echoing their own call for an X.

The moment is everything. And it stands for even more, crystallized in admiration.

Jaxston is on the shore, his ear-in monitor on, holding a wireless microphone, and he looks up to see Huxley and delivers his thumbs-up. Huxley knows what that means.

It's showtime.

Speakers line the perimeter of the island. Searchlights straddled with cameras emerge from the waters outside the cloak, as do large holographic projections for an enhanced viewing experience. Veiled behind the camouflage, Jaxston embarks on the Partyboard, wearing his costume of glitter—his hair gelled to perfection and his feet tapping, ready to spring into action. The Partyboard soars high, and the water beneath caves to its rise.

Standing behind the cloak, he calls out, "Ladies and gentlemen, boys and girls, and everyone young at heart ... welcome to Planet Next."

Every person on every boat shifts their attention to the melody, uncertain of its source. The drum thuds, as does the beat of the music, opening the show. Suddenly, the Partyboard pushes through the cloak, and Jaxston appears, hands in the air, clapping and tapping his feet. "C'mon, everybody," he says, bidding them to join in. "It's party time."

Inside the cloak, the citizens begin their march toward Jed's yacht. They're unmindful of Jaxston, knowing what awaits them.

"How long d'you think we'll be away for?" Coco asks, boarding the ship.

"Not too long, I hope," Chandler replies. "Once they appreciate what we accomplished, what we were able to overcome, the challenges, the corruption, the greed ... we'll be back."

The only obstacle, of course, is the two-billion-dollar reward, and Chandler knows better than anyone that the world can't look past that, even if they tried. What's more, they won't allow the yacht past them, even if it could fly.

There is a pink elephant in the room, and it's time to either move the elephant or paint the room pink.

On that note, it's also time for Huxley to visit Mr. Wickly. They'll be the last ones to board the ship. He knows Mr. Wickly must be kept in safe hands until his departure to a correctional facility. As always, Huxley has a plan in mind.

To the backdrop of the music, he descends his tree house, walks along the suspension bridge, and arcs around the island in a nostalgic tour. So many wonderful memories, but right now, so little time.

When Huxley arrives at Cell House X, he stands outside and stares. Something feels different, though he's not sure what. He stares longer, but the tree, the door, the steps, the exterior walls, the compartment, they all look the same. It must be his imagination. After a moment, he looks at Chester and nods, and as before, Chester flies above and perches on the rooftop.

There's no time to waste. Huxley picks up the lantern beside him, opens the door, and steps inside.

Looking into darkness, he holds the lantern above his head, squinting to see as far as he can, and calls out, "Mr. Wickly?"

There is no response.

He stares harder. No one's visible.

Shifting his lantern—left, right, above—and rocking there for a moment, he repeats, "Mr. Wickly?"

He waits but hears nothing.

Opening cell door after cell door, he punches through and arrives in the third square. Suddenly he hears something.

He stands still, shifting his lantern, listening for breathing sounds. "Mr. Wickly?"

Amused, he ducks his eyes. *Where's the sound coming from?* He's not certain, but it's there. His eyes rove the dark, searching for what he can't see. He listens again ... and finally, taking a deep breath, he spots Mr. Wickly sitting on the ground, balled up in a corner. Relieved, he shakes his head. Calling out to the principal again, he opens the fourth cell door.

No response.

"It'll be time for you to leave soon," Huxley says, opening the next set of doors, drawing closer.

Confused, he stands there, holding the lantern. He can see Mr. Wickly's shape, but he's not moving. *Is he all right?*

"Mr. Wickly?" Huxley examines the principal, worried now. Mr. Wickly's eyes are closed, his body is still, and his chest is rising and falling—*He's definitely breathing.* Nodding, Huxley adds, "Don't worry; you'll have plenty of time to sleep later." He opens the next cell door and walks around, arriving outside Mr. Wickly's cell.

Huxley stops and watches him. *This is strange.* Undoubtedly, it's not the most opportune time to sleep. "Wake up," he admonishes and bangs at the cell bars ... The clang echoes, but there's no reflexive response. "This isn't a good time." No, it's certainly not. He stares at Mr. Wickly's eyelids: not a flicker. His body refuses to move.

Huxley mulls the situation over for a second—*What to*

do? Debating his options, he shakes his head. *There's no choice, is there?*

"Really ... you're not going to get up?"

In disbelief, he places the handcuffs in his pocket, opens the last cell door, and steps inside. Huxley looks at his lantern—*Where to put this?*—and stares at the floor, left, then right. Finally, he decides, *Beside Wickly*, on the ground. As he lightly places it on the floor, suddenly he hears a click. *What's that?* He's not certain, but he's certain of one thing: something is now tugging on his arm. *That doesn't feel right.* Confused, he tries to pull it forward. He can't. He tries again. A strange feeling overtakes him.

Huxley looks at his hand. It feels ... *Oh, no* ... It feels ... *Stuck!* He tugs again ... He's handcuffed to the cell bar. Anxiously, he yanks at the cuffs again and again and looks down.

Mr. Wickly has vanished, replaced by darkness.

What ...? Where did he go?

Silence festers ... Then a snotty voice croaks behind him, "You're not so clever after all, are you, Mr. X?"

Panicked, Huxley fixes his eyes on the handcuffs, tugging back and forth, trying to break free. "You won't get away!" he shouts, ignoring Mr. Wickly's sermon. "You can't open the doors."

Mr. Wickly stands and looks at him. "You really think you know everything, don't you? I have to admit, as foolish as you are, you have your charm. Just like your parents, your predictable patterns are what betray you. It's a shame you'll have the same fate."

Huxley continues to tug, staring at his hand, words having escaped him.

"Where is your magic now, Mr. X?" Mr. Wickly tilts his head sideways, and a curled smile dawns on his face. "I wish I could watch you struggle. It would be amusing, of course, but I really must go," Mr. Wickly chirps as he begins to climb. "You did ask if I enjoyed the view." He lifts the bars above and looks back. "It was delightful." Adding his nod, he pulls himself up to the rooftop, taking the lantern with him.

Huxley slides his arms up and down, trying to free himself, and though it's hopeless, he tries again, his eyes flushed with fear.

Mr. Wickly gazes at Huxley from above, watching him wrestle with fate—the scared expression, the frantic movements. "Don't worry; you'll be seeing your parents soon. I know you miss them." He smiles and then tilts the lantern to light a loose branch, admiring it glow. After a beat, he waits to meet Huxley's eyes. Then he waves before throwing the branch inside the cell house.

The walls immediately catch fire, and smoke floods the room, rising in clouds of gray. Standing atop the cell house, Mr. Wickly gazes about and admires the dense rug of trees waving through the island, curving around the pi. "It's a shame this must go," he whispers and lifts a hand to light the leaves above.

Pushing that first domino, the tree is torched, and after a breeze, the trees around it begin to blaze in sequence. "I just wish I had a marshmallow." Mr. Wickly grins. "It'd be a fitting end."

Inside, Huxley coughs, starved for air, his wooden cell house burning. Mr. Wickly smiles at the struggle and then enjoys it for a little longer before taking out the key to the handcuffs. He looks at Huxley, no mercy, and throws the key up and away, watching it soar into the heart of the blaze, deep in the jungle.

Engrossed in his pleasure, he would like to stay there longer, but his motorboat awaits him. *Never underestimate a Wickly,* he reminds himself. Lost in those thoughts, he sees something from the corner of his eye, and he isn't sure what it is. Then, in a sudden moment of understanding, his head cocks north, and his smile deflates: *It's that bloody bird.* Never underestimate him. He emerges, bursting out of the flames, flapping with force—a key chain in its beak.

Stunned, Mr. Wickly lisps what his thoughts scream louder: *How is it possible? It shouldn't be. It can't be true.* It doesn't matter—there's no time. Overwhelmed by the fire's heat, he rushes out, climbs down, and races to the waters.

Back in the cell house, the fire rages, and Huxley, barely conscious, struggles to stand. His eyelids heavy, he attempts to pull his arms free again. There's no hope. The fire crackles and begins to devour the structure … A loud pop and then an explosion, and the side wall crashes, freeing a torrent of fire.

Battling to stay alert, his vision blurs from the smoke. Suddenly he sees something checkered cutting through the flames, flying toward him. *It's Chester.*

The bird descends to the bars and nudges Huxley's hands, prompting him to take the key. For his part, Huxley, fighting nausea and fatigue, flutters his eyelids, too weak to understand.

Chester taps his finger again, urging him to fight. Huxley is waving away the cloud of smoke, struggling to

find the strength he doesn't have, when suddenly—
boom!—an explosion occurs at the front door. Sparks fly.
Flames billow ... and oxygen floods in.

Coughing now, Huxley's eyelids flick open once, and
then again. Fighting his own demons, this is a battle he
must win. He takes the key and struggles to find the lock,
tapping at the key post. Then, feeling the groove, pushing
once, pushing twice, he fiddles a third time, and the key
finally slides in. One turn, and he opens it.

His eyes roving around, he knows there's only one way
out. Without a second thought, he climbs, pulls himself up,
and emerges on the rooftop—*Oh ... my ... God*—he stands
there, stunned, watching with unbelieving eyes. The fire is
ravaging the island, nothing is untouched, it seems. He
hears a loud snap and looks up. *The tree!* It's about to
collapse.

"Chester!" he yells, and then he takes one step and
jumps ... The bark comes crashing down behind him,
breaking in half ... and sparks fly up like a fountain.

The fire roars like an angry dragon—crescendos louder
and louder—unwilling to compromise, unwilling to relent.
Its heat: suffocating. The noise: deafening. Huxley's skin:
baked red.

Then he hears a faint call in the distance, "Huxleeeey!"
He knows the voice. The call is repeated.

Like a compass, his head turns and navigates to the
sound, searching for Chandler. Surprisingly, he sees a
torrent of students running out of the yacht, like a wild
stampede. *It's on fire.* A collapsed tree fell on it.

"Off the ship! Off the ship!" an anxious voice echoes.

Panicked feet run past Huxley as he battles upstream

toward Chandler, with Jed, Coco, and the Dragon Dale brothers arriving in sequence. Like a series of news flashes, everyone frantically issues their concern.

Chandler: "We're losing the island!"

Jed: "We don't have a vessel!"

Dragon: "Jaxston needs to know!"

Huxley: "Mr. Wickly has escaped!"

Coco: "All we have left is a motorboat!"

Dale: "What are we gonna do?"

Sure enough, all their boats, big and small, are burning to a crisp. Silent now, they swap looks, knowing each point is as valid as the next. After a pause, a second round of bulletins resumes.

Chandler: "There's no way out!"

Dale: "Jaxston has to come back!"

Coco: "We hafta do somethin'!"

Dragon: "Look! The outside ships are movin' in."

Everyone's eyes dart around, wondering how they're going to manage their way out of this. Then Huxley shouts, "We're going to plan D! Except ... we'll have Jed surf it." Without question, plans A, B and C are already off the table.

"Oh, no!" Jed shouts, his voice squelched in the surrounding howls of the flames and his own doubt. "We can't. The waves aren't strong enough, and my Vibeboard doesn't work."

Huxley eyes the twins, who look back at Jed.

"It works!" Dragon shouts above the noise. "Dale and I worked on it ... It's fixed."

Jed is suddenly quiet, though he's inexpressibly delighted. "You did wha ...?"

"It works, Jed." Dale nods as well, smiling.

A tree topples and lands behind the group, startling them. Sparks explode everywhere.

Rushed to action, Huxley yells, "I'll turn the searchlights manually! The controls are too far!"

Dragon turns to Jed. "Come back from the northeast side of the island. No one will see you. Huxley will turn off the searchlights there."

Chandler screams, "Let's get movin', then!"

Everyone runs.

Dale dashes to the sand, pulls out the Vibeboard, and hustles back to Jed.

Keeping a close eye on Huxley, Chester flies above him as he sprints madly to shore. Feeling the weight of disaster, Huxley calls out, "Chester!" and even before the bird has a chance to answer, Huxley yells, "We're playing *Ches*!"

THE WORLD AWAITS

The time: time to leave … and quickly.

It's dark. The fiery tempest rages. In sequence, the trees, tree houses, farms, solar panels, windmills, and devices burst into flames, many sparking fireworks of black, gold, and red.

The outside ships, in unison, move closer. Jaxston is unaware of the change in plans and carries on, staying in the spotlight, dancing, singing, performing to script.

Vibeboard in hand, Jed emerges in gear to the backdrop of Jaxston's music. He lays it on the water, within the pi, and when he turns the device on, its perimeter lights flash on. He's set. One, two, three, and off he goes, braving the water, still within the cloak.

Near the shore, away from the fires, Dragon and Dale start the wave engines, and like in a wave pool, the water begins to rise—and then stirs the accelerated start Jed needs.

As the wave surges, the Vibeboard accelerates, and

using the wave's energy, it charges forward. It tilts but does not flip; he's now embraced by the arc of fresh water—refreshing, no doubt. Two hundred yards remain before he emerges from the cloak.

The wave rolls higher, and spreading his arms open, he closes his eyes and taps the Jed within to the fable of his youth, where the unthinkable met his legend and lost. Searching where only he can go, where only he can survive, he's in that underworld where the lore of his Jules Rules lies. He looks for him, deeper and deeper, in every corner, every crevice, and at last ... he finds him.

Jed's eyelids flick open; his hair blows in the wind, as it should. He has that look. The ocean is his, and he holds court. An amalgam of clarity and rebellion crosses his face. He knows better than anyone that he's the favored child of the sea, the wonder of Santa Monica. His only challenge: the jury of his inner voice.

There are a hundred yards before the end of the cloak. Feeling the rush of truth—his heart racing a million beats per minute—Jed rides the wave and, without blinking, bouncing once, bouncing twice—*Oh, man!*—he curves ... Thirty yards remain, then twenty, ten, five, and he punches out of the cloaking barrier, his confidence swelling, as it must.

Bursting forward, he threads the needle of the wave and arrives to a mind-blown gush of *oohs!* and *aahs!* before everyone's breath is ransomed to wonder.

His hair moist, his chest bare, his tan baked to expectation, the viewable experience is as overcooked as it is perfect—just as Jed demands it to be.

Roused up as much as one can imagine, the crowd

cheers and senses something more, that this might be …
that this could be … that perhaps … and sure enough … it
is: Jed's coming-of-age moment.

Doubters be gone, it's a beauty of the ages, conquered,
no less, on the wave of an age-be-damned, I'm-coming-
full-tilt crusade.

Battling on, he throttles forward, risking everything for
his peers, risking everything for the greater good, risking
everything, well, because he wants to … and he searches
for what he knows he must find: a new ship.

Meanwhile, back on the island, Coco sprints up the
docks and then spins a corner and hops into the motorboat.
She turns the ignition on, and the engine hums, and then
she pulls out, riding off, yanking a towrope.

Huxley chases behind in his bare feet, waterskiing
handle in hand… two steps, he jumps, and he's on the
water.

The boat roars forward, and Huxley hangs on, barefoot
waterskiing, moving faster and faster—a bump, a pull, it
bolts forward, and water arcs on each side. Just as he
pushes through the cloaking barrier, he combs a hand
through his hair—*It feels much better*—and picks up speed.
As he passes by the northeast searchlight—a reach, a pull—
he turns it off.

Then, at lightning speed, he rides around the eastern
searchlight, puts an arm out, swings it to the southern sky,
along with its camera, and without missing a beat, he glides
to the next searchlight, and the next, and then another,
pointing each to the southern sky.

Chester flies along, flapping his wings vigorously,
keeping pace, awaiting Huxley's command.

Meanwhile, the surrounding ships draw closer, and Huxley, glancing at Chandler, waits for the signal. After a second, she raises her fist.

One nod, and then Huxley shouts, "Chester!" After a heartbeat, he asks, "What must be done to capture the queen?"

Chester lifts off, soaring into the night sky, aiming for the converging point of light in the southern air.

Jaxston's surprised at the series of actions. His eyes roving, he's unsure what to think. He looks down and sees Huxley nod, and he realizes that plans have changed.

With no time to discuss things, Huxley disappears and blasts back through the cloaked barrier, hidden again.

Chester now takes the spotlight, and Jaxston glances up. Then he looks back at the audience and says, "Ladies and gentlemen, young men and women, friends and foe ... if I may draw your attention to our next performance." He points to the sky. "Born from the genus of Falco and Cacatua, and of noble lineage from the European, African, and Australian continents; this storied treasure has traveled the world more than five times, has averted more crises than civilized nations ... warmed more hearts than global warming. He's faster than disaster, the wonder in the thunder ... and, truly, a mandala of the skies.

"Gracing our eyes tonight, I present to you the one and only, that majestic bird of everything marvelous ... the talented Mister Chester."

Completing his part, Jaxston's Partyboard descends and retreats, disappearing behind the cloak. Turning around, he's gobsmacked ... *That's fire!*

"What happened?" He looks to the waters. Coco rides

by with Huxley sitting beside her.

"Jump! There's no time!" she shouts.

None.

Huxley looks back and sees Dragon raise a two-finger salute. They're almost ready.

The show is now Chester's. The moment is his, and he knows it. Under the stars, where he belongs, he flies in circles with his wings stretched, shortening and lengthening them in intermittent sequence. Gazing above, the audience is mesmerized by the checkered black and white wings, watching the squares morph into diamonds, back and forth in reciprocal series.

With each round, Chester flaps slower, then faster, before gliding, winding … again and again. It's as calming to the eyes as it is breathtaking.

Chief Ross, eating a donut, is entranced. "It's beautiful. I can't make up my mind if it looks more like a chessboard or checkers."

His lips quiver on the cusp of the answer, but then they close. The accompanying officers are already mute. The heads of the crew point up, tongues still, eyes glaze—fixed on one target: the charming marvel in the skies. Lulled by its splendor, benumbed by its display, some boats slow to a stop. A few vessels stagger and drift by, almost asleep, the minds of the people onboard floating somewhere on Chester's wings.

Silence soaks the moment with awe. The parrot-falcon bird swirls as much as he must and looks for his master's signal. Like the thief of time, twenty minutes pass unnoticed. No Huxley, no signal … Chester glides above, waiting.

Then, suddenly emerging from nowhere, a ship bursts out from within the cloak, sailing forward.

The ship's captain: Jose.

Not to be forgotten, and standing at the ship's bow, are Huxley, Jed, Chandler, Coco, Jaxston, and the Dragon Dale brothers.

Behind them: everyone else.

Cutting through a headwind, the ship sails forward, gaining speed, gaining momentum, and unhindered, it passes by vessel after vessel.

"How long will they stay hypnotized?" Chandler wonders.

"Until the cloak holds up ... The visual storm of the fire will snap them out," Huxley replies, and then he looks back up to Chester to signal *his* good deed is done.

Minutes later, sailing peacefully, they pass the police boat. The chief is at its bow, his hand embracing a donut just inches from his mouth.

Huxley writes something down on paper as Chester finally descends to his shoulder.

"Chester." Huxley nods and points to the chief.

With the last phase of Huxley's plan, Phase VII, now completed, Chester takes the necklace with the recording device in his beak and then flies over and places it around the chief's neck.

It has an attached sign: "Please give to MI5."

The chief doesn't know it yet, but this evidence will unravel one of Britain's greatest unsolved mysteries, most certainly leading the MI5 to a host of revelatory truths. Known as a man with shrewd instinct, the chief's savvy explorative techniques will eventually crown him with a sundry of accolades and awards; he'll be known as the transformative investigative mind of his time.

Pressing on with no resistance, Jose's ship accelerates and passes every vessel one by one, and then it sails alone, surrounded by nothing but dark water.

Relaxed and refreshed, relief sets in, and the cool breeze soothes the citizens after the earlier heat of battle.

The students are quiet. It's been an interesting day, and more than anything, nothing went as planned.

Huxley, feeling his necklace, remembers a small but pertinent detail. Indeed, there's an important matter that needs attention. He looks at his friends, and they nod. They know what he's thinking.

Then he turns and walks back to the cockpit and stands next to Jose. After an understanding exchange of looks, he reaches out a welcoming hand. "We owe you a debt of gratitude. Thank you for coming."

Jed contacted him earlier this morning, knowing they might need a second hand and, if their enemies ever managed to confiscate his yacht, a second boat.

A good call—one that came in handy. The only challenge: where to find him in the myriad of boats. Surfing out into the ocean, his Vibeboard finally delivered as Jed had always hoped it would. Upon spotting his friend, they sailed back together, from the northeast side, where the searchlights were turned off.

Nodding, Jose stretches out an arm and shakes Huxley's hand. "Not a problem, my friend."

After a moment, Huxley reaches for his necklace, removes it, and lightly holds it in his hand. "This belongs to Chandler. But I'd like for you to hang on to it until we get to shore." With a knowing smile, he gently places it in Jose's palm.

Jose doesn't know what to say. This isn't something he was expecting. He'll take it. Clasping the chain with his hand, he grins, at a loss for words, and once again, he nods in appreciation.

After nine months, 751 victims, 147 episodes, and more than two hundred countries enlisted, the victory bell has finally been rung.

No doubt about it, the two-billion-dollar question has been answered.

VOYAGE TO HARBOR

The night is cool, the winds cooler, and the waters still unsettled. Waves splash against the ship as Huxley starts to tread back to join his friends.

He wonders about Mr. Wickly on his walk. Most certainly, his prisoner believes he had the last laugh. And who can argue? Mr. Wickly's motorboat is fast, it's small, and it's hard to spot. Perhaps Huxley should be worried. But he's not. How can he be so calm leaving without his coveted goal and trusting his unfinished task to the chief and MI5? Huxley lips curl to a smile recalling a fond memory. With numerous joyrides, the twins had reduced Mr. Wickly's fuel to only ten miles of mileage remaining. This much he's been reassured.

And so, when that expected distance arrives, Huxley gazes out and sweeps the ocean surface with a flashlight. Its glow is not as powerful as a searchlight he doesn't have, and while he sees nothing, he senses Mr. Wickly must be close, sitting in his fuelless boat, *alone*.

Stepping up on the taffrail, he has a hunch Mr. Wickly can view him from somewhere in the darkness, but where? His eyes hunt for what it can't see. He won't find him. *Not tonight.* Then, Huxley closes his lids, chin up, and gestures as Mr. Wickly had done, so many times, cruising past Planet Next. He draws in a deep breath and exhales, and a beat later, he inhales once again. Is it refreshing? How can it not be? Like a curtain, his eyelids lift skyward. Huxley smiles—this time for Wickly. And, perhaps, he'll just leave it at that. Indeed, his prisoner of the island is, for now, a prisoner at sea.

Huxley's friends line the edge of the bow, looking to the horizon with pondering faces. Behind them, the island is now just a speck. At last, the black veil drops, and they can see its distant blaze.

Gazing in silence, no one says a word. Its memory is still fresh in their minds, and their hearts are full of appreciation they didn't have when they first arrived. The planet was host to the secrets of their hearts. They know that. They also know that a secret unraveled is clarity, and clarity unraveled is belief. Tonight they believe—in themselves, in each other, and in the beauty of what they've discovered.

After a moment, they turn away and look forward. A new horizon awaits. It's dark now, but the light will come. It always does.

Jed, Chandler, Huxley, Coco, Jaxston, Dragon, and Dale look ahead, waiting, anticipating. Nobody wants to speak; they're lost in the secrets of their thoughts, and they stay there for some time, enjoying their questions, enjoying their answers.

While uncertainty marks the moment, certain feelings accompany it. The Dragon Dale brothers gaze nowhere, content. They know they're returning to a home rich with everything but love. And that's okay. The twins be all right. They have Jed. They also have their higher education in the Jules Rules scriptures. With the coming of age of their hero, his sacred mandate is now theirs, and they know they must now be the torchbearers for *his* genius.

Jed looks on, unusually silent. His mission is finally accomplished. And he's proud that it was completed at sea. Pondering dreamily, he fancies if his coming-of-age story could possibly have a sequel. He abandons the thought, only to find it reappear, louder and more vivid this time. Though he knows it's not possible, he resigns himself to one verity: if it can be done, he'll be the one to do it.

Jaxston's tired from the evening's performance, dangling in his memories. He wonders how much practice awaits him in the morning. He smiles. It doesn't matter. Not anymore. Having had his respite, at last, he's rediscovered a forgotten love: his music. And tonight, for the first time, he enjoyed it. He's good, dang good; how can he deny it? He can't. So why give it up? He won't. But he understands that he must have that all-important discussion with his parents—what he desires and how much is too much.

Coco knows this is the last night she'll be with her friends before joining her team and pursuing gymnastics full time. Having spent the time she's had with her friends, she's at peace with herself, knowing what tomorrow promises. She understands that a *parting* of ways is a *part* of life. But more than that, she realizes that true friendship never ceases. She nods. This is just the beginning.

Chester is perched upon his master's shoulder, grateful to have played *Ches* like never before. Not unlike his human companions, he covets more. He knows it's dark. He knows it's late. But he looks longingly at the skies and imagines if, perhaps, he'll play *Ches* once more before the night is done.

Huxley ruminates on a cherished memory of his parents. For years, he was overwhelmed with shame, carrying the burden of their death, and was never able to feel anything more. Alas, his magic could make everything disappear except his guilt. Tonight, he's free, and he remembers them differently. He remembers their love, and he remembers their kisses, too, dotting his head. Then, abruptly, he recalls something else. "We forgot to send the letter."

Chandler nods. "It's already been sent."

Surprised, Huxley's head tilts sideways, his eyes narrow with intrigue. Indeed, there's a member on this ship who has endured through more phases of a plan than he has. And as always, she's a step ahead of trouble ... and him.

Chandler smiles and says nothing more. She gives Huxley a cryptic look and smiles again, just to be sure he didn't miss it. She's happy about something. Life is good. Then, with anticipation, she opens the letter, one she'd scanned and sent earlier on the ship, enjoying her own Huxley-esque moment.

With her head held high, she looks off into the distance,

waiting for the horizon to stand up, and she dreams, excited as one can be while staring into the darkness. Suddenly she sees a twinkle, and moments later, she sees another, and then several more. After a few seconds, she sees the shimmering lights of the harbor rising in the distance. She grins, as do the others, the moment etched in their collective memories.

Then she sees the assembled crowd and deciphers the silhouette of their waves. Drawing closer, she listens to their distant hum and a few rippled cheers and reflects on the many marvels of this world—its mysteries, its oddities, and its heavenly delights—and she wonders if, perhaps, she experienced one of them. Holding the letter, she glances at it and nods. She knows. Phase VIII of Chandler's plan: now completed.

Truly, what else could she have hoped for?

Dear world,

You're beautiful! And you're quite messed up. We know that. And by now, with some reflection, introspection, and mindfulness, you've probably figured that out, too.

Naturally, the only reason we know is because we were messed up, too. It may seem brilliant ... Surely, it's not. But then something happened, something curious, something we unveiled, and now you've unveiled it, too, something we called Planet Next.

Amazingly, and much to our surprise, we worked together shoulder to shoulder, side by side: one community, one people, diverse cultures, diverse nationalities, all striving toward the common good of the first, the last, our planet, and everything else in it. And, sure enough, the results were charmingly magical: discovering our world, discovering each other, and discovering our families—fused, no less, on the crucible of justice.

Isn't that what life's all about?

Take it from us, it wasn't easy. Well, that's not true. It was pretty simple once we saw past the greatest obstacle known to humans: the person standing in the mirror. Perhaps that was the secret, or perhaps we chased a rainbow and actually found it.

Indeed, Planet Next hosted a number of secrets. Some were unmasked, others had to be discovered, and of course, a few had to be confessed, but by far, its greatest secret was its vision—a vision of hope, a vision of beauty, a vision of humanity, and a vision of our fated and collective destiny.

So, for now, we're coming back ... back somewhere,

but really, it's not home. Not the way it is. Needless to say, that's not news, is it? What happens next is. Be ready. The storm is coming: the storm of imagination, the storm of change, the change of direction, and the direction of everything good and valid we can imagine.

After all, if we don't address our direction, the universe will—history's anointed equalizer. Whether or not you're on board is actually inconsequential. The authorities couldn't stop us, and neither could their empires. And they can't stop you and the liberated voices of those who seek to join us. And therein, our faith lies—in the invisible ring of heroes ready to unloose their indomitable forces.

We'll be arriving at Meyersville Harbor at midnight. Please come and see us. We'd love to meet you, and we'd like for you to meet *your* winner. But it goes without saying that the winner here is us—and *us together*—and, most certainly, wherever else we build our Planet Next.

From the ocean of fire and dreams,
The united citizens of Planet Next, on behalf of,

Made in the USA
Columbia, SC
22 December 2021